Murder by the Broads

by Anthony Tamiozzo

For Jean Dorothy,
You're only a thought away

Chapter 1

Wolves, two of them. Watching, circling, teeth bared, dripping saliva. Snarling and sneering at each other. They sense my terror – smell my fear like an open wound.

Saturday 29 August 2015

A pale face stared up at the young detective, the eyes following him as he searched the body. The crimson flow reduced to a trickle as the boy gave up hope. A knife poked out of the wound in his throat, twisted by the thrashing in a fight to survive.

***

A fretful Adam Burnt made his way down the embankment, edging sideways like a crab as he approached the crime scene. The stifling summer heat appeared destined for interruption, a thunderstorm lay waiting to quell the humidity. The clouds grumbled and rolled behind him, rested their weight on the detective's shoulders, already sweating under his beetle-black waterproof. He approached the nearest SOCO.

'Ashley?'

The Scene of Crime officer nodded over to the paramedic van. Ashley, bent over, vomiting against the wheel arch, was splattering his suede Ted Baker ankle boots.

'That bad, eh?' Burnt stomped to the van, surprised that it had managed to park so close to the crime scene.

Detective Constable James Ashley was steadying himself, holding the side of the van for support, waiting for the shooting stars to subside. He looked up, saw the familiar face of Detective Sergeant Burnt gunning towards him like a bull, and took a deep breath. Ashley's ashen face revealed how his stomach felt. He fumbled in his faux suede jacket for a handkerchief.

'What do we have?'

Ashley began to speak but turned away to spew the remainder of his lunch.

'Don't bother yourself. Bloody newbies,' Burnt muttered, shaking his head. He perched on the bumper of the paramedic van and fished out a pair of blue overshoes, straining as he pulled them over his size nines, hoisting a thickset leg over each knee in turn. He had the suppleness of a length of pine. He growled as the polythene ripped. 'Bloody cheapskate, cost-cutting, micro-thin crap,' he grumbled, his fat fingers tearing at a second pair.

The next couple of hours would be vital, as images were already on social media courtesy of voyeuristic locals even before the police could isolate the incident. Support still arriving, Burnt needed witness accounts.

It had taken some time to get the ambulance and equipment within proximity of the incident, entertaining for the locals who gathered around the edge of the embankment – a disused rail link that sliced through the town.

Burnt's recent record was not great, he was feeling the pressure. Two murders in seven days. The first was 'a disaster', his superior had told him. Unjustly perhaps, but he was in no place to argue. Never mind, move on, get the formalities right. A crime like this would typically go to a detective inspector to head up. But resources were stretched, so the crime rate was not slowing. Hence, Burnt was first in line.

Burnt's experience of murder investigations brought him to East Anglia. The sleepy town was changing. Offences were growing; not just theft, violent crimes on a regular basis occurred and not necessarily finalised into prosecutions.

Seconded from Nottingham, the detective worked on an operation that linked the Midlands city with the seaside town. It soon became apparent his experience of gang crimes might be a great asset to the Norfolk police. The secondment became permanent.

The media would remind the police department about the growing crime rate on many occasions, and today provided another test for the force. The control centre described this as a possible gang-related murder. The public, however, didn't want to hear the words 'gang' and 'murder' in the same sentence, but preferred to dismiss such a statement as something that only happened in cities far away – not on their own doorstep.

Burnt knew today's events would cause a stir; the small-time gazettes wanting something more than gossip to print would be all over it, maligning the police pushed up sales.

With Ashley still saying hello to his lunch, Burnt called over to a forensic.

'Any weapons?'

'Weapons? Oh yeah. Quite a pantomime if you ask me. Easy to find as it's sticking out of the boy's neck.'

The young forensic officer grinned with enthusiasm, pleased to be working on something other than the usual wife-bashing gone wrong. This was exciting stuff.

'Yep, this one's worth the overtime for sure,' he continued, motioning over to the lifeless body. 'Guess you seasiders have got a bit on your plate then?'

'As soon as you've done your job, we can get on with ours,' snapped Burnt. There was always banter from paramedics, but Adam was anxious, and he wasn't keen on being tarred a 'seasider'.

The duty of collecting information in preparation for a press briefing, prior to the evening news, had fallen to Burnt; the superintendent's way of keeping the tabloids onside, any leverage with the media would be helpful. The police, under scrutiny, had more questions than answers.

Burnt turned back to Ashley, now a better colour. Ashley, marked with mud and puke, knees of his slim-fit chinos streaked with grass stains, had clearly been ruffled by his first ever visit to a major crime scene.

'Night out in a cow shed?' asked Burnt.

'Male, teenager at a guess, knife to the throat which is still intact.' He glanced over at the frail body. 'Footprints suggest a struggle, with two or more.'

'Witnesses?'

'One so far, a dog-walker who made the call. He was escorted home, here's his name and address. He said he saw a struggle between a couple of youths and that one ran off to the bridge. I guess the perpetrator's lying up there on the road.' Ashley pointed up towards the bridge.

'What?' Burnt exclaimed, whirling round to face the busy road over the top of the embankment.

'Yep. First impressions are that the two lads had a scuffle. One ran off in a panic, straight into a fifteen-tonne lorry. An eyewitness gave us the name of Drew Trench, identified by a friend of the family at the scene.'

'Jesus,' said Burnt. 'Is it secure?'

'Yes. I got the call to go to a traffic accident. No sooner had I got there than I get a second call to come down here, and … wham, I got a big surprise. A young lad lying stabbed to death looking like one of Dracula's empties. The dog-walker was standing by, trying to restrain his dog from licking up all the blood, he looked pretty calm if you ask me. There was a mobile phone in the pocket of the deceased. I tried 1-2-3-4 to unlock it, but no such luck. All this was the wrong move, according to the pathologist. She gave me a right mouthful in fact.' Ashley held up his hands. He was finding his first serious crime investigation a baptism of fire. 'And I thought I was doing my job.'

'The pathologist wasn't my idea, probably came from the super, that one.' Burnt untucked his stone-grey T-shirt, flapped it for air. Sweat formed on his brow.

It wasn't standard practice to have a pathologist at the scene, but with unusual incidents, the Chief or Superintendent might find it worth the extra budget to have the expertise present. They may spot something the SOCOs would ordinarily overlook or consider trivial.

'Yeah, they get twitchy if you start handling the evidence before they've started,' Adam replied, feeling a little sympathy for the young copper.

Burnt remembered his first dead body, and it still made his stomach churn. It had been a suicide by hanging. The rope had sheared from the ceiling sometime after the death. The body lay rotting on the floor until concerned neighbours called the police. Burnt had knocked down the door to the small flat in Nottingham, falling over the lifeless body. Lying eye to eye on top of a stinking corpse had been Burnt's initiation into the 'first dead body' club.

'I don't recognise the name, it's not on our radar,' Burnt muttered half to himself. Trench couldn't have been that dangerous if he'd had no previous, he thought. Maybe the small police department was starting to lose its grip, as the press liked to portray.

'I checked, no previous,' Ashley answered, reminding the preoccupied DS he was still there.

A familiar clicking sound interrupted them. Burnt turned, looked to the top of the embankment.

CID had requested the press to keep away from the scene, but the location was impossible to isolate from busy snappers, the small green valley giving good vantage points on either side of the embankment. Word was spreading fast, courtesy of mobile phones and social media. There must have been more witnesses. He gave orders to the police officers to interview everybody within the surrounding area. He trudged the underside of the bridge, to the body.

'DS Burnt,' he said, by way of introduction to anyone who might be listening.

'Grumpy pathologist so keep back,' said the back of someone's head, who was trying to construct the habitat with the help of a uniformed officer. 'Five minutes I've been here, and already you want answers. I've got size ten boots from the first copper on the scene right through any evidence, along with someone's puke. I've got criminal evidence tampered with, along with half the town and their dogs' crap and saliva. The mobile phone of the victim handled, pockets rifled through. It's about to piss down over anything we can find. So in brief to answer the question you haven't yet asked, no, I haven't got anything for you – other than, guess what? He's dead.'

Wow, thought Burnt, catching himself before he made a clumsy PMT joke.

He crept over to the body, ignoring the abuse as SOCOs constructed the tent, and looked down. His stomach turned. The hollow, wide-open eyes of the corpse glared back.

In the Victorian age, detectives would look at the eyes of the victims, expecting the retina to hold an imprint of the murderer's image. Burnt expected no such truths, but perhaps current police techniques would be regarded as humorous in another 100 years.

Muddied prints around the body indicated movement and struggle. There would be a lot for the forensics and short-tempered pathologist to go on. Burnt suddenly felt nauseous and backed away while the pathologist barked more complaints.

'Okay,' he said, 'but just do me one favour, would you? The kid's mobile … see if you can unlock it with his thumbprint.'

The pathologist turned to face Burnt, about to make another verbal assault, then paused. The request was worth a try. A positive ID this early would help keep the pressure off. She nodded to the nearest SOCO as a way of granting permission. The SOCO took the phone out of the evidence bag and pressed the bloody thumb against the start key, then gave a twisted grin. 'Bingo,' he said, and handed the phone to the detective.

Burnt pulled latex gloves from his pocket, stretched them over his chubby fingers, and grabbed the phone. The banner read 'Tom's phone'. He noted down half a dozen numbers in his notepad, including 'Dad', along with the 'recently called' list.

'That was lucky,' said the pathologist. 'Around twenty Pico farads of charge is needed to activate a smartphone. Within about three hours the body would have lost all energy. The murder was just a few hours ago.'

The pathologist looked from the body to the detective, camera in hand. She had calmed. 'The body loses 1.5 degrees an hour until it reaches ambient. This body is still above ambient, and there are no signs of any rigor mortis which sets in after a couple of hours at the earliest.'

'Thanks,' said Burnt, handing back the phone. 'I'll keep out your way and let you get on with your job.' The pathologist's report would be essential – along with any witnesses. He moved away from the body, turning his attention to the onlookers. 'Ashley, get rid of the clickers,' he ordered, trying to take more control, instil urgency into the assembled officers; the authorities were the last on the list invited to the party full of gate-crashers. Crowds of people milling around the top of the hill for a nose inched closer. Christ, any minute now the entire town would take over the place. This was turning into a fiasco. 'Right,' he shouted to all officers within earshot. 'Anyone with a uniform, set the barriers thirty yards back, both ends of the bridge. Not you, Ashley, warn the clickers. Threaten them if you have to, just get rid of them.'

'Threaten them with what?' Ashley inquired, bewildered.

Burnt had to think about this. After a moment he shouted back, 'Disruption of the peace,' which caused a giggle amongst the SOCOs behind him. Turning his back on the crime scene, Burnt called control and requested an address check, gave numbers and names from the dead boy's phone.

A bystander shouted out, 'Find the one with the blood on his face.'

Burnt scanned the crowd, resting his eyes on the woman who had made the remark. Burnt thought the face was familiar but had no time to place it. No sooner had she spoken, than the crowd swallowed her. Was she genuine? It was common for a crank to take the opportunity to get in the news, trying to snatch some limelight. She might know more, shouldn't be dismissive at this stage. 'Ashley, find her. Get a statement.'

Unfortunately, this encouraged others to chip in with advice for the police, but none so cryptic or helpful. The crowd started jeering, like football fans on the terraces, abusing the poorly performing team and taunting the referee, complaining about the cost of a season ticket. Or, in this instance, the taxes they had to pay and what they got for their money.

Ashley pushed his way through the thickening crowd towards her. His first thought was someone had used a pair of shears to cut her hair. She was middle-aged, had a small nick on her cheek, potholed skin. Her stare was hard and she was long overdue a brace. Ashely took her details, checked the palms of her hands for blood.

Burnt barked more orders to Ashley, commanding him to assist the SOCOs, which he did, after entering the name Julie Caulk in his notepad.

Adam Burnt dodged debris strewn along the hillside, glad he wore boots today – unlike Ashley, he'd never get the sick out of that suede. *No problem, he's got twenty pairs to choose from. The guy treats each day like he's on the pull, still he's young, maybe he is on the pull. Grumpy pathologist? Good luck with that, Ashley.* Sharp dressing wasn't Burnt's best attribute, he'd wear tatty tracker bottoms and his faded Van Morrison T-shirt if he could get away with it. But the missus wouldn't let him, even if the force would. She practically dressed him, more from embarrassment, she'd given up taming the beast long ago.

Burnt was thirty-five years of age. His rugby days, not far behind him, had helped to mould his shape. He had thickset, rounded shoulders and strong, stubby legs. He was a short, squat man who seemed to take on the appearance of a bull as he made purposeful strides across the grass, snorting through his nose.

He intended to speak to the single eyewitness, whose evidence he hoped would wrap this up as quickly as it had started. A fight between two lads ended in tragedy. This would quell notions of a gang-related crime.

The rolling clouds shed their first drops of rain on the detective, who mopped his forehead and prayed the change in weather would deter the onlookers. A crack of summer thunder echoed around the town. Burnt clicked his fob, clambered into the BMW, sank into the seat and rolled down the window, closing his eyes just long enough to consider if his week could get any worse. The sky wept on the windscreen.

Chapter 2

Burnt rapped on the door of sixty-five Oak Street, pushed his hands into his bomber jacket, rocked on his heels, and waited for an answer. A pixelated figure approached the frosted glass, a dog barked, the figure barked back instructions. Why people chatted to dogs, Burnt would never understand. It was not possible to teach a dog to obey any more than one or two words, expecting them to understand a conversation was pointless. Burnt did not have the same level of empathy as most, his wife had pointed this out on many occasions.

'Mr Haines? DS Burnt. Norfolk police.'

'Eric,' replied Haines. He motioned Burnt to enter.

Surprise. Burnt recognised the face, Haines had a fresh wound on his forehead. 'Weren't you a witness at Bells Road last Sunday?' He had been smacked across the skull one week earlier. Burnt had discovered the man, face down in a car park. Burnt entered.

'That's right. Quite a week it's been,' answered Eric, with a subtle country accent.

'It has,' Burnt agreed. *Remember, he's not a suspect. Not yet.* 'How's the head?'

'Oh, the hospital patched me up fine. No damage that isn't there already,' Eric joked, knocking on the side of his temple. His short grey hair poked out in tufts. He stooped over Burnt, had gaunt, hollow cheeks that never fattened in all his sixty-one years. Dressed in a well-worn grey sweater, faded denim jeans, and slippers with a hole one of his big toes poked through.

They walked down the hall. Burnt scrutinised the surroundings. He observed some relics and pictures on the wall, stopping at two samurai swords mounted above a bureau in a recess under the stairs.

It had a glass top cover, and displayed dozens of intricate carvings and artefacts made from wood and stones. 'Are you a collector?' enquired Burnt.

'Not really,' replied Eric, placing his hands in his back pockets, offering no more detail.

'Impressive,' Burnt said, scanning the bureau. After an uncomfortable silence, Eric motioned the detective through to the small kitchen diner.

'Quite a scare you've had today by all accounts, Mr Haines. Twice in a week.'

'It's a while since I've seen a corpse.'

'You've seen this sort of thing before?'

'I was in the army until ten years ago. Saw a bit of action, but I'm retired now. I did see a few corpses, yeah. But none since I left.' Burnt eyed an aged scar down the side of Eric's neck and wondered how much and what he'd seen. That would have to wait.

'Ah, I see. Do you travel a lot?'

'Yeah. I travelled around quite a bit in the Middle East and Asia. Tea, coffee?' asked Eric.

'No thanks.'

They sat down at a pine leaf table littered with books from travel to science fiction. Adam wanted to know more about this guy. 'Quite an eclectic taste,' he said.

Eric rested an elbow on the table. He spoke slowly, mindful of his words.

'Yeah, I do like a read. There's not much else on my plate these days.' Eric's hand rested on a book entitled *Collected Works of Mahatma Gandhi*. His long scrawny fingers tapped the cover.

'Are you a big Gandhi fan?' Burnt was not sure why he was asking this, he just wanted to know more. How could one person witness two serious crimes in a week without being involved?

'We can all take something from his life, I think. He was some guy, by all accounts,' he added, looking down at the book, Post-it notes scattered through its pages. Tap, tap, tap.

'Some guy indeed,' agreed Burnt, who knew nothing about the Indian legend. He had fallen asleep through *Gandhi* at the cinema, and was nudged by his wife each time he'd started to snore. She explained later what he missed, he took it on her authority that Gandhi was 'some guy'.

'So today,' said Burnt, getting back to the point, 'this afternoon, just after twelve pm, you phoned emergency services. Please take me through what you saw.'

Haines cleared his throat, pausing to rest his palms on his knees. 'Yeah, although my eyesight isn't the best anymore, that's for sure. And I'm a bit forgetful with wearing my glasses like, so I didn't see anything that clearly. I only wear them for reading. I don't bother when I'm out walking.' Still the tapping, one knee at a time, a metronome for his words.

Burnt waited for him to continue, as the Springer spaniel sat in the corner tearing at a play snake with an inbuilt squeaker. Not good for Burnt's anxiety.

'Well, I was walking Madge along the embankment, as I sometimes do.'

'Sometimes? Every day?' interrupted Burnt.

'No, not every day. Usually, I take her to the woods or something, but today I just wanted to get my paper. I'm a bit old-fashioned, as you can tell. I can't do the news on the tablets or computer. I like to read a real paper, as you can probably guess.'

The veteran tried a smile, took the hint that the copper wanted no more small talk. 'Well, I just passed down the side of the bridge to give her a bit of a run, and was walking along the edge of the embankment by the school. After about two hundred yards or so I spotted these two youngsters. They were knocking the crap out of each other.'

'Did you know either of them?'

'No. I walked past, trying to mind my own business, but Madge is the friendly type, so as she was off the lead she ran over. I called her back, but she wasn't having any of it. I ran after her.' He scratched his head, returned to the knee tapping.

'Well, by the time I got to the bottom of the valley, one of the kids was on the floor writhing around under the bridge, the other standing over him. Madge ran up, which startled him, I guess. He panicked and stumbled a bit, then ran straight into me. Knocked me clear off me feet, got blood all over my coat.' He nodded towards the hall.

'I see. We'll need to take the coat for a forensic test.'

'Of course. I don't know what else to tell you. I tried to help the boy on the ground, but when I got to him, he had stopped moving. I took his pulse, but there was nothing. I phoned for an ambulance and waited. In hindsight, I probably shouldn't have touched the body. I guess you're supposed to leave a corpse to paramedics and not tamper with it, but it just came to me, probably from my army days. The first thing with a casualty is to check for a pulse.'

'Don't worry. There's a queue for the wrath of the angry pathologist, and the police are at the front of it, I can assure you. So, there were only two people involved in the incident under the bridge?' Burnt was hoping he could rule out a gang.

'That's all I saw.'

'Is it possible there was a third person or some others?'

'Maybe, but they would have had to run off before I got to the dead boy, and I wasn't that far away. I would have seen if there were more than two.'

'And after this?'

'I waited by the corpse. After five minutes or so the police showed up. I saw the other lad running away, climbing the hill to the road at the top of the embankment. I told all this to the police when they arrived, then a constable took us home – Madge and me, that is.' Eric shrugged, nodding at his dog.

'Thank you, Mr Haines.'

'I much appreciate your time and help. Please phone this number and arrange to come down to Gorleston police station to give a formal account.' Burnt stood, and handed Eric his card. They walked down the hall, and once again Burnt stopped at the bureau to peer at the bizarre collection of carvings. Eric towered over him. A brutally ugly, bearded face peered up at him from the bottom corner of the velvet lined display.

'Where are they from?'

'Mainly the Middle East, but some are from Asia and South America. That's Mustapha, carved by a five-year-old boy in Petra, Jordan.' His tone lightened, suddenly interested in conversation. 'It wasn't for sale, but I gave the family some money for it, it must have taken the boy weeks to carve.'

Burnt stood captivated by the tiny scratches outlining the beard, the figure looked so imposing. The red Jebel stone glistened from under the glass. Once more, 'Impressive,' was all he could manage to mutter. His attention then moved to a large ivory piece of sharpened bone in the top right-hand corner of the collection. 'Is that a tusk?'

'Could be. I'm not sure. I found it on the beach when I was walking Madge.' He nodded towards the dog. 'I'll get it looked at one day, take it to a dealer or something. I'm not sure what the pattern is, but someone's spent a lot of time on it, I guess.'

'Yes,' replied Burnt bemused. He hadn't seen such a collection of random artefacts before and wanted to ask more about them, but none of it related to the case. He forced himself away, plucked Eric's black overcoat off the rack for forensics. Next to a small black waterproof jacket with a sports logo.

'You have company?'

'No, I live alone, but my nephew visits from time to time.' He looked away, checked the fake Rolex that hung from his wrist like a dead weight.

'I see. A bit of company doesn't go amiss.' A blank stare from Eric. 'Goodbye, Mr Haines. Oh, and where were your tours of duty?'

'Ninety-two to ninety-six in Bosnia, then various tours in the Middle East, ending in Christmas 2005 when I was sent home … er … well … we … rather, we were sent back in January 2006.'

Burnt noticed the stammer. There must have been a trauma for this man, it was the first time he had heard him falter. He had just explained a murder scene word for word without stopping, used the word 'corpse' to describe the body when most would say 'the boy' or 'the body'. He'd seen death before.

'And afterwards?' Burnt couldn't help but ask.

Eric placed a hand on the doorjamb. Tap, tap, tap. Once more the blank stare while he chose his words. 'I retired after that. I took my pension and came back for good. I was fifty, which is over the hill for combat. I didn't fancy an office job. That sort of thing doesn't suit me, so I came back to the wife, God rest her soul.'

'I see.' There had to be a story with that scar down his neck, but too soon to pry.

Burnt zipped his jacket up to his chin and stomped into the rain that had begun to lift the summer heat. The sky creaked thunder.

Eric closed the door behind him, peeled back the net curtain in the side window, rounding his shoulders, eyeing the short dumpy man clamber into a BMW and drive off. He walked down the hallway, stopping at the antique bureau. Carefully opening the glass panel to handle his latest find – carved whalebone, moulded to form a sharp bowed weapon. He rubbed his thin, bony forefinger across it. The tiny black markings told a story, could just make out the profile of two people facing each other, scratched in a naive style, it fascinated him all the same. Swirling lines around them snaking their way to the tip. 'You see nothing, blind man,' he muttered under his breath. He turned his head at the sound of footsteps.

'Has he gone?' A soft voice in a whisper from the landing.

'He's gone,' confirmed Eric.

A boy padded down the stairs, and stepped into the hall. 'I heard wolves at the door.'

Chapter 3

The humidity rose. Steam layered the window inside the pool car, the rhythm of the windscreen wipers a metronome for Burnt to ponder his meeting with Haines. Old scars, new scars, witness to two crimes in a week, seen death before, no family, and something unpleasant to hide.

His mind moved on to Jackie, his wife. Like it always did. Was she? Wasn't she?

The traffic lights stopped him. A young girl no older than six sauntered across the road, drenched in a T-shirt, blinking into the rain. *Christ*, he thought, *she's too young to be out on her own, there's just been a boy carved up not one mile away*. He wound the window, pushed his head out. 'Hey, young 'un, you lost?'

The girl turned, shook her head. Stopped at the side of the road.

'You need lift home? It's okay, I'm a police officer,' he said, flashing his ID.

She considered this, shook her curly locks. Shouted, 'Dad says cops are just like the baddies.'

The lights turned green, Burnt got a toot from behind.

'Not all of us. Where do you live?'

She pointed to a block of flats across the green.

'Well, you get inside, quick as you can.'

She nodded, sprinted over a stretch of grass. Burnt saw her disappear into the ground floor of a tenement.

Another toot.

He connected his Bluetooth, eased away and called for Ashley. *It's turning into some downpour*, he thought, cranking up the air conditioning, staring into the beating rain.

'Sir?' the reply came after two rings.

'Has the body been moved?'

'Just doing it now, sir. Oh, crap.'

Burnt gripped the wheel. 'What is it?'

'We've dropped the body.'

'What?' Burnt smacked the wheel with his fist.

'Up the bank getting to the ambulance. It was too slippery. I don't think anyone saw.'

'Oh, I bet they didn't, you bloody clown. Christ! Any developments? Any more witnesses?'

'A couple. I've got statements, names and addresses, but a bit cranky.'

Burnt could hardly hear Ashley through the noise of the drubbing rain. 'What?'

'I said they're a bit cranky.'

'Relations of yours then? Okay, I'll leave you with it. Meet you at Lowestoft Road.' He killed the call, pulled away from the lights, as his phone rang. He glanced at the caller ID, rushed his hand through his thick black hair, grey sprouting from the temples.

'Burnt.'

A smooth voice oozed from the speakers. 'Super needs an update.'

'When I'm ready he'll get one.' Burnt terminated the call. As usual, it was Ross's pet, DS Griffin, doing the super's laundry. Burnt pushed harder on the accelerator, twisting his hands round the wheel, gripping harder, as if it was someone's neck.

***

Superintendent Ross sat in the makeshift crime incident room in Gorleston police station. Ancient, compared to HQ in Wymondham, the locale more convenient for interviewing suspects and holding press conferences.

Ross was feeling the pressure, still unsure of which detective should head up the case. Burnt had the experience. It was Ross who had requested to make his secondment from

Nottingham permanent. The change in location had halted Burnt's career, no doubt he would be DI by now if he'd stayed in the Midlands, but his lack of local knowledge of the area meant it would take a couple of years before he could expect promotion. Those two years had passed, and Burnt proved a valuable resource, one who needed rewarding with a promotion.

But Griffin was an equally good candidate. There was only one DI position available, and the two longest serving detective sergeants no doubt wanted it. Griffin reminded Ross on a regular basis – too often, perhaps. Griffin was a local lad, born and bred, had grown up with the criminals he put away. Also, he kept Ross informed. He was neat and punctual with his paperwork, whereas Burnt was a bloody loose cannon. No one could be a law unto themselves in modern policing.

Ross tapped the desk; only a week earlier Burnt had driven to the wrong location in response to an emergency call. It was a fire at Bells Road. Ideally, he would choose one of his DIs to head this case up, but they were all busy with court appearances – the need to finalise prosecutions a priority.

Decked out in full regalia in anticipation of the press conference, Ross took out his antibacterial gel and rubbed his hands, nervous of what news Burnt would bring, hoping on enough evidence for a good start. At forty-nine, Ross was still a tidy dresser, no mid-life crisis slouch, a well-manicured individual who kept himself in shape and well clipped. Perhaps giving too much attention to detail, his coiffured side-parting rarely out of place. He checked his face in the camera on his phone; he would be briefing the press soon. The smooth skin helped chip off a few years, he worked on keeping the moisturised lines under his eyes to minimal creases. When under pressure, however, these lines would reveal an uncertainty, a lack of self-confidence usually masked with an all-important reassuring smile.

Ross's private life was just that, he gave little away to his fellow workers, which made him appear aloof. Distancing himself helped to maintain respect but created gossip. He never spoke about his partner. It was rumoured she lived estranged with their daughter abroad.

Burnt tapped at the open door and stuck his head through the gap.

'DS Burnt. Come in, give me the news.' Ross, formal as ever, motioned for Adam Burnt to sit down. Adam strolled in, put stress on an overused hard-plastic chair, plucked out his notepad, and leafed through the notes. He brought the superintendent up to speed. A constable had notified the parents of Drew Trench, and an ID arranged at the morgue once the pathologist had finished her work.

'What about the victim under the bridge?' Ross asked, tipping forward on his seat.

'We managed to unlock his phone, sir. I have his father's number.'

'Well, that's a good start. You'd better inform the parents. If I'm to do this press conference, the parents need to know, even if we don't name them publicly.' Ross relaxed back into his chair and pressed his fingertips together in an arch. 'I want you to visit both sets of parents as soon as possible. Take Rawlings with you, and make sure there is a liaison officer present.'

Burnt looked at his watch, aware he was off-shift in half an hour, but he couldn't leave this hanging until tomorrow. It wasn't a job he wished on anyone else – well, except maybe Griffin. He stood to leave.

'Oh, Burnt, I'll be heading this up, but will split the investigation between you and Griffin. I haven't a DI free until next week, so do all you can. We'll meet again in the morning. Are you on tomorrow?'

Sunday. 'I am now,' Burnt sighed, wondering how Jackie would take it.

'We're going to need everyone on this until it's wrapped up.'

Griffin poked his nose round the door, Burnt's cue to leave.

***

The marked police car eased to a halt outside the Hackets' house on Baliol Road. Burnt took a sharp intake of breath before running through the protocol with the constable and family liaison officer. Burnt, the designated notifier, knew from experience what followed was never easy. It was a situation you could never make better, but easily make worse.

'Okay. To recap. First, I'll make sure that we are talking to Mr and Mrs Hacket. Second, ask if his son is Tom Hacket. If we have the right place, the next thing is for the father to ID the phone number we've discovered on the victim's mobile. If at that point we have all the correct information, I'll tell them to sit down and I guess I'll proceed to turn their world upside down.'

The liaison officer murmured agreement, and the three stepped out of the car. Burnt caught the neighbour's curtains twitching as they walked through an unhinged garden gate, wedged permanently open. Burnt weaved through the littered garden, plastic debris from an upturned bin. Paint peeled from the windows, splinters of wood giving way to years of weather.

Burnt pressed the doorbell, no sound, no answer. He rapped on the door. A tall, wide-eyed skinny teenager opened up a few inches.

'What is it?' the teenager asked, peeking through the gap.

'Could I speak to Mrs Hacket?' asked Burnt.

'You'll be lucky. What's she done now?' The boy barked into the house, 'Dad, it's the law, they want Mum.' He slammed the door. It was then reopened seconds later by the father. The hallway and stairs looked no better kept than the garden. No carpet, half-stripped wallpaper. A minimalistic decor greeted them, not in a Feng shui kind of way either. A musty odour to complete the ambience, belonging to a house without dignity. Burnt made introductions, requested they move to the living room.

The father looked dreamy, he slurred, padding back from the hall. He wore a woollen cardigan, the pockets holding his roll-ups and lighter, which he tapped as he muttered, for comfort. The twitchy teenager sat, almost bouncing on the couch, an oversized Timberland hoodie hanging off his skinny frame, sleeves pushed up to his elbows, and baggy jeans showing his knees. His father sat beside him, the pair could not have looked more incongruous. The teenager bounced his knee, stared down the constable who switched off the TV, Burnt waited for the father to confirm his phone number and his son's name and age.

Burnt delivered his speech, trying to appear sympathetic, but paying careful attention to their reactions. The father, speechless, the twitchy teenager wired to the moon – a fresh wound on his lip, and scratches down the side of his face.

The liaison officer explained how the crisis support unit operated, how it might benefit the family, giving her unreserved sympathy. The father nodded, wiping away tears while sucking on a roll-up, the ashtray next to him littered with more. The teenager was spoiling for a spat.

'So what happened then? Who was it?' he asked, getting more agitated as the minutes passed, his voice rising in pitch the longer he spoke.

'And you are?'

'His brother, for fuck's sake.'

'I mean your name,' said Burnt.

'Graham. Graham Hacket. Who else?'

Burnt made a note, continued in a rehearsed manner. 'I'm very sorry for your loss, but there have been two boys killed and a lot of evidence to gather. I'm afraid it's very early into the enquiry, and we don't know who is responsible. We will inform you as soon as we find anything conclusive.'

'Two?' both the bereaved repeated in unison.

'Yes, Mr Hacket. Did your son know a thirteen-year-old boy by the name of Drew Trench?'

'Yeah, yeah, they were best pals.' The father was glazed. On medication, Burnt guessed. *This guy suffers depression.* Burnt would bet his house on the answer to the next question 'Mrs Hacket? Is she…'

'Long gone, the slag,' piped Graham, jumping out of his chair like a jack-in-the-box.

'That's enough,' shouted his father. The emotions of the bereaved in the first hour or so of someone's death paint an optimal picture of their personality. It is the best time to ascertain if the mannerisms seem guarded, consistent throughout the interview.

Graham Hacket was aggressive and unconvincing.

'I'm afraid I have to ask, did Tom ever carry a knife?'

'Course he didn't.' A bit too quick.

'How did you get those cuts, Graham?' Burnt asked, pointing to the teenager's face.

Graham stopped bouncing his knee, searched the room briefly. 'I fell off my bike. Why?'

Find the one with the blood on his face.

'I'm afraid we are going to have to search the house, Mr Hacket, to allow us to gather evidence. Can I have your consent?'

Family liaison squirmed in her seat. It was not the direction she was expecting the enquiry to take. This wasn't helping to console the bereaved, it was intimidating them.

'Detective?' she started, but Burnt was already instructing the constable to help him restrain the youngster and call for forensics. With no warrant authorised, the occupier had to give permission. Luckily for Burnt, the father consented without objection – unlike his son.

Drew's bereaved parents gave a more straightforward interview. Although only a five-minute drive from the Hackets' to the end of Crab Lane, it took him to a homelier environment, where a female constable was consoling two weeping parents. The soft, dowdy furnishings and school photos were a contrast to the Hackets' home.

Burnt requested the same level of forensic tests at the Trenches' house, which was again met without resistance. He didn't expect it to throw up anything. The signs so far showed that an altercation had taken place between two friends that escalated to tragedy.

Chapter 4

Delayed check-in times at Singapore airport. Some took the option to sit at the outside lounge in the beer garden, watching giant birds take to the tarmac. Greenery entwined the ornately decorated archways providing welcome shade. Passengers could easily forget they were at an airport, the impressively modern building exceeded expectations for both attractions and distractions, as passengers waited for their long-haul flight.

Fiona Pendle knew the airport well. She had used it many times, but never with such a burden to carry. She felt duty bound to make this trip. Too late to reconcile with Agatha, her sister, she wished more than anything else she hadn't slammed down the phone on her yesterday – Agatha was in her hour of need, Fiona as stubborn as ever. But she had time to do the right thing.

She sat at a table sipping mineral water, scratching her hands. Checked her manicured nails, pulled invisible creases from her cream cotton dress, tugging her ponytail tighter. She looked at the photo taken over ten years earlier. Where had the time gone? Why had she not patched things up sooner? Guilt consumed her, annoyed by her stubbornness. On reading the news, she knew she must fly to the UK at once. Fiona had talked it through with her supportive husband. He told her blood is thicker than water, and the water has long gone under the bridge.

She finished her Perrier, pushed the photo into her leather satchel, adjusted her dress, made her way inside. With an hour until check-in, she decided to visit the butterfly garden, she always did when at the airport. She watched a young family taking in the surroundings as she passed through the large glass doors. The youngest, a small girl, attracting the attention of the butterflies and laughing hysterically. Fiona pointed to the child's T-shirt, showed the information notes, the colour purple attracts Monarchs. Thanked by the parents for the information, she moved on around the garden, envious, nervous, guilt gnawing away at the inside of her stomach.

Her husband's connections provided them with the opportunity to make a life in the Southeast Asian city. Financially it had turned out to be a success. As for settling down and having children, the settling down had certainly happened, but the children never came. After numerous consultations they had come to realise they would never have offspring. Her husband had sharp business skills, the ability to make vast amounts of money, but a rare disorder – primary ciliary dyskinesia – had rendered him infertile. Although they led a more than comfortable lifestyle, there was a gap. Maybe she could bridge the gap, ease her guilt at severing ties with her sister ten years earlier.

***

The sun rose over the marshland, smiled through a haze of mist that eddied towards a clear blue sky. The sleepy village yawned itself awake. Haddiscoe, less than a village, more a hamlet, swamped by the meandering broads. Swapping city life for a rural retreat had been an easy decision once they had children. A modest three-bed semi, enough for his two boys to bump around in, it was a well-worn home. Outside of work, there was not a lot needed to fill his time. His family gave him enough distractions, apart from the occasional sailing trip and an ongoing boat renovation project. He suggested they live on a barge, plod along the broads at a whim. She wasn't having that. The kids would grow up like gypsies, she felt. Shook her head and laughed out loud. 'No way am I living on one of those things.'

He didn't give up, slipped it in on occasion, just to remind her. For him, it was the idyllic counter-culture. The rebellious cop.

Her mother would go ballistic; then again, he always found her lot a tad snobby. Another reason to turn to life on the broads, he would hardly ever see the in-laws. Or, was the real reason he wanted to isolate *his* family? Contain Jackie.

His two young boys played noisily in the conservatory, the voice-over of motor cars and space ships echoed into the kitchen. Burnt sat at the table in tartan pyjama bottoms and a 'Motorhome – born to be mild' emblazoned T-shirt, sipping freshly made coffee. He was looking forward to tucking into a much-needed Sunday morning fry up, albeit earlier than anticipated; his youngest had come into the bedroom, pushing his eyelids open at five am.

His phone rang. 'Burnt.'

'Good morning, Adam.' Ross as courteous as ever, always called him by his Christian name when he was off duty. 'Have you seen any of the morning papers? I'm looking at the *EDP*.'

'Can't say I have.'

'There's a front-page photo of the stiff rolling down the hill.' Burnt put down his coffee mug.

'It doesn't put us in a good light, Adam.'

'It was raining.' Burnt had hoped they had got away with it. No such luck.

'I know, but journalists like to sell papers. We have been the brunt of the *EDP*'s joke two weeks running, do you get my drift?' continued Ross. Burnt's indiscretion at the Bells Road fire a week earlier drove to the top of his mind.

Burnt moved through to the lounge, flicked the TV to the *Look East* morning report. A picture of the medics sliding down the hill, the dead body tumbling off the stretcher, a message of 'Calamity cops' beamed out below the news reader. He didn't need or want the sound up. 'I get your drift.'

'No more mistakes, Burnt. There's overtime signed off for the next two weeks – do as much as you feel necessary. I want you at the pathologists at James Paget. There should be a report ready by midday. Catch up at Lowestoft.'

Adam hung up, padded back to the kitchen. Jackie was at the cooker, frying pan in hand, dressed in a heavy towelling bath robe. Not the most attractive get-up; kids do that to you she would say, she used to pad around braless in some baggy T-shirt and knickers. Not anymore. Though, underneath, she still had it. Burnt was punching above his weight and knew it, at the school gates she was top of the yummy mummy list for sure. *Not that the bar's raised too high in this area of the world.* First day Burnt dropped the kids off at school, he checked out the other mums and wondered if he had stepped into the *Planet of the Apes* film set.

'Problems?' she asked, pushing blonde hair away from her face. She stood at the oven, moving fried bread around the pan. He wanted her.

'I have to go in, I'm afraid.'

'You promised. It's your first day off in two weeks.'

'I know, but this is serious, were all over the news, we're stretched – and clueless. Just a couple of hours,' Adam lied, looking at his watch. Eight am.

'Back by midday,' she insisted, 'I want a day out with the kids. Like normal people have.'

Not the 'normal' conversation again. He backed off. She was a very understanding wife, he knew that, but you can push it only so far. Right now, he wanted nothing more than to crawl into her bath robe with her, feel her warm skin, hide away from the world. She knew it, knew him inside out, traits and all. Which was partly why they moved from Nottingham. Before the chump with two black eyes and a broken nose found out her jealous husband was a copper.

A sex pest who wouldn't leave her alone got more than he bargained for. Burnt followed him home, dragged him out of his car and left him bleeding on the cobbled street in St Ann's. A talking to would have been enough, but that would have taken diplomacy. You can't train the beast.

'I promise,' he hoped.

She turned to the pan, stabbed at the bacon.

'Bloody work. Sodding Ross. Fucking Griffin.'

'Whose Soddy Fucked?' asked an inquisitive four-year-old from the conservatory doorway.

'Adding more words to your son's vocabulary?'

'It could be worse.' It usually was, but this was a great moment to change the subject. He edged away from the cooker where Jackie held a spatula, she'd do more than flip bacon.

'It's good to give them an all-round education,' he added, returning to the table. 'Let's face it, when he meets the angry brat who's been moved from school to school with antisocial disorders, and any other mental health issue they diagnose kids with these days, reels off the foulest words known to man, our son won't be shocked or intimidated. He'll be able to deal with it.' He tried his knowledgeable look. 'And may even know how to speak his language.'

'Stick to the day job, honey, and eat your brekkie.' Jackie piled his plate with enough calories for him to forget about work ... for the next ten minutes.

***

The corpse of Tom Hacket lay on the cold steel table. A gaping wound to the throat, duly swabbed and cleaned, a lot less gory than the last view Burnt had. Something that always surprised Burnt, maybe the clinical environment, but laid out naked on the slab, prodded and sliced by the pathologist, the sight was never grotesque, just a matter-of-fact hunk of meat.

But a loss, to someone, and another statistic. Fifteen years he had served in the force. Not a long stretch, but enough to see the progression from child to the morgue. At first, petty crimes, just kids having fun. But they turn into cocky teenagers, pushing a bit of gear, which always gets ugly. Patches, turf, gangs, habits. Next, a proper stretch inside which should wake them up. But no, they get educated in there and come out with big ideas.

Then it's all over and they're on the slab.

Burnt listened over the two-way intercom, the pathologist giving her report as he looked on at her through the glass panel in the viewing room. DC James Ashley stood beside him, decked in a Hugo Boss light brown tight knit jumper, and slim mauve chino trousers. He'd changed his footwear, Barbour deck shoes.

'Sharp instrument, puncturing the larynx, trajectory shows the assailant was slightly smaller in height than the victim and the perpetrator. Right-handed. The bruising to the back of the head, scratches on the arms and back more likely to be from the fall, and subsequent panic of the attack.'

Veronica Esherwood paused the monologue as she moved around the body to the instrument table. 'As for the weapon, a sharp six-inch knife, still embedded in the neck on the discovery of the body. But what is strange, is that there seems to be alien collagen in the wound, a tiny amount that doesn't match the type from the deceased. We're running a DNA scan on the samples and waiting for the results to come back, which may provide a clue as to the perpetrator.' She peered at a small deposit on a tissue swab.

Adam scratched his head, shuffled a little on the spot, not sure of her meaning and not wanting to sound ignorant.

'Someone else's bone?' interjected Ashley over the intercom.

'Ten out of ten for the young detective,' smiled the usually grumpy pathologist, which was the first time Adam Burnt had seen her anything less than surly. Ashley gave a bashful look in return.

'I'll be with you shortly.' Veronica concluded the analysis and left the laboratory, picking up results from the graduate running tests for her on the specimen. She marched to the viewing room like she owned the place, she certainly commanded the space, pushed open the double doors at the end of the corridor, and greeted the pair who looked down at the corpse, waiting for it to tell them something.

'I'm afraid he's dead,' she said, smiling with sarcasm. She wore her blonde hair in a bun, the lab coat now lost, a slim-fit jumper and jeans augmenting her slender shape.

'Humour? From a pathologist? Never,' countered Burnt.

'We have our moments. Here's what we have. I'll mail the report electronically of course, but I know you boys struggle a bit with the technology. So, here's a good old-fashioned manila folder, hot off the press.' She plucked out her large-rimmed glasses, and with one hand on her slender hip, she studied the notes out loud.

Adam was beginning to warm to her. Ashley had certainly warmed to her, it was looking a bit too obvious. *She's the controlling type*, Adam thought. It made sense now. Irritable when not in control of the situation at the embankment, but now, in her environment, relaxed. Personality types were Burnt's speciality. He studied people without realising it.

'Let's have a look at what we have on the DNA report of a few foreign fragments found on the body – minute as they are.'

The two detectives eyed Veronica like two schoolboys waiting for their exam results. She enjoyed the attention.

'This is the part we were waiting on, and looking at this the closest known match for the collagen is …' She fingered down the sheet of paper. 'Baleen?' she questioned her answer aloud.

'Baleen,' the three repeated in unison, this time Ashley couldn't hope to score any points. Veronica removed her rose-rimmed glasses once more, part of the act.

'Of course. Baleen. I remember. I should do after spending three years part-time at the aquarium.'

'Aquarium?' Burnt pressed for more. The pair stood gripped, she let it hang.

'During my student years,' she continued, and smiled at the two guppy fish.

'It's whalebone.'

Burnt and Ashley looked at each other and back at Veronica, who now wore a smug expression, a puzzle for the police.

'Are you sure?'

'Sure as we can be. I'll re-run the tests myself to confirm.'

'Could it have been there already, before the attack?' Burnt knew this was a stupid question but had to ask it. Telling Ross they were looking for a whale in connection with the murder would be career suicide.

'Not a chance.'

***

The pair strolled across the car park, Adam clutching the manila folder as if it were sacred. They climbed into the pungent smelling Mondeo, Burnt threw the folder onto the backseat. It sat between polystyrene cups and takeaway boxes that had accumulated from an all-night surveillance operation.

'She took a shine to you, *young detective*,' quipped Adam.

'You think?'

'Oh yeah, I'm sure. You got anyone else in tow?'

'Er … can't say I have.'

'Well then, what are you waiting for?' He watched Ashley blush for the second time that morning. 'But I'd be careful,' he said, turning the key and revving the engine, 'she wears the trousers. She's a control freak, that one.'

'Oh?' That was Ashley's charm, his naivety. He just didn't know it. A tall athletic young guy, with a great career ahead of him, he should be knocking them dead.

'Anyhow, I'm not looking,' he said, scratching at his neatly cropped auburn hair.

'Course you're not.'

Their favourite DS interrupted them, Griffin's smooth voice. 'Meeting twelve pm, Lowestoft road, incident room.'

'Coming right over, Simon. Ten minutes.' He hung up. 'Can't stand that guy.'

'You were screwed with the chemist job. It wasn't your fault, and everyone knows that – Griffin too. He's exploiting you to win promotion to inspector.'

Ashley, loyal as ever.

Burnt revved the engine. 'All week he's been reminding everyone I went to the wrong address, and I don't get why he's so up Ross's arse all day.'

'You don't mean literally, do you?'

'Let's not start rumours, Ross is married, remember?'

'She lives with their daughter in California.'

Adam pulled away from the parking spot and eased to the exit barrier. 'You're a gossip, Ashley. Anyway, Mr Ten-out-of-ten, where are you taking her, and which shoes you gonna wear?'

Chapter 5

With the post-mortem report in front of him, Ross had enough to start the investigation. He extracted a couple of photos, fixed them to the wall with other notes of interest. He turned to the small team in the cramped, crime incident room, which consisted of Burnt, Griffin, Ashley and two constables. The unit only had six detectives at its disposal, and Ross hoped with the evidence they had so far, the two in front of him could tie this up.

'Around eight am this morning we arrested Graham Hacket. He's the older brother of the murdered Tom Hacket. Griffin, Burnt – I would like you both to interview him after this meeting.' There was a responding nod of approval by Griffin. He sat cross-legged, tapping his foot.

'But,' interrupted Adam, 'two witnesses stated they only saw two people, and there's evidence to suggest it wasn't a knife. Possibly some sort of whalebone.'

Griffin answered the question for Ross. 'One, a mentally unstable woman who spends half her life at the Saint Nicholas psychiatric hospital, and second, an old man without his glasses. We won't be able to take that to court, will we? It was a shambolic start. We need to maintain our reputation, and an early arrest calms the public,' Griffin said, not even facing Burnt, looking to Ross for reassurance.

'The fingerprints on the knife belong to Tom Hacket's brother, Graham. That alone is enough to bring him in,' said Ross.

'There's no way it was him,' Burnt said, arms outstretched. 'The pathologist said at the scene, the crime was committed an hour or so before we got there. We would have found blood at the house, soiled clothes, anything. I know there's a connection, which is why I got the place turned over, but it's not him. You think he would kill his brother and then be sitting on a couch an hour later with no blood to show for it?'

'It's worth an interview,' insisted Ross. He looked towards Ashley. 'I want you to speak to the neighbours, find out if anyone saw Graham Hacket at all that day, and what state he was in if they did.'

Ross dispatched duties to the remaining officers. With a lack of available chiefs at his disposal, he designated himself as the senior investigating officer. The deficiency of high ranking officers was something he brought up with superiors, but his charges would never hear him complain. He thanked everyone for their efforts so far, and requested 100 percent commitment for the case.

***

Burnt stood with his back to the wall, waiting on Griffin outside Interview Room two. No way was he going to collude in finding a scapegoat. Graham Hacket was an obnoxious teenager, maybe a crim, but not a murderer. You couldn't go ruining people's lives for convenience. Hacket had been inside for the last hour, before that in a cell for two hours, with no clue when the interview would start. The delay routine was an old but useful trick – especially effective with newbies. The room sat next to the boiler which piped out excessive heat, making the questioning uncomfortable for the suspect.

Griffin strolled up, straightened his lapels, clicked his pen, prepped Burnt for the interview. 'Okay, this is going to be good cop, bad cop. He's only a kid, so it's bound to work. You get the honour of being the good guy,' he said, sweeping his thick blond fringe across his forehead.

'Right, you are,' said Burnt. It suited him fine. They entered, the accused sitting at a table in the centre of the oven.

How different the boy looked after twenty-four hours; dishevelled, hollow-eyed, wearing a pleading look.

The aggression and defiance he displayed yesterday had vanished, sweated out of him. Graham had come down from the cloud he'd been bouncing around on. Loss replaced the spite – along with guilt.

Gregory Ravel, the solicitor requested at short notice from the CPS, sat next to his defendant, waiting for Griffin to start the interview. Burnt didn't recognise Ravel. He knew most of the solicitors the Crown Prosecution Service sent through the door, but not this one. Griffin, however, had known him for some time. It helped to scratch each other's backs now and again. The pay these public civil servants got for defending people who couldn't afford better, it was no surprise some of them would look the other way in an interview. For Ravel, a prosecution was another piece of trash in the bin. He sat – dressed in a formal, cheap, slate-grey suit – leafing through his briefcase for nothing in particular. He finally pulled out a pen.

The recorder started. Griffin was looking forward to getting his teeth into Hacket. It was moments like this Griffin cherished. His piercing blue eyes bore holes into the teenager; he paused before speaking, it was a skill that needed practice, no one better than a boy to try it out on. Griffin was tall, with the frame of an Olympic rower. Bullying petty criminals into confessions was becoming his forte. He removed his blazer, hung it over the back of the chair, swept his fringe.

'You know why you're here, Graham?' The teenager stirred, nodded. His short, thick brown hair stood up in tufts. Rushed out of his pit first thing, no chance for a freshen-up. Still wearing an *I Love Vegas* T-shirt with stains on the front that he'd clearly slept in. Love Vegas? He'd never even been near it. His goofy teeth carried a sheen of dull yellow.

Ravel, who looked positively bored, reiterated the charges, almost yawning as he spelt them out, smoothing his side parting. 'Do you understand, Graham?' he repeated.

Christ. What sort of defence is this? thought Burnt as Graham gave a slow nod.

Ravel sighed tiredly and nodded to the DS to carry on. 'My client is ready for questioning,' he said, like a mother sheep disowning its lamb.

'Let's start at the beginning. Where were you yesterday at around twelve noon?' Griffin walked around the table, unnerving Graham. On seasoned criminals, this technique would not work, but it would keep someone like Hacket, who was just starting out, on edge. Unfortunately, it would also serve to strengthen his resolve to counteract intimidation at future interviews, harden him in dealing with his unchosen career path.

'Just riding around the woods on my bike.'

He'd had time to make up a better alibi, had racked his brains for the last three hours. The boiler room had drained his courage.

Griffin paused for a moment, rested his hands on the back of Graham's chair. 'Of course, you were,' he said quietly. He continued his slow pace, circling the table.

'Just stopping to feed the ducks, no doubt, and do a bit of shopping for your poor old grandmother.' Griffin smashed his clenched fist down on the desk with such force, the boy jumped in shock.

'Then what!' he screamed.

Burnt flinched. The creepy solicitor almost fell off his chair.

'I wasn't anywhere near the place. Honest,' yelped Hacket.

Griffin pointed his finger at Graham, and made stabbing motions with each accusation. 'We have your fingerprints. We have a witness who placed you there. We know you had a fight, just look at your face.'

Graham looked with pleading eyes, 'Fingerprints?'

'On the knife, and we found similar knives in your house.'

'What witness? I wasn't at the embankment.' Hacket didn't want to explain his scars from the previous night.

Griffin ignored the question. There was no witness, Hacket wasn't to know that.

'You like knives, you like showing off with them, don't you?' Griffin leant across the table and stared hard into the face of

Graham. 'And you hated your little brother because …' He paused, walked round the back of the boy once more and whispered in his ear, lowering his voice before he verbally twisted the knife. 'He used to go see your mother. He spent time with her, and you didn't. She didn't want to see you, did she? She didn't have time for you, did she? But little Tommy. He was there all the time. She loved him, and after a while you got all jealous.'

Griffin paused and moved to face Hacket. 'It all got a bit carried away, didn't it Graham?'

Hacket's round, hollow eyes filled with tears. He searched the hot room for help. 'But I wasn't there. No one could have seen me,' he pleaded.

Griffin brushed this aside as mere detail. Circling again. 'Oh yes. We have witnesses, and your fingerprints.'

Griffin took his seat, ran a hand though his hair in self-congratulation, and made some notes. 'My colleague here, who's a bit nicer than me, will tell you how you can make things right.'

Adam took the cue. But the game was a bit sickly for his taste. Couldn't watch it anymore.

'Graham, did you know that if you're not happy with your solicitor, you can always ask for another?'

***

'What the hell was that for?' shouted Ross, glaring at Burnt. They were in the chief's office, Burnt under the spotlight. It was rare for Ross to lose it.

'Well, Griffin told me to be the good cop,' tried Burnt, although he knew he had overstepped the mark.

Ross sighed, lines under his eyes. 'My God, man. You're making things very difficult.'

'The boy was being bullied into a confession, sir. There is no evidence.'

'There were fingerprints on the knife,' returned Griffin.

'So he handled the knife at some point. Forensics confirmed that the perpetrator was smaller than the victim, plus there was no blood or soiled clothes found at the premises. It's not right – and who the hell was that freeloading CPS creep?'

'Ravel, if you must know. Gregory Ravel.' Griffin turned to Ross. 'He's our preferred solicitor, and willing to come along at short notice. He's ideal for defendants who're unprepared.'

'Most people don't *prepare* for being accused of murdering their brother. You want to give him a record that he will carry for the rest of his life to make your job simpler?'

Burnt was face to face with Griffin.

'This is getting us nowhere,' interrupted Ross. There was a tap at the door.

'Ashley, come in, join the party. Anything from the neighbours?'

Ashley trotted in, a little breathless. 'No one saw Hacket either leave or return to the house. But there is something you might want to know.' Ashley had their attention, and not because of his attire. Burnt was sure Ashley had changed clothes since this morning.

'I've got a bit more information on the coat worn by the dog-walker, Eric Haines. If you remember, his coat went to forensics.'

He pulled out his notes. 'The bloodstains examined don't match up with the scene as described by him.'

'In what way?' Ross asked.

'I haven't spoken to forensics directly. I know, however, that there was more than just blood splatter from the attack. There were markings on the coat consistent with a knife wipe. There would be no reason for the man to wipe any blood, he was about twenty metres away. Apart from Trench running into him, there should have been no interaction with the victims.'

'And they've just told you this?'

'Well, no. I spoke to Esherwood the pathologist, but she works closely with them.'

'And you followed up. Very proactive, Ashley.'

Burnt smiled to himself; he knew why Ashley had spoken to the pathologist in the first place, and why he had changed into a white polo shirt. Then his mind wandered back. 'Wait a minute,' he said, searching for his notebook. He pulled it out, flicked through the pages, stopped at the notes he'd taken at Haines's. 'Haines said he'd called 999 straight away – well, once he'd got back on his feet, after being knocked over by the other boy, Trench.'

'Yes,' Ross said, waiting for an explanation.

'Well, the first 999 call was for Trench's death – the road accident, not the embankment murder. There were a couple of minutes between the two 999 calls. That must have been, what? Three hundred metres to the bridge? About three minutes difference?'

'Easily,' agreed Ashley. 'It must have taken me five minutes to get there from the bridge. And it would have been another minute or two for someone to make the call from the traffic accident.'

'What was he doing all that time? Why did the call come in *after* the traffic accident?'

'Well, that's good enough for me,' said Ross. 'Let's get him in. Burnt, you stay away from that bloody interview room. Griffin and I will question him. I'll sort out a search warrant, you two have a sniff around his house.

***

Eric Haines sat in the same seat Graham Hacket had occupied an hour earlier, surrounded by dull, nicotine-stained walls and observed by a bored constable. It was a cellar, he'd experienced much worse, but the pair about to interview him didn't need to know that. It was a typical interrogation room, no natural light, little oxygen, hot and uncomfortable. Haines had seen it all before, but the pair of so-called experts on the other side of the door working out who was going to be good cop weren't to know. It wouldn't be that hard for them to dig out his history, maybe they would, but he wasn't going to help. He was taught anti-interrogation techniques in the army, today it might help. Talk clearly, don't slur, look the questioner in the eye when answering – especially if it is a lie. Make like you *want* to help, enthuse, don't look away from the bad cop. Hold his gaze. You're supposed to shy from the bad cop, and look to the good guy for help, reverse it, try your best to help – shame you don't know anything.

He waited, eyes closed, back straight, slow breathing, in a better place, hands on knees. Tap. Tap. Tap.

The interrogators entered. 'Before you ask, this isn't an arrest, but we are searching your premises in case there is anything we find that might be useful to our enquiry,' Ross said, with a beaming smile. *The good cop*, thought Eric. The pair sat opposite Haines, one wore a smile, the other a frown.

'Remind us of what you saw on Saturday afternoon, please, Mr Haines.'

Eric repeated his account. The bad cop glowered, cross-checked Eric's story with the notes made by Burnt. There were no contradictions and little else to tell. The blood markings on the coat must have been from Trench running straight into him. Yes, he did walk up to the victim, he had to put his dog on the lead and pull her away. Whatever the eyewitness saw from fifty yards could quite easily have been him crouched over poor Tom Hacket, and, no, he didn't know either of the deceased. He held out his arms, shook his head. He wished he could have done more.

'Why did it take you so long to make the 999 call?' asked the good cop.

'Shock, I guess. It took me time to get Madge back on the lead. Then I checked the boy to see if I could help him. I took a pulse.'

'Yes, of course. Live alone, do you? No wife or children?'

'My wife died of cancer five years ago. I have no offspring. My nephew stays over now and again, but other than that, I'm alone.' He drummed his fingers on the desk, blinking at Griffin.

'Why was there so much blood on your coat?' asked Ross, leaning over the desk.

'Must have been when I was checking the boy for a pulse. Before that, the other boy who ran away, bumped straight into me, knocked me off my feet in fact. He was covered in blood.'

'Mmm. Yes. Rather a lot of blood. What did you do in the army?'

Haines considered how much to give away.

***

Burnt rifled through the kitchen, rummaging in drawers and cupboards. It was a tidy house, not too neat, just a bachelor with a routine.

Constable Rawlings kept the spaniel amused, playing tug with a toy. It grated; Burnt wasn't keen on dogs, even the 'happy' ones. He glanced at the books on the table. Gandhi, a Post-It note wedged between the pages. He picked it up, no writing on the note, and read the first paragraph of the marked page.

'Forgive me but how can I redeem myself?'

'You took the life of a Pakistani?' asked Gandhi.

'I did,' replied the Indian man, on his knees in shame.

'Then give one back. Find an orphan who is destined for the grave and take the child as if your son.'

'Bloody heavy stuff,' Burnt said aloud, tossing the book back on the pile.

Ashley appeared from the stairway. 'It seems like he's had company. A nephew by the looks of it. A few clothes and CDs in the spare room, along with a "good luck with the new job" card, "Love Uncle Eric".' He waved the card in the air.

Burnt walked through the hall, stopping at the bureau to glance over the ornaments. He could hear the officer in the kitchen shouting baby names to his canine friend. Then he realised – the bone was missing. A gap in the velvet cloth that lined the display unit. 'Now why would he do that?' Adam asked anyone listening.

The answer was easy. It was between Rawlings' hand and the dog's teeth.

'Give me that,' ordered Burnt. He rushed to the kitchen, snatched the bone off the dog. 'It's evidence.'

The bone had been gnawed down somewhat, discoloured since yesterday, but worth taking back to the forensic lab. It might be a close connection to Haines and the murder.

The spaniel gave the constable puppy dog eyes – the constable gave Burnt the same. Looking at them both, Burnt felt he could explain better to the puppy. 'Bag and tag it.'

Rawlings, remembering he was on duty, placed the bone in an evidence bag, while Burnt and Ashley combed the rest of the house. Nothing – but a half-gnawed bone.

***

'Why would he do that?' asked Burnt in the car. They made their way back to the station. 'If it was a display piece that you liked, why give it to your dog? We'll have to see what comes back from forensics, see if it gets a DNA match.'

They scanned the streets in silence.

'I wonder,' murmured Burnt eventually.

'What?'

'Well, he has a nephew. Nothing unusual about that, but the Gandhi book is a bit strange, you know.'

'Oh?' replied Ashley.

'All that about protecting someone, he's marked it as though he needs to remind himself.'

'So we question the nephew?'

He shrugged behind the wheel. 'Can't do any harm.' The perpetrator was smaller than the victim, Burnt reminded himself. 'Yes, the nephew,' repeated Burnt.

They turned into the car park at Lowestoft Road police station. Eric Haines was leaving the building, mobile phone to his ear.

Chapter 6

Sunday 23 August 2015

One week earlier.

It was the actions of two men a week earlier that had contributed to the murder of Tom Hacket and Drew Trench. Actions these men might never account for, and that would affect the lives of others forever. Like most crimes, the cost never calculated, the victims never compensated.

***

The courier van ambled its way up the A12 from London. The headlights cut through the morning darkness, the driver stared intently in front with a pained expression, squinting through the early morning rain, using the rear lights of the vehicle ahead as a compass to Norfolk. One hour into the journey the dashboard had collected an empty packet of cigarettes, two cans of Monster, and an assortment of confectionary. Fag ash added to the litter, smoke hazed in the cabin of the van.

Safe FM played easy hits of the eighties and nineties – a genre of stereotypical white pop rock music, the bland radio station of choice for white van man.

A dank, musty smell clung to the pair, especially the passenger who didn't feel the need for regular washing, hygiene not on the top of his priority list. He was explaining to the driver, who was by far the more intelligent of the two, and had adopted the mantle of being 'in charge' when 'at work', now he had found himself a new title.

'So what I thought was, *the dice man*.' The passenger looked at his colleague for approval.

'Oh yeah?' the driver said, slightly interested. Anything to keep him awake, the caffeine had worn away too soon. It had been a late night and an early start so any conversation would be welcome. His sidekick could add comedy value on occasions.

'So this is how it works, right? When someone's wronged me, I give 'em a choice of how to take punishment. By throwing a dice.' Ronnie smiled at his new idea.

'Right.' *Play him along for a while*, Frank thought. He opened the window slightly, letting the stale air escape.

'What are the choices?'

'Ribs, fingers, nose. The higher the number, the worse it gets.'

'So what's a six?'

'Er … a broken leg.'

'How ya gonna do that, then?'

'I dunno. It don't matter. It's the point that counts,' Ronnie said, with self-approval.

Frank tapped the wheel. 'And what if they don't want their punishment?'

'Well, they ain't got no choice, have they? After a couple of doings I get a reputation, don't I? And then no one wants to try it on.'

'So you'd be the dice man?'

'That's right,' Ronnie replied, nodding.

'That's a book, you know. Not sure if it counts as plagiarism,' Frank gave Ronnie a hint of a smile.

'Oh.' This stumped the thug. Ronnie didn't want to associate with anything like that.

'Well, I don't want anyone thinkin' I'm wishy-washy.' He thought some more while Sting sung about a message in a bottle.

'Ronnie the Dice. That's it.' Pointing to the roof like he'd cured cancer.

'Ronnie the Dice,' reiterated the driver, nodding in approval. 'Sounds menacing.'

Ronnie was beaming. The driver repeated it, but this time with Ronnie's surname, he knew he loathed it.

'Ronnie the Dice, Lesley.' He grinned, taking his eye off the road to see the reaction.

Ronnie squirmed in his seat. 'Well you don't need the end part. Keep it short, like.'

'And if they call you Lesley, you can throw the dice,' Frank said, laughing.

'I'm gonna change it anyhow, by deed poll,' Ronnie countered, 'it's only fifteen notes. As soon as I get a chance, I will.'

There the conversation stopped for a while. Ronnie deflated into his seat, knowing he would never change his name, that would require a certain amount of form-filling and basic literacy. Writing eluded him.

Instead he kept quiet and listened to Meatloaf churn out 'Bat out of Hell' for the millionth time since its release. Ronnie's long, black greasy lank hair stuck to the side of his face, his big, tired eyes stared blankly into the emerging sun. He grabbed some nicotine and a hand full of fruit chews off the dash, lit a fag, pulled slowly on the filter, letting the burn settle inside. The smoke poured out of his nose, he looked like a baby dragon.

Ronnie's life so far had been unfortunate. He'd started out his petty criminal trade at an early age. Taught by his stepdad, it was not a good start. Trying to impress his adopted father, who gave most of his tips from the other side of bars, Ronnie soon became a juvenile at a dead end. After a couple of short spells, there was never any other way. The only real work he had done was labouring on a building site, which hadn't lasted long, caught breaking into containers at night and helping himself to tools. By the age of eighteen his future seemed assured. The route and cycles between jail terms were like a bad game of Monopoly. The dice would never roll kindly for Ronnie, struggling to make it past 'Go' every week to collect his £200. Apart from a few successful jobs, he found himself turned over by colleagues, and more often stabbed squarely in the back. Looking for the next father figure to impress usually cost him another stint in jail, another layer of contempt for all the successful crims that he'd heard about on the inside.

Ronnie was not exactly bad through and through, more misguided and let down by those around him. Crime was the only way for Ronnie, like a compass that points in one direction. He had limits. He hadn't taken a life, had a certain amount of decorum and decency – at a criminal level.

There was one bungled petrol station job where his colleagues were screaming at him 'to finish the bitch'. She had heard their names and seen their faces, he was in prime position with the right tool to smash in her skull. His co-worker had to take over and finish the job. Ronnie found himself out of work overnight. For some time, his reputation was tarred as someone you could not trust with serious work, lucky not to be serving a lengthy prison sentence after that caper.

That encounter forced the hapless rogue to work solo for a good while. Self-employed work was hard going and not so well paid. Reducing his criminal appetite to petty theft, a hard winter ensued. The highlight of that cold December was probably mugging Santa on Christmas Eve, who was on his way to a charity gig at a hospital. Ironically, Santa had stolen the goods himself, from John Lewis a week earlier, so without realising it, Ronnie had given Santa retribution that year.

The driver, Frank Allen, had a happier story, not just because he could drive legally. He was more astute than his counterpart – he was doing the stabbing in the back. Frank made it all look easy, keeping away from Her Majesty's, dodging Mayfair with the big hotels, passing 'Go' week after week.

Frank had no real excuse to be pursuing his current career. He'd had a steady background, a leg up into the family business, even if it was just working the market, there was a future there for him. But he knew better. Frank's problem was simple – he was a romantic. He watched too many gangster movies and yearned to be part of it. He mixed with crooked people, but only the professional sort. This was what set him apart from Ronnie.

Frank hooked up to crims with real jobs, who wanted to invest the clean money they had made, make better returns than the interest offered by a bank.

He liked explaining this to Ronnie, who was always keen to know more about their 'clients.' This imparting of knowledge gave Frank the mantle of authority. He could make the inroads, do the talking – get clients.

'Is it gonna be the same as before?' Ronnie asked, hoping for a bit more than instructions.

'Not exactly. Okay, we do the pickup and get to work at the lockup, but I've had a tip. If you want to make a bit of extra coin then we can make a right earner today, but we don't tell the doctor. Just keep this one to ourselves, a bit like claiming expenses.'

Frank smiled, adjusted his coiffed blond hair in the mirror; he was dying to explain today's job, but bided his time. He looked all of ten years younger than his unlucky counterpart. Ronnie tried not to appear interested, but couldn't help himself.

'What's the tip?'

'There's a little chemist that I've got plugged into my satnav. And there's no buzzer on it. The doors are wide open for us. There's something in there that will come in handy.' He looked across to Ronnie, waiting for a bite.

'I'm not believin' that, not for one second. Every chemist in the country is buzzed straight to the nearest grill. If not, there's some security firm that does the dirty work for them.' Ronnie loved to push the crim slang, it was his only area of expertise.

'Fair enough, we'll give it a miss then,' Frank said, knowing full well that Ronnie couldn't resist.

'How do you know?'

'I've got contacts. I've cased the joint without having to move a muscle, all from my lappy in my flat,' Frank explained while admiring his profile in the rear-view mirror. 'We don't do it in the dark, that just attracts attention. On Sunday afternoon in a dopey seaside town we pull up in our business van with our overalls on, and have a sniff round. We knock through the back door and help ourselves, it's a snitch. If we get alarms, we fly. I've got a kid up there who's been doing some sniffing for me, looking for a bit of extra, so I put him to work.'

Ronnie thought about this for a while. 'It's all a bit small time, innit? There won't be anything in the till, a few boxes of prescriptions won't fetch much.'

'We don't waste our time with any of that. It's the raw ingredients, Pseudoephedrine, that we're after. We can sell it back home. There are a couple of kilos in this chemist. It's not often this happens, but, as I say, my little helper has told me exactly where to find it. It's worth about a grand a kilo to any cook. That's it. Simple. We go straight to the locker room, no need to go near the till or the shelves. We lift and leave. No one will even know til they need to use it next week. We'll be long gone by then. Easy.' Frank tapped the steering wheel, brimming with pride.

'This *soo-do* whatever, what is it, and how do you know it'll be there?'

'It's the raw ingredients for crystal meth. It'll be there, and I'll find it. I know a cook who'll hand over two grand for it tomorrow.' Frank let the cogs whir round in Ronnie's head for a while.

'You see it's all a bit carefree up here, isn't it? No one's as suspicious like at home.' Frank hummed to himself as Bono reminded him of a street with no name.

'All right, it's worth a look, I guess. We'll see if it's an easy pickin', if not, we leave it.'

'That's right, we can walk away. We'll check it out after the pickup.'

'Yeah, so this doctor, then. What's he got to do with the pickup?'

But that was more than Frank was willing to give away. Ronnie knew this and resented it. He could never make such connections with anyone like his accomplice could. People like Frank would never share their knowledge with him, so he just shrank back, finished his fag, gave his brain a rest.

Daylight started to emerge. The clouds and drizzle gave way to the sun, which burnt through an early morning haze, leaving a crystal layer of dew over the marshes. Cattle meandered in the chilled air. This view, however, was wasted on the pair of onlookers.

'I couldn't live up here,' Ronnie said, looking out at the giant hay bales and ambling cows. 'There's nothin' to do.'

Kurt Cobain sang 'Dumb' to them both as Ronnie stared blankly out of the window. He wondered if each pig knew which hut was its own, or if it was content to sleep in any pen.

Chapter 7

Gorleston seafront. A crisp day with bright sunshine. The sea murmured, lapping at the shore, clawing at the sand. The tide marking a snaking veil of foam, glistening with each receding wave.

Timothy Levin focused on sculpting a life-size mermaid from the sand. Agatha observed her thirteen-year-old with admiration. His gift for art had always made her proud, she had passed it on, just hoped he could nurture it into a profession. The boy used a washed-up stick to give life to the figure, meticulously carving out detail. Beachcombers ogled the mermaid, astonished. He stood back for a moment, observed his work, considering what to add next. Bare feet digging into the sand, black cargos rolled up over his ankles. 'Wings, she needs wings,' he said, fell to his knees and began carving.

Agatha Levin sat on a blanket reading her magazine, constantly looking up to admire her son's work, brushing back that long black hair. The last ten years hadn't been easy, but things were improving.

Her husband's death had rocked her. It had taken time, but slowly, mother and son had fashioned a life without Gary Levin. Timothy had asked questions about his father's death, the nightmares came regularly, school was a drag from the start – the school bell would never come soon enough. The professionals explained his nightmares were natural. They said, 'Timothy has a deep fear of losing his mother. He is an only child with a withdrawn personality, which compounds his condition.' Counselling helped them both, time healing the wounds – as long as the scab wasn't scratched too hard.

Timothy joined his mother on the blanket, nestling in. His long dark locks flicked across her face, and she instinctively drew him close with a hug. The pair looked out to sea, large brown eyes narrowing into the sun that pulled away from the clouds. It was moments like this she knew she could speak to Timothy. About things that troubled him. When younger, he would keep his problems buried, but as he grew his talent for drawing channelled his feelings. At just five, while other children were drawing naive pictures of a house on a hill, Timothy illustrated figures with clawed hands dripping blood. The teachers complained his imagination was scaring other children. What he created was way beyond his mental age, but the content too disturbing to display on the classroom walls.

Years passed, the themes changed. An infatuation with drawing war scenes developed. Timothy created a character called 'The Taker', which moved across a battlefield in a hooded robe, searching for bodies to drag to the afterlife. His therapist said this was natural, his father was killed serving his country.

At primary school, children were scared of Timothy, although if asked, a child could not explain why. He was timid, but possessed a vivid imagination. On one occasion, at a birthday party, the clown asked all the children to draw him. So, Timothy scribbled away, just like the others. But revealed a character with fangs and tentacles – Timothy said the man looked like this behind the mask. Agatha took him home, giving embarrassed apologies to the family and clown.

A change of schools at aged ten helped for a while, but his classmates soon discovered Timothy was different, and it wasn't long before the bullying began. Fortunately, his art flourished. The theme changed from war to Nordic mythology, something the therapist recognised as a sign of improvement.

'So, Timothy, what animal am I today?' asked his mother.

Timothy rubbed his chin with amusement, looking his mother up and down. 'A polar bear.'

'Ha. Have I put on weight?'

'I read they're the most loving mothers.'

'Well, I never knew that.'

It was common for Timothy to substitute people for animals, depending on their characteristics and personalities. A few years ago, it worried her senseless, relating people to animals, but as he grew, it happened less frequently and only for fun.

'Well I think it's time this polar bear bought us some ice-creams,' she said, squeezing her son tightly. They jumped up, brushed sand from the creases in their clothes, packed the blanket into the rucksack, and walked along the curved tide line. They dipped in and out of the water, the cold sea biting at their ankles.

A spaniel bounded up, jumping around them both, wet paws all over them, tail wagging. They giggled and fussed the pup.

'Eric. I haven't seen you for a while.'

'Hi, Agatha. I've meant to pop round, but I've got my hands tied up a bit with this one,' Eric said. He tried a few commands to calm Madge, but failed. She was having none of it.

'I give up,' he exclaimed, flapping his arms by his side, grin on his face, unzipped coat flailing in the wind. Squinting into bright sunlight.

'Harder than kids, they reckon,' said Agatha.

'I'll have to take your word for that. How's things anyway, everything okay? You need anything doing?'

'Well, as you're asking.' Agatha tightened the scarf round her neck, 'I've got electrics on the blink, and as usual, the landlord won't move a muscle. You know any sparkies?'

'None that are genuine, to be honest. I can take a look. I've got a bit of work to do for my sis, I'll drop by after that.'

She veiled the sun from her eyes with the back of her hand, 'If you're sure, that'll be great, Eric. Thanks.'

'No problem. How's young Rembrandt?'

Timothy ran in and about the water's edge with Madge, the tide clawing at his ankles, the pup yapping in the foam.

'Just great. The last three months or so I've seen him open up so much more. You can tell from his artwork, he's leaving the dark stuff behind. His teacher said it's GCSE standard, the best in his class.'

'That's great. I can't remember Gary being much of an arty person.'

'No, though he always said he would like to swap a spanner for a paintbrush.'

They fell silent. Conversations always came back to Gary Levin. The waves and playful sounds of the living filled the gaps. Ten years on, Eric still found it difficult to look Agatha in the eye at the mention of Gary's name. He was there – with him when it happened, next to him. He spared Agatha this detail.

Agatha tugged a floppy woollen hat from her pocket, stretched it over her ears, asked if Eric wanted to join them for a walk. He made excuses, offered him round for a bite to eat. He refused – she knew he would.

'I'd better get going. I'll catch up with you later this afternoon, to look at the electrics.' He whistled. 'Come on, Madge.'

'You're a star, Eric. Thanks.'

The spaniel spun round and bounded over to her owner. 'Catch up soon, Tim, show me some of those paintings later.'

'Bye, Uncle Eric.' Timothy's voice swept away with the breeze.

Timothy returned to the curling edge of the incoming tide, lost in thought. His mother following, looking out to sea, hopeful gulls drifting overhead. Eric wasn't Timothy's uncle, but he didn't mind the mantle if it made the boy happy. Tim needed the security, having no father; his mother could only provide part of it.

Chapter 8

Endeavour cruised into the industrial estate on the outskirts of Norwich. Ronnie woke with a yawn.

'Wake up, sleeping beauty. There's work to do,' said Frank, shaking his head. He checked his blond streaks in the mirror.

The van stopped at the entrance to Zenacare. The security booth was unmanned, as promised. Frank plucked out his pass, displayed it to the sensor on the security post, and waited for the barrier to lift. Once through, Frank crept towards the mostly empty car park to the rear entrance, keeping his speed below twenty.

'Get the dispatch note then,' barked Frank, scanning the factory. This part always made him jumpy. Relying on others.

'Alright, alright.' Ronnie pawed at his baggy eyes, black hair stuck to the side of his face. He rummaged in the litter on the dash, 'Where is it?'

'It's in the glove-box, else it's down the side.' Frank padded his pockets while driving one-handed, stopping at his chest pocket. 'I got it, it's 'ere.'

'Calm down,' said Ronnie.

'Don't tell me to fuckin' calm down. Else I get me a new dwarf, and not Dopey. Just remember who set this up.'

Ronnie slumped into his seat, crossed his arms with a 'fuck-sake' sigh.

The paperwork was for back-up, in case they were spotted, or some jobsworth doing overtime got nosey. They show the dispatch note, stamped with Friday's date, explain they didn't know Sunday was out-of-hours, that they'll return tomorrow. A fresh note to courier some PC accessories, printed for them every week – never used.

Frank reversed into position, and the pair hopped out. Ronnie opened the rear doors of the van, and Frank stooped under the half-open roller into the deserted building. He pulled on a pair of rigger gloves, jumped into the seat of the forklift, started her up, and lifted the forks that were holding a pallet. A voice sounded behind him.

'Half an hour late. A bit sloppy, aren't we?'

Frank flinched. He made out the shadow of a figure behind a nearby container. His employer, he knew better than to argue. 'I had a bit of trouble.'

'The security guard'll be back any minute. I've always said that for this to work out for all of us, we must be like clockwork. In and out in ten minutes.' The man finished his cigarette, stamped it out, turned, and walked away. 'Get a move on,' he ordered over his shoulder.

'Will do, won't happen again,'

There was no more conversation, the pair moved the goods to the van and left Zenacare, just as they had every Sunday for the past month.

***

Within an hour, Endeavour trundled along Great Yarmouth seafront towards the outer harbour. It turned at a large monument of Nelson that stands scarred by the weather, the colour long drained from the statue, peppered in white from seagulls, even so, looking out to sea with dignity. Like the town, the monument stands degraded but proud.

Frank crawled to a group of lockups operated by small steel fabrication businesses, and eased on the brakes at the far unit, whilst imparting his wisdom. 'It's about being seen, you see. That's the best way to stay inconspicuous – hiding in plain sight. You think about it, right? If you go creepin' about at night in an unmarked old banger, that raises attention. But you turn up in the middle of the day in a company vehicle with your overalls and a tool bag in one hand, people just see two guys going about their business, they don't see anythin'.'

Ronnie nodded in agreement. He always did, but found the advice patronising. He had the most experience, although Frank would remind him he'd gained most of it on the wrong side of the bars.

Sure enough, no one took notice as they jumped out. Frank unbolted the lockup, stepped in, flicked the light switch, and barked to Ronnie over his shoulder, who stood posing with a tool bag, chin stuck into the air, doing his best 'work-like' look.

'Unload it.'

Ronnie sighed, dropped the bag, walked to the rear of the van, and wrenched the doors open, muttering under his breath how this work was beneath him.

The unit was the size of a residential double garage, with a half-height mezzanine deck. It had a tiny makeshift office-cum-kitchen at the back.

Once inside, Frank plugged in a portable set of halogen lights. They hummed to life as white light illuminated the room, making him wince.

Ronnie slammed two boxes onto a steel table with a groan.

'Be careful. And hurry up, we need to clean up,' Frank stated, wafting at floating flecks of dust. Before they unpacked anything, the area had to be spotless. He had spent his first week scrubbing walls and floor, applying industrial paint to reduce the build-up of dust, it was the hardest graft he'd put in for years. Maybe he should have dragged someone along to help, but it was the early stages. He'd only met the client once, so didn't want to scare them away with a dopey twat like Ronnie blundering around.

Ronnie trudged back to the van, slumped shoulders, wheezing for breath. Frank flicked the switch for the overhead extraction, and it whirred into life. The preliminary tasks were straightforward and carried out every time they visited the building. Once they had vacuumed, the pair dragged the steel table with the pill press to the centre of the room from under the mezzanine, and scrubbed it with detergent.

Frank, a little calmer now, stretched, adjusted his fringe, and checked his phone. He had couple of texts from his new, barely legal girlfriend. He'd played her along a treat. She thought she was dating Scarface. He sent a blunt reply, letting her know he was away all day on business. Keep her keen.

Ronnie brewed tea from the makeshift kitchen out back, Frank climbed the stairs to the mezzanine, fished out a few tools, and brought them down to sterilise.

The pair sat, supping their tea, listening to the noise next door.

'Sounds too much like real work, all that,' said Frank.

'Too right,' agreed Ronnie with a shudder. The grinding and welding echoing through the wall made him shudder. The last time he held a grinder he served two years – caught red-handed hacking into a safe after a messy post office job.

Frank slurped back the last of his tea, and slammed the plastic mug on the table. 'Time for work.'

The instructions were simple. Their unknown colleagues at Zenacare had carried out the complicated part of the process. Their task was to unpack the powder labelled with a medical trial name, add a mixer, then compress to a ten-milligram pill. The mixture needed turning through the press, its form in tablets placed into separate bags, 100 pills at a time.

The pair created a new identifier for each one-kilogram pack of pills with a label tool. They marked the bags with a brand name, along with the name BetaPharm. Some packages were already in tablet form, just needed stamping with the BetaPharm logo, even simpler. Today there was a slight change to the format. One package read 'DO NOT RE-LABEL'.

Frank had received explicit instructions about this. 'There will be one bag labelled HAL31. Pill it, and leave it at the lockup in the safe. Do not deliver.'

Frank turned the bag over in his hands, HAL31 plainly inscribed on it.

It was after the pilling when Ronnie indulged himself. He knew helping himself to the powder was a no-go, their employers would know how many pills should be in each bag. But powder caught up around the inside of the crimping section of the press, the bottom of the hopper never fully emptied when the cleaning took place, so a little waste was inevitable.

Ronnie swiped the dregs of the last pills on the press into his metal cigarette case. A dirty little treat. A sweetener for having to work a Sunday shift. Frank, however, was no user – that was a fool's game. He turned a blind eye to Ronnie's habit, if he kept it to himself, the excess not enough to sell.

Ronnie never knew what to expect, the effect of the powder was subtle. Last week, there was no buzz – no bonus. Week before he got a warm glow, week before that he slept the journey home.

Unbeknown to the opportunist, most of the powders were simple anti-depressants, a form of serotonin restrictor. Serotonin, the body's own chemical that gives the feeling of well-being. When its emission is suppressed, the natural supply increases over time, and the user is slowly lifted out of depression. Hence, regular use of the antidepressant is required – ideal for the pharmaceutical industry, not much fun for the occasional user, such as Ronnie.

The package labelled HAL31 was not a slow release antidepressant. It was in trial phase, and administered under supervision.

Frank was putting the HAL31 package into the safe, and setting the code, while Ronnie finished up in the kitchen, washing the cups and glugging back a pint of water. He reached into his breast pocket and pulled out the dented, tin cigarette box, opened it, licked a finger and dabbed at the gleaming bright powder. The crystals sparkled like fake diamonds.

Ronnie rubbed the chemical on to his gums, felt a tingle, and the back of his throat went numb. Better than last week. Pleasantly surprised, he took another dab, his lips burned, a hot shiver ran down his spine. Result. He necked another pint of water, walked back with a spring in his step to the van. Frank locked up behind them.

'Right, let's deliver to the hospital, but first a detour to a special little place. Let's see if we can score a little extra for ourselves,' Frank said, enthused.

'Fair enough, it's been a hard day's work,' replied Ronnie, a sheen of sweat appearing on his forehead, an extra layer of pungent smell added to his aroma.

Chapter 9

'Fiona, it's me, Agatha.' She gripped her shawl.

A moment's hesitation, then a cold reply. 'Hello, Agatha, it's been a few years.' Fiona, sipping on an iced tea, lay out on her couch, hair still damp from her shower. It had been a long session with her fitness instructor. The phone was on loudspeaker by her side.

Agatha felt a chill, rubbed her arms. Always a draught in this tiny kitchen. 'Twelve, before Gary's death.'

Fiona put down the cosmopolitan, stretched out and took in the view over the harbour. She liked to watch the yachts moor up, jostling for position, spotted the yellow catamaran and wondered if it was her husband's. Said she had meant to phone.

Agatha's voice trembled. 'No you didn't, sis. Don't lie. You still haven't forgiven me – after all these years.'

She waited. Thought she heard Fiona sit up, take note.

Continued. 'Christ, Fiona, you were missing for six months. What were we supposed to think?' It sounded weak.

'So you decided to shag my fiancé?' Still got that sharp tongue.

'That's … that's not how it was,' Agatha stammered, circling the phone, rubbing the side of her head. 'We were both worried sick, and it, well, just happened, we got close, you know. I'm sorry, honest I am. He would have had you back, too. You know that, don't you? We both wanted you back, just like before.'

'I can't talk …' sighed Fiona. She stood, paced over to the full-length window, arms crossed over her silk gown. She searched the Singapore harbour for a distraction.

Agatha wouldn't let it go, not after it taking so long to summon up the courage. 'That's just it. We *have* to talk. We haven't spoken for years, and where's that got us? I'm dying here, from the inside, Fiona. I can't do it anymore.'

'You need money? I'll wire you money.' Fiona's voice, faltering.

'I don't want charity. I want you back. I want you to visit, you need to meet Timothy. My God, he looks more like you than me.' Agatha's voice rose as she tried to patch things up with her twin in Singapore. A migraine crept up behind her neck, clawing the back of her skull, a panther pacing around her mind.

'I always wanted a boy,' Fiona said after a pause. 'Came so easy for you.' Fiona's voice, softer now. Maybe missed her sister more than she wanted to admit.

'Please... keep in touch, and next time you're over let me know so we can meet. Just come and see us.'

There was no other reason for Fiona to come back, their parents had died long ago. Deep down Agatha knew why she clung on to Gary after her sister went missing doing charity work in Sierra Leone. It was because there wasn't anyone else. He was the closest thing to her sister.

'He was all I had,' she said.

'I know sis, I know. I just felt, well ...' She couldn't finish, the call had come as a shock. She choked back the tears she had kept deep for years. Stubbornness her biggest weakness.

'Just give me a bit of time. I'll phone, I promise.'

Fiona cut the call, unable to carry on, stared out into the intense Singapore heat, put her head in her hands – then burst into tears.

***

'Mum? Are you alright?'

'Yes, darling, yes of course,' Timothy's mother said, faking a smile. 'I've just had an emotional chat, that's all. I've got one of my headaches coming on.' She brushed her hair back from her face, and pulled her woollen cardigan round herself.

They hugged for a while on the couch, his mother reassured him about all the things she needed reassuring about herself; the things she wanted someone to say to her, empty as it might seem, soothing as it always was, the comfort of sweet nothings.

She ran her fingers through her son's hair and gripped him tight. She needed him as much as he needed her. She had told herself year after year if they'd got this far, it would be okay. She couldn't blame her sister's resentment, she had taken her fiancé. More like clung to him, when all hope of finding Fiona had gone. Gary had been the closest thing to her.

'I'm going to lie down for an hour. You watch TV for a bit, and wake me if I'm asleep for too long, okay?'

Agatha slipped off the couch, and padded wearily upstairs, clutching the creaking banister. The two-up two-down terrace had character, but age with it, and was overdue a facelift. She was an artistic woman, the décor was eye-catching. The duck-egg blue paint, and soft, shabby chic furnishings covered the tired plasterwork, papered the cracks. Long forgotten electric cables jutted out from the wall, begging for attention.

Timothy walked to the kitchen and fixed himself some supper. Apple, cheese and biscuits. He took the plate into the living room, humming a tune to himself. He settled into the couch, and sat in near darkness, plate on knees, just the light from the TV bouncing off his face. He scooped up the remote, and flicked through the channels. Sports reports – old men droning on and on about what could have been. News – always ugly and unhappy. Soaps – people not behaving real. Reality TV – people being very unreal. Chat show – more pretence, more un-reality TV – dull, dull, dull. Where were the cartoons? Jumping endlessly through the channels, he finally found something to pause on – a documentary on wildlife in Canada.

Immediately captivated by the scenery, Timothy let the remote slip out of his hands, and fall between the cushions. He took in the incredible landscape. His imagination whirred. He and his mother camping wild in the mountains, him foraging for them both, supporting his mother as she had done for him all his life. That's what they needed – a move to the wilderness, to fend for themselves, and live in an old log cabin.

The vast open landscape welcomed Timothy to the mountains. The narrator's warm monologue gave the boy insight into a part of the world he could only hope to see in real life. But hope was enough, and the screen had it in abundance.

Caught in a warm spell, he nibbled on the light snack, the TV glare bouncing off his face.

The colour and scenery changed from mountains to the undergrowth. The animals from bears to magnified millipedes crawling over each other. He paused, slice of apple in hand, but stuck with it.

'Canis lupus – the largest wild member of the dog family, commonly known as the wolf.'

Timothy, defending his mother from wolves, hunting down their next meal.

The narrator continued in an intriguing, yet whispered, tone, 'The pack has a hierarchy, and is always with a dominant alpha male. Most game can outrun the wolf, so they use cooperation and cunning to catch their prey.'

Timothy watched as a deer grazed on the borders of a forest, nibbling away at the grass, unaware she was stalked by wolves, circling in silence.

Chapter 10

Must make an effort, he told himself.

'Here's one,' Burnt said, trying to make himself heard over the chatter and scraping cutlery. He sat at the corner of the ten-seater canteen bench preparing to deliver his joke over the clatter and rustle of his colleagues, yapping and scoffing. They hardly turned a head. Rawlings picked away at his lunchbox, discarding the lettuce with a grumble. 'It's all bloody green crap these days,' he said, over Burnt.

'Crime in a multi-storey car-park,' Burnt started, giving a smile, craning his neck, looking down the table.

Beano, or Super-ears to everyone else when not in earshot, cut in. 'Mine's taken to quinoa. If not it's couscous. Tastes like bloody sand.' He took a gulp of tea, looked to the other side of the table, left Burnt hanging.

'That's wrong on so many levels….'

Burnt *couldn't* fit in. He blamed Norfolk people, joked to Jackie they were living round simpleminded bumpkins, that it was a cultural difference between the Midlands and the East Coast. Deep down he was papering over the truth that caused him to ring-fence his family and isolate them from the big bad world.

Griffin strolled in, which cut the tumbleweed. Super-ears made room. Burnt, almost off the end of the bench, stood and made his excuses. Took his tray to the dispenser, feeling like a schoolboy with *kick me* stapled to his back. No Ashley to laugh at his jokes, too busy sniffing round Veronica. Burnt swiped his half-eaten burger into the trash and padded away while raucous laughter filled his ears – Griffin delivering his latest tale.

On the outside Burnt was the big bad cop. On the inside he was Mr Insecure. If anyone probed his childhood he would deflect it with a joke. Dig deeper and the humour would turn to anger. Persist and he would break down and melt in front of you. Only one had gotten this far.

He was the son of a crack addict and it had scarred. Dragged up by his grandparents from the age of six, he grew up a loose cannon loaded with anger who didn't know who to trust.

Through the double doors, stare fixed to the floor, he felt Jackie's phone rumble against his chest. The phone she thought she had lost – the one he'd taken without asking.

Jackie had him figured out. Had probed him to the point it had ended in tears. Burnt's tears. She had slowly stripped his outer layers of routine comedy and found the vulnerable boy underneath, the scars as fresh as yesterday. The scars of his earliest memory. Four years of age, waking on his stained mattress, jaundice streetlight peeping through the window cutting a silhouette of the stranger at his door. The stranger who knelt by his bed and told him to keep quiet.

A passing female constable flashed him a smile and asked why the long face. He just stared into the phone, felt a lump in his throat.

Another sly text.

Still thinking of Jackie. He couldn't trust her but he couldn't bear to lose her. No way could he face spilling his guts all over to another. The problem was, Burnt hadn't figured out Jackie.

Should he respond? His hands shook, he had to get out, get some air. He pounded across the foyer scratching his head, eyes glistening with fear. Hands now in pockets he barged the doors open with his shoulder and stormed onto the streets.

Not the familiar salty sea air, like when the wind is just right, coming off the east coast. Today, the smell of trash clung to the streets. Bin day. Gulls cackled, circling Burnt, spewing and crapping in his path.

A garbage truck rounded the corner and wheezed to a halt. Two trolls in high vis trailed it. They grabbed wheelie bins two at a time and hoisted them onto the truck; the shorter one, bottom teeth showing, was yelling about his weekend, about the creep he was going to break in half when he found him. Just waiting to catch him at it, he said. Told his pal, 'She can watch me crush his bones.' Said it with a grimace, and that she could keep the creep after that.

The giant with a bald head nodded as he grabbed the remote panel from the rear of the truck, square stubbled jaw jutting out as he considered the two buttons. The black wheelies flipped vertical.

He never knew how to approach it with her. It always came out wrong, his emotions getting the better of him, always ended with shouting and scaring the kids. Then it was the silent treatment for a few days afterwards, leaving Burnt to chew on guilt.

Burnt edged past the trolls, taking in the advice. If he wanted to be certain he had to catch her at it.

His phone reminded him he was a copper.

***

Two men in grey overalls, the gangly one clutching a tool bag, made for the steel gate.

Frank tugged a pair of large-handled pipe cutters from the bag and snipped the two padlocks. Ronnie covered his back. After a glance over the shoulder they were at the rear triple-locked door. The device for this was a little more bespoke. A large ratchet screwdriver fitted with a diamond-tipped drill and an eighteen-volt battery. Ronnie seized it, and with a scowl, powered through the lock in seconds. Frank gave the door to the tired chemist a nudge and it swung open.

Inside, they studied the control panel – 'alarm unset'. Frank mumbled praise for his informant, although more congratulating himself. The excitement started to replace the pre-job nerves, the buzz that never leaves even the most seasoned professional – the rise in emotion that can throw a newbie into hysteria, have them crapping all over the floor, leaving calling cards.

Frank woofed instructions. 'Pseudoephedrine. It could be in a bag or a drum. Don't go near the windows, stay away from the till, we're looking for a storage cupboard.'

The instructions irked Ronnie, he didn't like a younger mind telling him how to go about his business. The crafty sniff of powder confirmed what he already knew – this was *his* territory – *his* world – *he* was the expert.

He tiptoed around the small chemist, leaving Frank to rummage around in the back room, mumbling about finding the cellar. *The last place I'd want to be if it all goes wrong*, thought Ronnie. He bounced up the stairs, drill in hand, senses heightened, the soles of his feet tingling as the drug played games with his nervous system. Reminding him how good he was at his job. He felt razor sharp, not a sensation he was familiar with from the neck up.

Two doors presented themselves to Ronnie, almost as a test. He tried the first – unlocked. He stepped in. Nothing of any value – books, paperwork. He had a quick nose around, as unimpressed with the contents he turned away – just folders of business accounts. Maybe he'd return if there was nothing else of value found. He might steal some paperwork to sell on to a hacker.

He tried the second room. Much the same, but for a tiny set of stairs leading to a padlocked, half-size panel door. It was a loft of some sort – certainly worth a look.

Still holding the drill, he crept up the few creaking steps to the half-height doors that sealed the loft. He was sweating now, a mixture of anticipation and adrenaline. He paused at the top before inserting the drill into the lock. What could he hear? Was that Frank shouting him, asking for help? The mighty Frank finally conceding that Ronnie was the expert and asking for his advice?

Ronnie imagined Frank must have found the basement, tripped in the dark, broke his ankle, lying in pain, waiting for Ronnie the Dice to return. And return he does, along with a discovered safe they take back to the van. Crack it open, they never have to work again.

He drilled out the shrieking padlock, tried the handle. Also locked – this was clearly worth a look. He drilled through the handle, shattering the woodwork in the process, splintering the doorjamb. He pushed the narrow door. It swung open.

Ronnie had to stoop. It was pitch, he pulled out his torch and attached it to his head, pulling the straps tightly around the back. He twisted the light to illuminate the dusty room, and entered on his knees, crawling like an inquisitive baby into the unknown.

***

'The young deer ambles around the edge of the forest, easily distracted, she wanders into the open. She must stay close to her herd, but her mother is not in sight. The wolves circle slowly around the prey, waiting for an opportune moment. The deer is ever cautious and has an exceptional sense of hearing and smell, but at such a tender age her senses are not as developed as her elders...'

Timothy sat in awe, sketching the scene in a pad on the coffee table.

***

The light beamed from his forehead, picking out particles of dust in the darkness. Nothing. Hoping for something to show Frank for his initiative, Ronnie scanned the tiny space and crawled further into the loft on his hands and knees. He was a futuristic cyborg sent to reccy a dangerous vault. A class A, state of the art cyborg. Ronnie was certainly first class.

Warm shivers tickled his spine. Patterns danced on the walls. Once closer, however, the swirl vanished. Just dust trails sent to play with his mind – drawing him further into the emptiness.

At the wall, he pushed his finger into the dust, spelt out his newly discovered sobriquet: *The Dice has been*. He stood, grinning to himself like a lunatic. His new calling card. The brick separator stopped at waist height. He perched over the wall and discovered the attic space of the adjoining terrace house. Better still, they all had the same half height wall, access to all the lofts in the row.

Frank would be impressed with his ingenuity. The chemicals gave him enthusiasm, boundless confidence. The A1 cyborg scanned the area of next door's hidden objects, moving the light across toy boxes, suitcases, discarded computers and stereos. It clambered over the small wall, placed its foot on a wooden beam, steadied, and placed the right foot on an adjacent beam, pausing only to tune its sophisticated hearing to the frequency of the room below, executing an audio scan of potential mutants. The TV was on.

Ronnie shuffled across the attic space towards next door's adjoining loft, sliding one foot at a time on the two-inch beam, holding the roof truss for support. He always fancied skiing. That's what he should do, when he made it big, take off for a skiing adventure, the Dice hanging out in Switzerland with all the big shot crims, necking champagne and swapping tales. Fitting right in.

He concentrated on his slow march, taking deep breaths. A sneezing fit took Ronnie unaware. Dust flew up his nose, tickling the inside of his head. He put his hands to his nose, sneezed into them, creased over, stepped back, missed the roof strut, and stepped through the plasterboard ceiling.

***

Timothy glanced up at the ceiling – was that Mother? The old house regularly echoed, but this was a large thump as if she had fallen out of bed.

The wolves had the deer surrounded, Timothy waited to see the fate of the prey. The deer looked up, she was in trouble. She darted in different directions, surrounded by danger.

***

Ronnie lay for a few seconds, arms either side of the support beams. One leg poking through the ceiling. Staring at the inside of the roof. He had no Plan B, Plan A was rocky enough.

He breathed deep and pushed himself up. He sneezed again – his hand slipped off the beam. This time he crashed to the room below, plaster and timber falling with him, smashing his head on impact.

'Ronnie?' shouted Frank. 'What the fuck is going on up there?' Angry, cursing his informant, whom he had briefly praised earlier, he slammed down the latest dud container. He'd better check what his sidekick was doing. He followed the crashing noise, bitching with each stomp up the stairs. He checked his phone was switched on, he might have to make an impromptu call. He had a get-out-of-jail-free number ready, just in case.

Chapter 11

The circle closed around the young deer. It panicked, darting into the pack.

Timothy jumped, called for his mother, his big brown eyes blinking with fear as he edged towards the door.

Ronnie woke and looked around, rubbing his head. He cracked it on the bedstead when falling through the roof with the grace of an elephant. Plaster stuck to his sweating face. He was on a single bed, in a boy's bedroom, the walls covered with drawings. A lamp on the bedside table lay on its side, flickering. Smoke mixed with dust and plaster smouldered on the carpet. He hauled himself off the bed, and shook his head.

The lamp cracked under his leather boots, the plug socket shorted. Veins of wires drew strength through the decaying cables, current coursed through the house. A series of sparks jumped out of the sockets, fizzing from the walls. The brief lightshow dazed Ronnie, along with the mesmerising hand-drawn pictures in the bedroom. Voices laughed. Mocked.

Agatha groaned, regretted the sleeping pill. She sat up slowly, climbed out of bed, and put on her dressing gown. What was Timothy doing in his room? She rubbed the side of her head, the migraine now reduced to a dull throb. She tied the cord of the gown, leant over the bedside table, fumbling for the switch.

The lamp sparked, and the bulb burst, sending the room back to darkness. Agatha shrieked, turned, and stumbled to the door, tripping over shoes, with her arms in front of her.

Timothy opened the living room door, and was met with thick smoke energised by a gush of air. The electrics throbbed behind the walls, as if it had been waiting patiently for years, finally breaking free to consume their home. He shouted for his mother and tripped at the stairs. The carpet burst into flames around him, the light bulbs popped above his head. The fire alarm hollered. He cowered back to the doorway. The deer caught by the hoof, the wolves dragging it down, the pack descending on to the kill, wading in with hungry jaws – tearing at the flesh.

'You stupid clown,' screamed Frank from the loft space, his long face creased in a frown. 'Get up here now.' He knelt down, gripping the roof strut, offering a spare hand. Ronnie didn't know which way to turn; he backed out of the boy's bedroom. Frank poked his head through the hole in the ceiling, squinting into the smoke. 'Where are you going? This way,' he snarled.

Agatha stood, transfixed in horror. 'Where, where's Timothy?' she whispered, louder, 'Where's my boy?' Now screaming, 'TIMOTHY!'

Ronnie whirled round, his sweating face streaked white. Flashlight, still on his head, pointing upwards. The fire ripped through the staircase at speed. Timothy raced through the heat, scorching himself.

'Stay there,' she shouted. Timothy halted. The intruder was staring wide-eyed at her in a daze, blocking the stairs. 'Out of my way,' she hollered.

The drug was like nothing he'd taken before. It was an experimental hybrid. After the enormous initial feeling of well-being and sharp-mindedness, the user's perception alters, the thought process slows. Ronnie's thought process was slow at best, now he was mesmerised – but dangerous.

Ronnie saw a mad witch bearing on him. He punched it in the throat.

Agatha bounced off the corner of the wall with a crack, recoiled, and lurched forward. Ronnie followed up with an elbow to the face. Her jaw snapped. She sagged to her knees on the floor. Limp and lifeless, her body slumped at the top of the stairs. Ronnie looked on her, fists clenched, gasping for air, foaming.

Timothy peered through the smoke, eyes burning, throat screaming, transfixed. The heat forced him back to the living room. He saw the deer ripped to shreds by the pack. Chunks of flesh sliced off its back as it conceded.

The killer glared through the flames, bulging eyes, black lank hair stuck to his face, flashlight pointed at an angle, mouth gaped and foaming. He backed away as flames consumed the house. Timothy curled up at the bottom of the stairs. Wild animals exploded as the fire caught the downstairs electrical circuit. He passed out.

The front door smashed open. Eric burst into the hallway, tripping over Timothy. He grabbed the boy, tried to haul him onto his feet, but fell over with him into the living room. The flames gathered momentum, the feed of the fresh air blowing orange life into the house. Upstairs roared. Eric grappled with Timothy, who felt like a dead weight. He hoisted him up with a yell, felt his back twinge, but threw him over his shoulder. Blinded, he closed his eyes, and let his years of training take over. He held his breath, shuffled along the walls, using the back of his hand to guide himself back. Scanning the air with his other arm and stamping a foot in front of him, he edged back to the front door along the walls. He felt burning heat behind, fresh air ahead. He blinked his eyes open, trotted across the road, and laid Timothy in the garden opposite his burning home.

Placed two fingers on Timothy's wrist, located the radial artery, found a pulse, counted to fifteen, and did the arithmetic. Steady. He tore off his jacket and threw it over Timothy – and returned to the fire.

He got no further than the front door, it was a shield of heat.

'Agatha,' he screamed. He dropped to his knees and put his head in his hands. Then, in a quieter tone, 'I've failed you – again.'

Sirens whirred towards them, at the end of the road a police car flew past at high speed. Eric gawked in disbelief as the wailing noise faded away. 'Where is it going?' Eric said, dragging himself to his feet.

He pushed past neighbours, heard a crashing noise from the back of the house – then voices.

'Agatha?' he called, trying to get closer without feeling the heat of the fire.

Shadows danced in the window of the chemist, orange bounced from the glass. Squinting closer, he saw figures through the back. Could be Agatha. He scurried with a limp across the perimeter of the chemist, feeling his injuries for the first time. He found the car park at the back, but stopped and doubled over in a coughing fit.

The familiar whirring sound of the emergency services returned. Eric stumbled on, passing a grey van, still choking as he dug out a handkerchief and blew into it. Glaring down at the dark mess in his hands, he hardly noticed two strangers in overalls approaching. He looked up and took a blow from a portable drill to the side of the head. He spun, dropped to the deck, blacked out.

Chapter 12

The Assault 700 hovered above the monitor, swooped towards the single bed where McLeish lay sprawled, then ascended in jerky fits. Alexander McLeish whooped with each loop, trying to beat his personal best. The motor juddered, stopped whirring and fell to the lino floor, sending the rotor blades spinning under the desk.

'Bloody batteries.'

He lay there for a moment, one foot on the steel frame, revealing his Wallace and Grommet socks to the world. He grumbled, dropped the handset, scooped up the mini-sized basketballs from under his pillow, and threw them one at a time, high and wide across his office. The net above his cabinet remained untouched, and the balls ambled back towards the smirking doctor. He was pleased, it had gone well, he'd made inroads. Not much longer and maybe he could be getting out of this town.

He'd just had an encouraging conversation with Professor Thomas. Told him just how much the esteemed professor's articles on schizophrenia captivated him, how he looked up to him. Thomas took the bait, like a salmon springing up a Scottish waterfall, mouth wide open, swallowing the praise.

Alexander McLeish had gained a PhD at Bath University five years ago. He never completed the research, this detail highlighted in most rejection letters. After a year, McLeish lowered his expectations. Even then it needed his father, a well-connected barrister, to scratch the right backs. McLeish's only interview was at St Nicholas Hospital in Great Yarmouth. The isolated location attracted little interest – McLeish bagged his first job as a psychiatrist. It was not the first time his father had steered his profession, at each stage of academia he needed a leg up.

Through university he used his inherited funds to furnish the pockets of the brighter students in his classes, to help him complete the endless dissertations. It was a degree well paid for.

McLeish mapped out a patient rehabilitation plan to his employers at St Nicholas, and promised a great deal. He requested more staff to execute his vision. He hired undergraduates, claiming it was cost effective. And within six months he had carved out a research department for himself. The remaining psychiatrists left soon after, disillusioned with the way the hospital allowed McLeish such freedom. Each group of undergraduates was replaced with a new set, they never stayed long enough to question McLeish's work programme. The last remaining act was to take the mantle of head of psychiatry. The coup was complete.

Washington DC – he could make some serious coin there. Thomas and McLeish's father went way back. Surely, that would help. Just the parting piece of advice, as he hung up the phone on the old codger, niggled him. Like a piece of meat between the teeth that needs a floss. He was at the mirror now, his favourite place, examining his pearly whites, practicing his grin. He used the tip of his Bic to scrape away the leftover food, then stood back. He swept down his wispy ginger hair, licked his index finger, and smoothed down his eyebrows. He gave them a wiggle, his thin lips turning up. Then the sharp pain in his temple, like a needle.

He hissed, rubbed the side of his head with a grimace, and plucked out his breath freshener. He gave himself a hard blast, gazed towards the ceiling, and rolled his head as he exhaled with a sigh. The pipework croaked, murmurs in the hall grew clearer. Then the idea came.

You need a really unusual case, something that has not been diagnosed in a classic sense. Publish this prognosis, and how you aim to get your patients back on their feet, then your peers will respect you. You will have the choice of practices. Thomas had pioneered treatment in schizophrenia for the last two decades, and, although had come under criticism in the early years, now was highly regarded by most in the business. McLeish likened himself to Thomas in his early years, bemoaning how his own hypnotherapy was met with sarcasm by the antiquated staff at Great Yarmouth. And reminded Thomas how he and his father went way back.

McLeish jumped into his chair, and logged on to his PC. He scrolled his inbox to re-read an email, earlier disregarded.

It wasn't obvious this was a doctor's room. Other than a few books on medication, a white coat hanging on the wall, it could have been a teenager's bedroom. The dartboard was for relaxation, the remote-controlled helicopter – an alternative therapy for some of the more dextrous patients, mini basketball court – therapeutic, single bed – when overworked.

He rubbed palms, and crouched over the monitor, conjuring a reptile as he took in Mrs Warrington's message.

Dr McLeish,

I am the social welfare officer for the Norfolk district and have recently taken responsibility for the care of Timothy Levin.

Timothy is a patient at James Pageant Hospital and was involved in a fire at his home. His mother, consequently, tragically died.

I am concerned about Timothy's welfare. Although physically sound, I am unsure of his mental state. He is not communicating and seems to be virtually catatonic.

Police are still investigating the cause of the fire. At present, the police consider Timothy as a potential suspect, until further investigations can reveal otherwise. So far, we have not permitted police to interview Timothy.

I am trying to determine any next of kin, but cannot find any living relatives. I have discovered Timothy has previously had therapy, and I am going through the legal process of gaining control of the case notes. Unfortunately, the therapist is no longer practising.

I hoped you could provide some support for Timothy, and assess his mental state.

I attach an assessment. If you think you can offer any assistance, please contact me at your earliest convenience.

Regards,
Emma Warrington
Social Officer
Norfolk and District Council

'Hmm…' hummed McLeish. 'What I need is an unusual case,' he said to the empty room, giving the mirror a smile.

He pushed back in his chair, picked out a tennis ball from the drawer, bounced it from wall to floor, catching it in a rhythmic flow. Finishing with a dunk into the mini basketball net.

He straightened and typed, the practised grin turning to a sneer. He returned the mail, requesting they relocate Timothy to his hospital. To carry out a full and accurate mental health assessment, McLeish would need the facilities of St Nicholas Hospital, this would ensure the best care for Timothy.

Once finished, McLeish stood up, donned his white coat in front of the mirror, and smoothed down his hair once more, pausing to rub at the flaking dry skin on his forehead, which floated briefly then rested on his shoulders as he strolled out to deliver duties to night shift.

Chapter 13

Timothy squeezed his eyes shut. He wanted no interaction, to explain nothing. There were no answers for *him*, so he felt no obligation to give any in return. The only person he loved was gone, forever. He owed the hospital nothing.

Since the catastrophe, there had been nonstop examinations and questions. At first, he had answered their queries as best he could, but he soon came to realise that no one really cared. The gaps between sessions became longer, each session a different person asking the same questions, each time turning their back on him – a one way street. He was alone.

Voices echoed around the ward, he felt the occasional prod and poke, something attached to his arm. He was lifted from his bed onto a patient trolley, wheeled through the corridors, bright lights shining onto his eyelids, briefly darkening at each set of doors.

Footsteps, electronic sounds, then a cool breeze on his face. He was outside. The movement stopped with a shudder, doors slid open, someone spoke into a radio, a metallic response babbled back. He was hauled into a confined space, and behind him doors shuddered shut. The ambulance drove from James Paget to St Nicholas Hospital.

Timothy sensed he was alone, but kept his eyes closed. The rocking motion of the vehicle relaxed him, the honeyed murmur of the engine slightly soothing. He fell into semi-consciousness, the present becoming more distant, his mind fixed to the only person he loved.

He recalled the warm memories of his mother's smiling face, held them lest they get lost. Sometimes, he would be talking away, babbling, explaining something, probably trivial, her nodding in her understanding way. He would look up to see her beaming with pride, which she followed up with tears and a hug. It had always surprised him, he would need to ask what he had said or done that was so special. He never understood the answer, so could never replicate it. It just happened, on occasion. Moments he now cherished.

She was dancing in the living room to one of her favourite oldies, him on the couch giggling at her moves. He drifted further.

She waved for him to join her. At first, he refused, but she goaded, so he stood and started clumsily moving his feet, trying to mimic her. She took his hand and held him close, spun him round, reeled him in, let him go.

That was when a beautiful sensation took hold of him. He saw his mother drift off the ground. He was mesmerised, nerves filling his heart. His mother's smile encouraged him to try it. He didn't know how or why, but he took to the air.

She turned and flew. He followed, through the roof. There were no boundaries, no limits to what they could pass or see through. They soared into the air, swooped in and around each other, laughing, playing like children.

His mother was faster, nimbler. She changed direction at speed, while he was gauche and inexperienced. He had so many questions, but she gave him no time, just turning her head to give a giggle. He wanted to catch her, to hug her. How long had she held on to this secret? This was euphoric.

They flew over buildings, skyscrapers, cathedrals and monuments with unbound freedom. Shadows lay on the ground, outer shells discarded. They left the cities, and descended onto a valley, the sunlight danced on the lake below. Over open seas, the spray on their faces. At a beach, Timothy felt the sand between his toes, pushed into the air, landed on the other side of a sand dune. Each hop boundless.

She took to the skies, he followed like a disciple. The scenery changed to a forest, his mother darted between the pines, looking back and laughing as Timothy snagged on the branches. He was losing distance, the greenery grew thick, the forest, turning to a jungle.

He lost sight of her, became anxious, and fell to the floor. The ability to fly suddenly lost, without his mother he just couldn't do it, as if he needed to feel elated, euphoric before he could take to the air. He needed her.

He lay crumpled on the floor, covered in pine needles. His skin started to itch, he felt trapped, couldn't move. He writhed, tried to scream, but could not make a sound. He searched for his mother, through the veil of green.

A spider crawled onto his leg and turned its head towards him. He thought he saw it smile. It crept further up his body, its hairy legs probing him with each step. Again, a glint of a smile, but not one that gave comfort.

It had a face, a small, human face. The spider grew, the eyes bulged, thin lips mouthed at him, wispy red hair grew out of its head.

'Medication time. Medication time, Timothy.'

Chapter 14

Timothy woke and searched the room in panic. From the ginger-haired man facing him, to cables attached to his body. His mouth was dry, his body ached. A monitor by the bed pipped his heartbeat.

McLeish finished administering the hybrid of ayahuasca, dextroamphetamine, and Lysergic acid diethylamide. He then placed the saline drip back into the boy's arm and watched the reaction on the monitor, noting the results.

The sine wave on the oscilloscope peaked and troughed. The gaps between fluttering signals held McLeish's attention. He scribbled, cocked his head, observing Timothy like a freak in a circus, who lay with sensors taped across his forehead, falling to his shoulders like plastic white dreads.

McLeish gave Timothy a blank stare. 'I'm Doctor McLeish. You are at St Nicholas Hospital. We're here to help you with your problems and make sure we can get you back to full recovery.'

Timothy glared open-mouthed, scanned the room once more, then back to the tubes, his panic turning to fear, then back to the man grimacing at him with thin lips. 'Spiders,' Timothy whispered.

The doctor, smiled, whispered to himself, scribbled. He huddled round his notepad with hunched shoulders, flecks of his dry scalp flaked onto his white coat.

Timothy turned, puked bile over the bed, and fell back, the burn settling in his throat.

'Nausea,' said McLeish. Timothy grabbed at the man's lapels. 'It's you.' His grip was weak, McLeish brushed his arm aside and stood up.

'Attacking me now?' he tutted, shaking his head. He scratched at his forehead, stretched his back and stood, hands on hips, white coat pushed back, showing bright red braces and showing a cold grin. 'We will have to restrain you then, Master Levin.'

McLeish dropped to his knees, pulled the bed harness from under the mattress, and began strapping the boy down. Timothy made no attempt to fight, but lay back slumped on the hard bed.

'Probably all those drugs you've been taking, Timothy.' McLeish, kneeling by the bedside, eyes lit up like two tiny worthless, fake, tin coins.

McLeish slipped the leather strap through the buckle over Timothy's legs, 'Wait till I tell Mrs Warrington. She thought you quite the harmless victim, didn't she?'

He stood, tightened the buckle. 'You had a feeding frenzy on recreational drugs and lost control.' He moved to chest straps and repeated the tugging, leaning over close. Timothy could smell his sweat. That-,' yank, '-will be-,' yank, '-my report.' He came close enough for the boy to taste his breath. Thin wisps of ginger hair floated over his reddened face. 'The drugs you have taken may have a permanent detrimental effect. You're not safe. You need my help.' He pointed a finger to the ceiling and gave a cackle, then took a moment to catch his breath. Feeling good, feeling alive. 'Oh don't worry. I've got the remedy.' Now at the monitor, playing with the dials, he captured the image, saved it to file, and tugged out the USB stick. He glanced over his shoulder. 'You're very lucky, you will be the first to try it.'

He thumbed his braces, swept back his hair and switched off the monitor. Then yanked the drip from Timothy's arm, tore the sensors from his forehead, all whilst humming the latest tune that had crept into his mind like an ear worm. He detached the cables and buried them in the bottom drawer of the caddy. 'Perfect, that should do it.'

Timothy couldn't speak. The mediation was taking hold, the room was swimming, McLeish dancing on the waves.

An inquisitive face peeked through the rectangle panel in the door. Julie Caulk had her nose squished up against the glass.

Greasy tails of hair hung over her pock-marked face. She glanced between the doctor and the bed.

McLeish opened the door. 'Mrs Caulk, what a pleasant surprise.'

He rammed the medical caddy through the doorway, blocking her entrance.

'Why is he here? What's he done?' she said, craning her neck round the doctor.

'He is here to get better, just like you.' He locked up behind him in a hurry. Caulk jumped at the door, stuck to it like a rubber stick-man thrown at a wall, and spelled out the notes on the edge of the bed.

'TIMOTHY…LEVIN. NO MEDICATION,' she spelt out slow and loud.

'Not yet anyway,' replied McLeish, turning to the corridor.

'Your coat is dirty, let me take it to the laundry,' shouted Caulk.

McLeish wagged his head, shoving the trolley, offering his sneering profile. 'You don't get to wear it that easy. You have to earn it, remember?' he returned over his shoulder.

McLeish had, on occasion, allowed Caulk the privilege of wearing his white coat. It was a little reward in return for good behaviour. She took it seriously. Checking all the patients had taken their medication on time, talking them through their problems. She took on the mantle of in-house agony aunt.

'I'll make sure he's okay,' she said, once more squashing her face against the glass, eyeing the helpless soul in the bed.

'You do that,' McLeish muttered to himself, head held high, as a few poor souls beheld him as he parted the thin crowd with the caddy.

Caulk slowly mouthed to Timothy, 'Don't worry. I will watch over you.' Which she did – right up until her next round of medication.

Timothy watched the colours swim in front of him. Shadows threatened, creeping across the wall. A creature at the window in the door resembling a drooling goblin spoke in a foreign tongue. Where in the hell was this?

He recalled the tragedy. The smoke, the fire, a man standing over his mother who lay crumpled on her knees. His mother – gone forever. He was alone with his demons. There to remind him of his failure, to punish him for being weak. Leaving his mother to die.

The twisted face at the door, melted. Shadows grew talons, morphed into trees, creeping to his bed, tugging at the covers, scratching at his feet. Cold breath licked his body.

Timothy, praying the image would leave him, closed his eyes. The room spun, clanging of pipes augmented and reverberated in his head as he slipped away.

Pulled backwards, scraping the walls of the narrow corridor, helpless. His mother stood at the far end, piteous, reaching out, pleading.

He tumbled backwards, weightless into a blanket of fog. Deeper.

He descended through mist, peering into the emptyness, searching for his mother. The outline of a face appeared from the grey, vague at first, detail emerging slowly. It was a face he recognised, but not his mother. His sketches. His impression of Valhalla, the nordic goddess, faced him. She smiled, but receded into the cloud. Another face formed, this time Odin. Again, a portrait Timothy made, pinned to his bedroom wall. The Viking god looked stern, said nothing, regressed into the bleak cloud. All his favourite images presented themselves in turn, Ran – goddess of the sea, Guthrum – the king of the Danes, Raven perched on his arm.

Grey turned to white, indistinct murmering changed to coherent sounds. Voices.

Timothy tried to sit up, but the leather straps gripped him – he sank back. He looked at the window, the sun spied through cracks in blinds, slits of light cut across the covers. Reality.

The viewing glass in the door now clear, apart from occasional heads that moved past, some fast, some slow. He needed to escape.

Timothy listened to the strange moaning of the pipes under his bed. Voices came closer, whispers of his name, the door opened.

Trust no one, remain silent.

Chapter 15

'Out! Out! For one last time – out!'

This time she threw his trainers. He stumbled down the stairs of the flat, retreating to the outside door as footwear bounced off the back of his head.

'And take all your crap with you.' Just in case he hadn't got the point already.

'Oh come on, Lola. It's just a bit of weed.'

'No. I told you, no more of that shit. The flat stinks of it, and as soon as my back's turned, you're at it, getting wasted, night after night with your mates,' she said, dragging on an imaginary cigarette.

She pointed to the outside door from the top of the stairs, her Italian tongue rolling into overdrive. 'I could smell it from outside before I even came in. You know I can get a spot check any time. I'm trying to get a job in a school, for God's sake. You gonna ruin everything.'

There was no stopping her, Mario knew that. Best let her cool down. As much as he loved her Latin flair, whenever she boiled over everyone got scalded, and at present she was furiously steaming. She stood poised at the top of the stairs, long, dark hair flying wildly around her face as she gesticulated wildly, arms grabbing imaginary hand grenades out of the air to hurl at Mario.

Her night shift had finished early. He had dozed off on the couch – as usual, hadn't got around to tidying up the mess – as usual. His pal had been around with enough recreational drugs to relax with into next year – as usual. That wasn't so bad, could be tolerated by his hard-working girlfriend, but finding two kilos down the back of the couch, which he should have hidden a bit better, popped the Italian's cork.

'Look, we can sort it,' he tried.

'I will sort it. Your stuff will be in the hall when you get back. Take it and go. That was the last warning.'

She stomped back into the flat, and slammed the door, leaving him standing in the stairwell, with the downstairs ginger Tom that had been sitting watching the fight, in between licking its legs, now content to stare at Mario with an 'I told you so' face.

'You too, eh?' Mario turned out into the sunlight, rucksack in one hand, his sandstone quilted Carhartt in the other.

He squinted into the early morning sun, scratched at his collar-length mop of wild brown hair, pulled on his Carhartt, pushed his feet into his All Star sneakers, and stretched with a yawn. He sat on the kerb, searching through his rucksack of worldly possessions. Nothing. Just roll-ups, his wallet, a smoothie – and two firmly bound cellophane bags of homemade marijuana. He only had time to pack essentials.

Mario remembered waking, Lola slamming the door, and before he knew it she was screaming at him – two bags of grass gripped in her hands. She had thrown them at the TV, still switched on to the repeating episode selection of *Breaking Bad*, he had been lulled to sleep by the lullaby.

In a hurry he had grabbed the necessaries – the grass. It was not his to lose, it was Frodo's, Frodo who lived at home with his mum. Being a pal, something he was good at, he promised to keep the packs safe until they could sell them.

Frodo's mother would check over all her son's possessions when he was out, regularly turn his bedroom upside down. It was like living in a boot camp, according to Frodo, whose few skirmishes with the law had cost him a criminal record from the age of sixteen. She was trying to look after him in the best way she knew how, but Frodo was trying to dodge being looked after the best way *he* knew how. Occasionally he turned to Mario for help, like last night when he discussed his new business venture. An endless supply of weed that needed shifting.

The pair had sat back on the couch, laughing about all the cash they were going to make, and like stoned magicians, tore into the merchandise, turning money to smoke.

Mario had had a few last warnings from Lola, so he hoped this was no different. They had met at the University of East Anglia two years ago. He, dropping out, she, completing her final year. He convinced her to stay in the UK.

She was taken by his carefree persona, he was an open book with arms spread wide to embrace the world, a true free spirit. She, more academic and studious.

Lola was expecting a visit from her mother in northern Italy, and Mario knew she would be jumpy leading up to that, the need to show what she had achieved since uni.

Mario intended to get a better job, but it could always wait until tomorrow. Lola had told him countless times to get his act together after flunking. He had told everyone about his master plan. 'Yeah, this internet business is starting to take off,' he'd say, just not telling how long the runway was. Anyway, he'd got a job. Delivering industrial paint. So what? 'It's a job,' he would cry, 'and I get a van. That's a company vehicle, that is.'

Right now he was glad for it. Ten minutes after waking up, he was homeless.

A truck full of scaffolding rattled past. The pierced driver with the window wound down poked his head out and wolf-whistled to a young mum in a short skirt pushing a pram. She returned a bashful smile.

Mario plucked out his keys and climbed into the van. Started her up, waited for the growl, and shook away the cloud behind his eyes. Ripped the foil lid off the now-warm smoothie, took a glug, and sat it in the beaker holder. Gave the diesel engine some welly, jacked his phone into the Aux-in, cranked up the drum 'n' bass, and drove off to work – early for once.

Chapter 16

McLeish stood with Burnt, staring through the two-way mirror into the recreational room. 'Visual palinopsia,' he declared with delight.

Timothy tapped at a touchpad twinned with a dual screen next to McLeish. A cognitive test to establish his mental age and IQ.

'In other words, visual perceptive abnormality disorder,' the doctor continued. More grinning.

Burnt took a guess. 'Hallucinations, you mean?'

'In layman's terms, yes, but it's more intricate than that. This is trauma-based, the child is dealing with the shock inwardly, probably due to his personality and previous experience of fatalities.'

Burnt scratched his temple with his pen, rocked on his heels. *Last thing I need is an egomaniac blabbing all day.* He wanted to speak to Levin. The doctor continued, wagging his finger at Timothy through the glass. 'I had a patient a few years ago with a similar disorder. Olfactory hallucination, more commonly known as phantosmia. The detection of smells that aren't present. The odours in phantosmia vary, may be foul or pleasant. Quite incredible. With Timothy, it's visual perceptions that become distorted. Like phantosmia they vary from person to person, depending on the personality.'

He paused for a response. 'But I haven't seen anything this acute. This is rare. The visions and perception manifest differently for every person, depending on the fears and problems. In this case, compounded with drugs use.'

Timothy stopped. The monitor beamed a bright green tick, along with his IQ score, higher than average.

A nurse removed the pad, and Timothy turned to his drawings that were scattered on the table. He lifted a charcoal, studied it briefly, as if unsure, then scribbled wildly.

Burnt raised an eyebrow. 'Are you sure? That he was using drugs, I mean.'

'We ran a blood test as a matter of routine when he entered the hospital. I can give you the report. It shows LSD, amphetamine, novocaine and more, a real cocktail. Was the mother a user, maybe? Unable to look after her child?' McLeish said, shrugging his shoulders.

'We have no reason to suspect that. There is no medical or criminal history in the family, and the "incident" was a bungled robbery.' Burnt thrust both hands into his suit pockets. It was the smartest suit he had, which was probably why he felt so uncomfortable. Jackie made him.

'At a chemist,' countered McLeish.

Burnt fixed McLeish a cold stare. 'Next door to the victims.'

A white coat, in her mid-twenties, came between them. 'We don't want to assume anything in too much of a hurry. I haven't had a chance to talk to the boy yet.' She had a floppy, lama fringe pillar-box red, and holes in her nose and ears. She wore brown Doc Martens – the dressed-down-punk-at-work look.

'I'm Bryony. Bryony Joy. I'm a junior psychoanalyst, how do you do?' The politeness surprised Burnt. She didn't wait for a reply. 'I didn't know we had a new intake until this morning.'

Bryony had been searching down McLeish, wanting to know about Timothy. As usual, McLeish told her nothing of his arrival. She perched by the observation glass and studied Timothy, pushing at her fringe, and scratching at the eczema on the back of her hand that flared when she became anxious.

'Yes, we have our very own graduate Sigmund Freud.' The doctor gestured to his understudy.

'This work placement is part of my doctorate,' Bryony returned, louder than necessary, still eyeing Timothy.

'Everything's solved with talking it through,' smiled the doctor to Burnt, but rolling his eyes at Bryony.

'And you're the psychiatrist?'

'Yes, and the head of the department.' McLeish straightened his back.

'I'm afraid us old fashioned ones prefer proven medication for the mentally impaired, but it's all a matter of opinion.' He held a canister of freshener to his mouth and gave a blast.

Bryony turned to them with narrowed eyes, taking the bait, scratching that endless itch. 'Well, it depends on the condition. If what you say is correct, and it is indeed trauma-based, then counselling is more likely the best course of action for the first few weeks.'

Nine months ago she wouldn't argue, would succumb to the patronising smile, but the McLeish act was starting to grate. Week one of her placement, he tried it on. Mistake. Anyone slightly enlightened could see it was inappropriate on more than one level. He was not her type. She made sure he overheard a close conversation with her girlfriend to spell it out.

So far, from what she could glean from the scant case notes of Timothy Levin, therapy was the starting point and best policy, medication, much further down the line, if at all.

Burnt nodded in agreement, although he would be the first to admit he was no expert in this field. Taking the evidence so far, one thing the boy needed was a hug, not more drugs.

'So, you have started treatment?' he asked, notepad in hand.

'Oh no,' insisted McLeish, waving away the notion, 'I was requested by social services to simply analyse Timothy, and asses his condition. Bryony will assist with that, I'm sure.' Bryony turned away, had another paw at the back of her hand.

'I will give a full report to Mrs Warrington,' said McLeish, resting his gaze on Timothy.

'Of course, I'll make my recommendations. I think there is every chance that I can help him – with the correct medication.' The thin smile made an appearance again.

Since the fire, Burnt hadn't been able to get near Levin, and had no leads regarding perpetrators. It had been all over the news that the police drove to the wrong address. He was trying to get any clues he could, make up for lack of progress – the timid boy on the other side of the glass was key.

'Can I talk to him now?' Burnt, already making for the exit.

'Of course. We are committed to working with the police.' McLeish hurrying behind, saying, 'Although talking is not what Timothy does a lot of.'

Timothy sat sketching on a pad of A4. A yellow wristband identified him as a patient, along with the blue, hospital issue smock, over his T-shirt and jeans. Charcoals rolled along the Formica, morning television blasted out of the corner of the room.

Burnt waited for McLeish to finish his elaborate introductions, telling the boy that the kind policeman needed to ask him some questions.

Timothy glared at them with dilated pupils. *Surely too young to be a regular user*, thought Burnt. He would be on the radar, have parents with history. If there was so much in his system, there had to be a reason other than being a regular. First time? Maybe he'd taken more than he could handle, started the fire by mistake. He wouldn't have the contacts to score LSD and novocaine, difficult contraband to source, unfashionable by today's standards to say the least. Maybe the boy *had* raided the chemist as McLeish had implied. Need to know who was with him.

'Spider-man,' said the boy, gazing at McLeish, eyes swimming.

'Oh yes, that's me.' McLeish laughed. 'Just watch as I climb the walls.' He acted out the comic book hero, his skinny arms and legs crawling up thin air. A few found it interesting. Not Burnt, or Bryony.

McLeish stopped, and cleared his throat, wiping down his hair. 'As I said, visual palinopsia, a rare but medical condition.'

Bryony was barely listening, she was studying Timothy, who wore a face of distrust, clutching the charcoal. She kneeled in front of him – getting to know him without intimidating him.

'Timothy, do you think the doctor looks like a spider?' Timothy turned to her, his look softened. His grip loosening. 'Course not.'

He turned back to his drawings, Bryony, Burnt and McLeish peeked at what he had concocted. In front of them were elegant sketches of Nordic mythology. Viking-styled warriors surrounded by a goddess.

'Well I'm making progress already – he spoke,' spluttered McLeish.

Burnt broke in, unable to wait any longer. 'Timothy, please tell me who you saw on the night of the fire.'

Timothy stopped his sketching, looked up. 'Wolves.' The swimming eyes returned to his swirling cloud that morphed into a female figure.

Adam breathed out loudly, gripping his notebook.

'I think Timothy needs some time,' Bryony said, giving Burnt narrowed eyes.

'Was anyone else with you, downstairs?' continued Burnt.

Timothy sat up straight. Burnt's hope rose.

'A bear.' Sniggers from the other guests. Burnt sank into his boots, McLeish looked delighted, Bryony felt her heart would burst.

'A man called Eric Haines rescued you from the fire, do you know him, Timothy?

'The bear,' said Timothy. He paused for a moment, as if to add some detail, thought better of it, returned to his drawings.

A ward nurse distracted McLeish, an opportune moment for Burnt and Bryony to sit with the boy.

'Did you have any friends round that night, Timothy?' pushed Burnt, putting pen to paper.

No answer. Bryony changed tack.

'They're lovely pictures,' she offered.

Again, no answer, Timothy was locked.

Burnt tried again. 'Did you have any friends over, on the night of the fire?'

No answer.

Bryony helped. 'Maybe, you could draw what you remember?'

More wild scrawling.

Burnt again. 'Were there any strangers in your house on Sunday?'

Nothing.

'We want to catch the man who killed your mother, Timothy,' blurted Burnt.

Bryony gawped at Burnt, open-mouthed. Timothy hissed, scrawling over his artwork with fierce strokes, tears in his eyes. Bryony put an arm around him, leant in, to catch his whispers. Timothy tensed, scratching at the paper, then stopped, dropped the pencil, and put his head in his hands. Tears rolled over his cheeks, his shoulders shook. Still, he said nothing.

Bryony cradled him, gave Burnt two daggers. 'That's enough for one day.'

'Of course, I'm sorry,' said Burnt, not quite sure who to aim the apology at, glad to leave as no hole was appearing to swallow him.

'But I have to say that Timothy's account of Sunday evening is vital. If there is anything he is willing to discuss, please contact me.'

He hovered for a moment, in limbo, awkward and ignored, studying the scrawled outline of a wolf salivating over a goddess.

From across the table came, 'We need to watch him.' Burnt glanced up, and thought he was looking at an undernourished goblin. Face – worn. Teeth – like she had been eating coal. Probably in her early forties, years of mental health issues scarred her face. The backcombed hair-do wasn't working.

She continued, 'In case he gets hurt, he's scared. Need to make sure he doesn't come to any harm.'

'Julie Caulk,' explained McLeish, hurrying to Burnt's side. He lowered his voice, turned his back on her, told Caulk's history.

'She beat and poisoned her son over ten years ago, blamed everyone since. Munchausen by proxy syndrome. The husband suspected her and informed the police. She took a hot iron to his face – the marriage didn't last long after that.'

He sniggered, while motioning for the orderlies to coerce Caulk away. Timothy had attracted a crowd. McLeish walked on, waiting for Burnt to follow; he wanted to conclude the meeting – sooner the better.

Burnt gave Bryony his card. 'Please let me know when I can talk to him again. I'm sure you understand it's quite urgent … tomorrow, I hope.'

Bryony snatched it. Snubbed him, returned her attention to Timothy.

McLeish gestured around the room as they walked down the corridor. 'It's a real uphill battle, detective.' Caulk followed – spying was her speciality. She listened to McLeish's commentary as he shuffled Burnt away.

She shouted from the end of the corridor, 'You shouldn't be here. The people you're looking for aren't here,' then darted, before orderlies could intervene.

Burnt paused, McLeish continued. 'We can subdue the problem with medication. The correct prescription depends on the genetic make-up of the individual.'

Burnt caught up.

The psychiatrist was in full flow, how he was transforming the hospital, his achievements paying dividends to the community. 'We are always learning here, it's the spells between medication sessions that tell us how well we are progressing.'

'Would the likes of Caulk ever be allowed out?' He searched the corridor.

'Oh, she already is. She's completed her custodial sentence – she's an out-patient.' Caulk wore no blue smock, no yellow armband.

McLeish saw the look of surprise, and happy to enlighten him, explained the Mental Health Act of '83.

'We have to have a strong case for keeping anyone secure here. There's "care in the community", with the community helping the patients,' he tittered. 'Most can come and go as they please. I imagine with the correct care, Timothy could be in a care home or with foster parents within three months. Thing is, it all comes down to cost. It's expensive.'

They were again interrupted by a female inmate, this one far from unhappy.

'Oh doctor, where have you been? You haven't come to see me for ages.'

An elderly lady, wearing a brown woollen poncho, came close, eyes for no one else. For once, McLeish looked bashful.

'Mrs Primrose. What's tonight's entertainment?'

'Opera, of course. I'm still waiting for that date, young man, and I want you to give me my medication again.'

McLeish made excuses, nodded to the nearest orderly to intervene, continued with Burnt at his side. Not far to the entrance.

'Pleasant lady,' he said, 'only a danger to herself, really. Constantly trying to find herself a partner. She changes her mind every week.'

Burnt almost forgot why he was visiting the hospital.

'You probably wouldn't believe it,' whispered the doctor, 'but it was syphilis, coupled with what was probably recreational drug use in the seventies, now she lives in a world of constant euphoric feeling. Not the worst prognosis I've ever given.'

'So, when Timothy arrived, what was his condition?'

'Just as you see him now, but aggressive and more delusional.'

'Aggressive?'

'He attacked me. Please read the introductory report.'

'And who was with you when this happened?'

'I was alone, I didn't want to intimidate Timothy on his first meeting.'

They sauntered through the corridor, McLeish running low on self-praise, Burnt letting the gaps speak for themselves. A lonely figure captured his attention, a teenager who seemed preoccupied with wiping his hands. He was pacing, flicking his fingers, shaking down his hands in spasms, ridding his fingertips of parasites known only to himself.

'That's Anthony, he comes here of his own free will. We've been giving him placebos for the last two weeks to prove the medication works. Once he is back to a steady medical routine, he will seem no different to anyone else. He holds a full-time job.'

A request for McLeish sounded out over the intercom, Burnt's cue to leave. He shook the doctor's hand, thanked him for his time, and left. Deep in thought.

Chapter 17

McLeish scurried into his office. 'That went well,' he said to his reflection.

He swept over wispy hair, was panting from all the stairs. Then he got a shock, the biggest of his life. An ugly hairy face with canine teeth was staring back at him from the mirror. He jumped, blinked, and saw his own face, reflecting with a startled look.

'My God. These bloody wolves are getting to me.'

He'd had subtle illusions before, never so vivid. He considered it an occupational hazard, comes with the territory for a proactive doctor. He rubbed at his forehead, as if to make all good. Red blotches gave way to dry shredding skin, revealing a pink under layer.

He hoisted up his loose synthetic trousers that puddled his laces, tucked in his shirt and jumped into his chair, swearing at the creaking floors and groaning pipework.

Then made a call. 'Leeman.'

'It's McLeish. Ready for tomorrow?'

'The meeting? In what way *ready*?'

'Are you on board, man?'

'Of course, I'm on board. It's simply a vote of confidence, yes?'

'That's right. A vote of confidence for the hard-working, ground-breaking psychiatrist that's moved this place forward,' reminded the doctor.

'Don't you worry, you'll have my vote. You can count on that. But I can't help you with dragon face,' said Leeman.

'No one can. Tomorrow.'

McLeish cut the call. Two out of five. And, of course, there was his secret ally, the solicitor. If that were the case, the two social workers' votes would go to the wolves.

***

'What made you draw these, Timothy?' asked Bryony.

No reply, more shading.

Now the pair were alone, Bryony looked over all his work, trying to engage with the boy. She asked questions without expecting an answer, chatting about herself, anything to try and make some progress and connect with the patient.

She had talked about the institute, which in hindsight was probably the last thing the boy wanted to hear. Then, on to how her art at school had been so bad that everyone had laughed, no one had known what she had been trying to draw. At least this made him smile. She continued, with her childhood and schooling, anything she could think of to gain his trust. She didn't make notes, attempted to be casual. Hoping for some – *any* – response, even aggression, some pointers on where to take the therapy. It was people like Timothy she felt compelled to help, those who can't help themselves. That was the reason she chose her vocation.

Her earliest memories were of caring for her brother when he so much as got a scratch. Any excuse, she would grab the first aid kit, tear into the plasters, and smother his knees in criss-crosses. He spent months with a bandaged arm, feeding his sister's fascination for nursing.

The traits of her vocation became more evident as she matured. Raw unguided diagnosis of her family was met with sympathetic smiles or outbursts of laughter. After spotting her brother squishing a spider, she would run to her mother in tears, crying out, 'Mum, Jack's a sociopath.'

Watching her father fighting with an Ikea wardrobe, and damning the Swedish for it, convinced her he had anxiety disorder. Every month she diagnosed her mother as bipolar, which wasn't met with such amusement. This unbound enthusiasm propelled Bryony to pursue her career path.

But crouching next to Timothy, she felt helpless. All the theory classes on assessments, reading body language, engaging with patients, felt alien. Comments from McLeish had chipped her wall of confidence.

She rubbed her eczema, twirled her rainbow friendship band.

Timothy spoke. 'People have to guess.'

'They do?'

'That's the fun.'

'Guess what?'

'What I'm drawing.'

She hoisted her sleeves up her arm, as if about to undertake some heavy lifting.

'What's that?' Timothy asked, staring at her wrist.

'It's Celtic. Means friendship.'

A welcome break from the catatonic state he'd been in until now. He outlined another sketch. Bryony asked about his family, if he had anyone. She saw him tense. She silently scolded herself for the impatient questions. Her nickname of GI Jane at college had stuck for good reason.

'I will come back for a chat later, Timothy. If you ever need to get in touch, and I'm not around, you can phone this number. Anytime.

She handed him her contact – she had to give him *something*.

***

Burnt, about to turn the ignition, paused, sat back, and considered the meeting at the hospital. Trying to ignore the stale smell of yesterday's half-eaten kebab on the rear seat. He studied the decaying ex-military building. Not quite a monstrosity, more an unimaginative built-for-purpose eyesore. The purpose had changed. The structure was more like an abscess on the back of the town, evolving into a tumour. Refurbished after the Second World War by order of the government, to rehabilitate casualties of war, and investigate mental traumas caused by warfare.

The years had passed, new patients replaced old, and the hospital gained a reputation as a centre of excellence. Then the burden on the hospital bloated. Year on year the workload grew, the expertise started to wane, the decrease in skill typical of an overworked system.

Adam, deep in thought, wondered just how unlucky you had to be to end up there – like Timothy. It seemed odd, even though a mental hospital shouldn't appear normal, the whole set up had a pantomime feel to it. The only person that seemed rational was the student – that was worrying. Maybe the whole lot of them were acting, half expecting a comedian with a microphone to tap on the windscreen, declare in front of TV it was a set-up.

And that crazy streak of piss doctor – what a joke. Seemed to find the place an exciting experiment. So comfortable with the environment he was oblivious to the pantomime.

This reverie was getting him nowhere. He shook his head of invisible fleas, placed his phone in the holder on the dash, and checked for messages. He sighed at the number of incoming emails, ignored them, turned the ignition and headed for his meeting. Ross and professional standards – his stomach knotted. He straightened his tie while driving one-handed. He had to explain why he drove to the wrong location on Sunday, in response to an emergency at Bells Road.

Although certain he was given the wrong address, he hadn't told the whole truth about his location, or what he was doing when he received the call. He couldn't tell Ross and co that he had lost the plot, gone hunting down a guy who was sexting Jackie. That he had him by the throat when the call came through, asking him how five years behind bars would feel.

And if Jackie found out she would throw a fit. She hadn't lost her phone – Burnt had taken it. And checked the messages.

That jealous rage that dented their relationship from the beginning was raising its ugly head. Norfolk was supposed to be a fresh start.

Every guy found Burnt's wife hot, they didn't have to say it – just that some did. Then some did a bit more. Big mistake.

She told him some creep was contacting her, sending a few dirty messages, and asked how she could block the caller. Burnt used his resources, see if he could get a name to go with the number. Then searched the name on the PNC. Got a hit. A sex offender with previous, ten miles from their house.

Burnt, with his built-in slow blow fuse that could take weeks or months to detonate, took it further. He pinched Jackie's phone, unblocked the caller and sent some texts of his own. Asked to meet the guy. Which he did, just as the emergency call from control came through on his radio that was tucked into his bomber jacket.

He was going to omit that part from his report, but for the formalities of the meeting he would explain an instruction to proceed to address is simple to follow – unless someone had intentionally given him the wrong location.

Chapter 18

Burnt entered CID headquarters. An impressive modern building, with a warmer welcome than older police stations, but the location isolated. Wymondham. A one-horse town, a drive through at best – unless you're a train spotter, or crazy about medieval history.

Burnt could sense something was different – no one could look him in the eye. Not that he ever received anything more than pleasantries from his colleagues. Everyone was on Griffin's side, backed him for the promotion, getting on-side with him, hedging their bets on a winner. *He's welcome to it*, thought Burnt. Griffin had a circle of admirers, Ross included.

Except Ashley, who remained loyal like a puppy that came back for more beatings.

Past reception where the duty officer searched for imaginary paperwork, down the corridor past two uniforms swapping stories, he pushed on the double-doors to the gents. With the few spare minutes available, best for a scrub up.

He unzipped, was taking a piss when it clicked – why no one looked him in the eye. A sheet of A4 tacked to the wall staring at him, a hand-scrawled note:

CONGRATULATIONS BURNT – YOU FOUND THE URINAL :)

He gulped, felt his stomach turn to lead, almost heard the laughing in his ears as he turned to the sink and rinsed his face. Then yanked a paper towel from the dispenser, pushed the humiliation to the back of his mind, kept the anger in the pit of his stomach. He had a hearing to get through.

Staring at his reflection and straightening his tie, he was relieved he had taken Jackie's advice. The petrol-blue suit, purchased for a wedding a couple of months ago, fitted well, much better than the old grey number he'd first pulled out of the wardrobe. He ran his hands through his thick dark hair, attempting a slight peak with his short curls. A habit from his teenage years, one Jackie warned he should lose. He creased his lapels, sucked in his stomach, and spat out his chewing gum. Ready as he would ever be.

Heading through the corridor, Burnt swapped a few pleasantries with his colleagues, superficial but necessary. Felt there was still resentment since he ruffled a few feathers on his first case.

He rapped a quick double tap on Ross's door, and entered.

Ross made introductions, calm yet clinical, explaining Hailey Pearson was following up on complaints, said she had their full cooperation.

'Thank you, superintendent.' Hailey took control. Briefed the pair, peering through her round glasses at her notes on the table. She was pushing fifty with a plum in her voice. Dressed in a tweed suit, she looked every bit how she sounded.

'On Sunday twenty-third at five-thirty pm, there was a call to emergency services concerning a fire at 3 Bells Road, Gorleston. The response time was unacceptable. DS Burnt was expected to be the first officer at the scene, but reports show his vehicle went to the wrong location. Fortunately, the fire brigade arrived within the acceptable time-frame of fifteen minutes. I'm trying to ascertain if further investigation is needed.' Here she paused, looked across to Burnt.

'Can you explain your actions?'

The palms of Burnt's hands turned clammy. 'I went to the location control gave me.'

'And how were you given this information?'

'By radio. I received a call from the central control room to head to Pavilion Road, not Bells Road.'

'There is no record of that.'

'Well, I know what I heard, and it was Pavilion Road.'

'Did you take the control operator's name or did you recognise it?'

'No, I didn't, and, no, I didn't recognise the caller. It's not the sort of thing you do in an emergency.'

He reflected on the voice he'd heard over the phone. It was not anyone he knew, had an almost electronic sound about it, but too difficult to explain, so kept quiet. That would make him look dumb.

'So you were never told to go to Bells Road?'

'Yes, ten minutes later by the control room.'

'Was it the same operator?'

'No.'

'Did you report this?'

'No. I presumed it was a mistake.'

'Could you have misheard it?'

'No.'

'Do you struggle with Airwave, detective?'

This caught Burnt off guard. Airwave, the new communication system recently deployed by Norfolk police. A hybrid technology, half-terrestrial radio, half-mobile telephony. The transition had not been without difficulties.

'On occasions,' he conceded, 'when it first came out a year ago, but then so did almost everyone.'

'And would you agree that your geographical knowledge of the area is limited?'

'I know how to find Bells Road.'

Who the hell does this bitch think she is? The only emergency she's ever had is changing nappies.

'So just to clarify, Detective Burnt, are you saying that a hoax call was made, sending you to the wrong address?' Hailey Pearson took off her glasses, paused to give Burnt a quizzical look.

This indictment, Burnt wanted to avoid. He glanced to Ross who was wearing a frown. Burnt knew it would be a huge allegation, and not welcomed by his colleagues – he would be accusing someone in the Force of gross misconduct.

'No, I'm not certain of that,' said Burnt, slumping into his chair with a sigh.

'Well, I'll omit that from the report.'

Ross attempted to rationalise. 'Is it possible that you misheard the location owing to static noise on the radio receiver? I know it can be quite severe when you're near the sea front, especially in this heat. It can play havoc with the communication signal.'

Was this Ross throwing him a lifeline? One he shouldn't have to catch?

'That was probably it,' muttered Burnt.

The interview ended with a slap on the wrist for the department, no need for further action. Burnt fully expected to be the butt of everyone's jokes for a while, Griffin asking if he needed help to find the coffee machine.

**

'What a stitch-up.' Burnt kicked back at his desk and put his feet on the windowsill.

'Sounds like nothing will come of it, though.'

'How the hell did Griffin get there before me? He wasn't even in the station. There's no way I heard it wrong.'

Burnt finished his tepid coffee, and started gnawing at the edge of the plastic cup. Ashley was leafing through case files in the cabinet behind his desk. Pulled out a burgundy tank top.

'How could a wrong call be made without it being a hoax? Why was I the only one that heard it, how can I prove it?'

'There should be proof. You say there was no log for the call, but you still received a radio call from control?' asked Ashley, pulling the sweater over his head.

'I received something from control, but it was weird. It was as if it was automated. It was a young voice. I didn't think much of it at the time. I just drove straight to location without question,' Burnt conceded, hands through his hair. Convincing himself.

Ashley was sitting down now, adjusting his collar, thinking. 'Anything over Airwave is recorded. That's what we pay for, the back-up of dialogue and sharing of confidential data. This was the point of moving from standard radio, that and the saving of manpower on form-filling and paperwork. The server stores any data to and from the control room.'

'Another one for your IT buddies, not that I want to talk to them,' said Burnt, who knew that if you wanted to get anything useful out of IT, you had to speak IT. Not his favourite pastime. A job for Ashley.

'I can try them, but if it's a lot of work they will need authorisation.'

'If it's more than five minutes they will want a bloody purchase order. Surely one of them owes you a favour? You spend half your time playing GTA with them,' Burnt jibed.

'Anyway, how is it recorded and where the hell is it?' he asked, searching the ceiling, arms outstretched. 'And don't tell me it's on some bloody cloud.'

'Well, everything's recorded, isn't it? In a manner of speaking,' Ashley said, twitching with interest, scratching his neatly cut auburn hair.

'I suppose so.'

'Well, all things being digital, it's all traceable, isn't it? Your voice is translated into a sequence of bits that are transmitted and delivered to the device at the other end and stored on a server. As for telephone networks, the data is buffered, then sent when less busy,' Ashley explained, shrugging. 'The telephone exchanges are upgraded all the time, so the capacity to buffer increases. Weeks and weeks of it.'

'Ten years behind the rest of the country.' Burnt liked to remind the locals that Norfolk was the last area in England to complete the transition to an all-digital exchange.

Unabashed, Ashley continued, 'With Airwave, the voice is stored in the same way as pictures and documents, just like voice over IP, but more reliable.' He finished his tutorial by way of tapping his pen on the desk.

'I'm sure it is, but where does that get us?'

'It can help us to discover if there was a rogue call, it should be logged. Everything digital is traceable. I just don't see how it could have come from outside our network.'

'You should get out more.'

Much as he liked to tease him, Burnt was in awe of Ashley when it came to technology.

'I'll speak to IT, see if I can find anything,' replied Ashley.

Burnt folded his arms in contemplation. 'If it were traceable, how would we know where the call came from? They would use a free SIM for sure, or a burner phone.'

'I don't know. I can't believe anyone from outside the police network would use their own phone to call in over Airwave. It would be such an elaborate hack that it would be very difficult to cover up. Why use it just to make a hoax call for a fire?'

'Unless they had an Airwave device,' pointed out Burnt. 'We had any units stolen, lost – sold on?' This suggestion silenced them both.

'I will speak to IT.'

'You do that, you bloody nerd,' taunted Burnt, happy to get off the subject.

'It's geek, actually.'

'What?'

'I'm not a nerd. I'm a geek.'

Adam burst into laughter, plucked out a clean ironed hankie to cough into, then pushed back into his chair. He crossed hands behind his head. 'What the hell is the difference?' He tapped his foot in anticipation of one of Ashley's monologues.

'Well,' continued Ashely, taking it seriously – he felt such detail needed clarifying. 'A geek is someone who knows a subject to the extent that it excludes them from a social circle.'

'And?'

'A nerd is excluded not by knowledge but by lack of personality,' he concluded, staring blankly at Burnt as if he'd just explained noughts and crosses.

Burnt had to take a moment to find a suitable reply. 'Only a well-dressed nerd would say that.'

A tap at the open door interrupted their bickering. Not waiting for a response, Veronica entered with a smile.

'Got to admit it, guys, you'd make a great husband and wife. If it helps, I'm a geek, too, James. Of all things dead, unfortunately – which is why I'm here. I've got some reports for you.' She plucked the paperwork from her satchel and threw it to the desk in front of Burnt.

She wore her hair in a bun, had on a tight jumper, along with slim-fit blue jeans that showed off her slender figure. Her appearance was a welcome sight to the two police officers in the cramped office, the subtle scent of perfume that followed her helping to overcome the fusty odour the boys had generated.

'I know this is forensics, but I can't keep my nose out. Boot marks suggest two intruders of average size. No DNA other than the occupants'.'

Veronica perched herself on the edge of Ashley's desk, crossing those slim legs, twitching her pointy little nose. 'The fire caught a big chunk of the evidence. It started in the upstairs bedroom from a bedside lamp. Mrs Levin had a broken jaw, a blunt trauma to the back of the head, and then suffocated from the fumes. Indicators show she was in the other upper bedroom, the boy who survived was downstairs at the time. She probably disturbed the perpetrator and they knocked her unconscious. The electrical wiring in the house seems suspiciously faulty. Interconnecting lofts, quite common with terraced houses built around the mid-fifties, allowed the perps to enter from the ceiling.'

She eased back, placed her palms on Ashley's desk. She was happy to do the officers' job for them, it was more exciting than her own.

'There's an update with Ross tomorrow, you can review and let me know your thoughts then.'

'Thanks very much, Veronica. What are your thoughts, Ashley?'

Ashley was staring at the pathologist as though she had just arrived from another planet.

He recovered. 'Was anything taken?' he said, with a squirm.

'A few prescriptions,' replied Burnt. 'But that's all.'

'Small-time, I guess, maybe looking for something to cook with?' posed Veronica.

'Crystal meth? In Yarmouth?' dismissed Burnt. 'There's nothing to cook with in chemists these days, unless they managed to lift a crate of Night Nurse. We're relying on witnesses Haines and Levin.'

'Not so fast.' DS Griffin filled the doorway. He parked an elbow on the doorjamb. 'Ross instructed me to do the interviews, remember, you two should be searching HOLMES for known addicts.' He swept his hand through his thickly gelled middle parting.

'Well, good luck with Timothy Levin,' replied Burnt.

Griffin moved over to Burnt's desk and snatched the forensic report. 'I'll give this to the Super. Sounds as though a couple of local druggies bungled it,' he said, ignoring Burnt's glare.

'Dr McLeish is worth a visit, though,' added Burnt.

Griffin changed the subject. 'I wasn't aware a pathologist's duties covered forensic evidence,' he said to Veronica, tapping the folder on his palm.

'I'm off duty,' Veronica countered, 'and I work very closely with forensics as it's necessary – especially in cases like this.'

She stood to face the detective. 'If you have an issue with that, go and see my co-ordinator. She will be happy to shift my workload.'

'I don't think that's necessary,' Griffin replied, backing away with an awkward smile. 'We all need to work together.'

He'd overstepped the mark and knew it. He had no jurisdiction over either pathology or forensics, these resources utilised by the criminal investigation department – and good, hard-working ones were hard to find. Veronica had put in the last twenty-four hours straight to get this report to them. He reversed through the door, thanked her for the timely information, and saluted as a way of apology as he left.

'What a cheek, the smug prick,' she said, not waiting for Griffin to get out of earshot, her face red. 'I've just put in God knows how many hours, and that's what I get. I don't know how you put up with him. I'm out of here. Find you own bloody perps.'

She grabbed her satchel, threw it over her shoulder, and strutted away, heels clanking on the laminate. Left Burnt and Ashley looking like blinking rabbits.

'I'd watch your step, Ashley,' whispered Burnt, 'she's a fiery one.'

'Too right.'

'It was funny, though, I mean Griffin couldn't look me in the eye.' Burnt sat back and continued, 'Body language. Have they taught you that yet? How people respond to a question they don't expect?'

Ashley, however, was miles away, although he was thinking about body language.

'Wake up, constable. It's HOLMES for us from now until the end of the shift, probably for the rest of the week.'

HOLMES, The Police National Computer, the database used by detectives across the UK to search for any perpetrators with a link to previous crimes, along with vehicles, or addresses.

'Let's draw it up,' enthused Burnt. He took off his jacket, threw it over his chair, loosened his tie, and undid his top button. Scooped a marker pen and sketched a structure for the search. Although something gnawed at him, deep inside his stomach. Maybe the answer was not in the database.

Chapter 19

McLeish logged on to FreeMe VPN. Then to HOLMES, entering his fake username password combo, and waited for the database to respond. It was a slow connection, the data was bouncing halfway across the world to the FreeMe server, and back to the police network. The connection was sluggish, but the information invaluable – and anonymous.

The IT at the hospital consisted of a single stoned teenager who never had the slightest desire to spy on the staff's web browsing, fully expecting the IT software to do that for him. He was doing enough special browsing of his own. Once in the database, McLeish carried out a search for Frank Alan. The results gave a small list of previous convictions dating back to the criminal's childhood. This was nothing new to the doctor – he had hired the thug. He was interested in the last time anyone carried out a hunt for that name. The software obediently gave him the time and date of the last search.

McLeish checked the timestamp against the one noted in his diary, it was a match to the nearest hour. It was the search he had done himself. The result satisfied McLeish; no one had carried out any checks, Frank Allen was not a suspect in the Bells Road fiasco. He repeated the task for Ronnie Lesley, which gave the same result, albeit with a much longer list of offences. There was no connection between the thugs and the fire.

He checked the companies BetaPharm and Endeavour, which gave the same negative result. Everything was still on track, despite the latest setback. For complete satisfaction, he typed 'Alexander McLeish'.

The search threw up one hit, a misdemeanour from his teenage years. He wished he could erase that – her at the same time, gobby bitch. The fairer sex had always eluded McLeish.

He logged out and sat back, staring at bubbles on the monitor. He listened to the groan of the pipework – it was getting worse. He rubbed the side of his temples that throbbed a little too often. A clanging noise reverberated around his head every time a toilet was flushed, the ache only quelled with medication.

Medication was his life – he believed in it. His remedy would transform the boy into a role model citizen. He still needed to convince everyone, police included, that Levin was mentally unstable and a danger to society. This discovery would allow him to prescribe the miracle drug that would inevitably cure him.

If it didn't work he could always find another patient. Although, this lad's predicament was ideal.

Fantasy filled his mind – the dull, throbbing headache receded. The protagonist doctor would rid the boy of his plagued demons and then work his magic. What a change – just think what he could do for all those other poor souls. He would have the choice of any practice for his endeavours. Endeavour indeed, which brought him to the present; check the bank details of his offshore account BetaPharm and make sure it was flourishing.

A silver mask appeared on the monitor in front of him and screamed 'Creep!' Locked to his chair, he felt cold sweat trickle down his back.

The hallucination was so quick, it made him wonder if it had happened at all. The phone continued to shrill. Five rings passed before he sucked in a deep breath, reached for his mouth freshener, scratched his scalp, and picked up the handset.

'Doctor, I have a Fiona Pendle on the line.'

'Oh?' He knew of no such person. 'Okay, put her through.'

'Are you okay, doctor?'

McLeish laughed. 'Yes, fine, just a bit overworked.'

Barbara Stamford didn't believe a word of it, but connected the caller without any more pleasantries.

Fiona Pendle introduced herself, she wanted to know about Timothy.

'I read that Timothy Levin was brought into your hospital recently.'

McLeish's ears pricked up. 'That's right, Mrs Pendle.'

'Well, I'm his aunt, and, as far as I am aware, now his next of kin.'

'Really? We had no idea he had any relations. Social services must have been mistaken.' Shit.

'I owe it to his mother to support him,' Fiona Pendle stammered, as she recalled the previous conversation with her sister, which she guessed was just hours before her death.

'I read about the fire online. At first, I couldn't believe it, seeing my sister's name. It said Timothy was at James Paget, but when I phoned they referred me to you. What is the process for this sort of thing? You see, I want to look after him.'

The cogs whirred. 'Well, social services would find an adequate foster home once we feel he is ready to leave our facility.'

'Could I take custody of Timothy?'

The doctor knew full well that the next of kin would get the first right to the patient. To find a foster home for a thirteen-year-old with mental health issues was a big challenge, not one the health authorities would want. Kids usually ended up in a safe house until they were sixteen, then were spewed out onto the scrap heap in a bedsit on benefits, becoming another statistic on the police national computer.

'I think we could facilitate that.' Course he could, but he didn't want to let it sound that simple. This was going to interrupt the medical trial, he would need to find another target.

'It's a bit complicated, you see I'm expatriated from the UK. I live in Singapore.'

'That does make it difficult.' He paused for effect, heard Mrs Pendle sigh, 'But there is a way. There are companies that deal with the sort of things required, such as the paperwork and legal side for the migration and repatriation of children. A company

I know called Endeavour would probably be able to help. But I must warn you that it's a bit frowned on, as you can imagine, as it may have connotations to trafficking and the like, so I would advise not to contact the police at this stage.'

'I don't want to do anything illegal.'

'It's not by any means illegal, it's just that you may come under some scrutiny, and Endeavour will contact the authorities at the right time when all the paperwork is in place.'

McLeish was thinking on his feet, winging it. He needed to make some money out of this, as compensation for stopping the treatment early. 'I don't know the cost of such an exercise, but I imagine it might be expensive.'

'I don't think that would be a problem, we are fairly wealthy.' Fiona spilled her guts to McLeish, told him her husband was CEO for a major oil firm. They had no children of their own, wanted to give the boy as much of a stable life as possible. It was her priority.

McLeish relaxed, reclining in his chair, imparting his worldly advice. He passed instructions, who to, and when. He needed time to prepare Endeavour.

He hung up, stood with a new air of confidence, took in the wilting breath freshener, and left the room. Ignoring the mirror – just in case.

Chapter 20

Like a rat in a maze, McLeish scurried down the corridor, bemused patients turning their heads. He could smell the route – to the basement.

He didn't see Julie Caulk spying from the alcove. She always did, spied most people, but especially the doctor.

'I can help them,' she muttered, watching McLeish disappear, coat tail flapping in his wake. 'I just need the white coat.'

McLeish swiped into the bowels of the hospital and marched to a small closet room located at the end of the hall. Only he had access, insisted on it to the contractors who carried out the security upgrade. An Achilles heel that added to the costly refurbishment.

He swiped the security block on the panel, waited for the familiar beep, and pushed on the heavy fire door. It was inside this cramped, six-foot square cubbyhole that McLeish carried out his own programme.

A workbench, a kettle, a sink and a cabinet. He unlocked the cabinet, and leafed through barbiturates and powders, all for trialling on his patients – and a little for himself.

Out spilled the plethora of chemicals. He checked and weighed, scrawled some notes on the inventory sheet, then rubbed his hands together. And pulled out the jewel in the crown – a packet labelled MR11.

This evening it was being trialled by Miss Primrose. The more beta-testers the better. He watered down twenty milligrams in a stainless bowl, flicked a lighter and heated it, giving a stir. It bubbled, his hand trembled, his long nostrils flared over the sour odour. He popped a new syringe out of a dispenser and, eyes narrowed, sucked up the taupe liquid.

'Do you ever feel bad?'

'Jesus fuck.' McLeish dropped the syringe, faced the mirror.

'Guilty, I mean. It's not good for others.'

Timothy Levin, on McLeish's shoulder, head tilted to the side, reflected big sad, brown eyes, as if ready to weep.

'You're not real,' McLeish called out, snatching the needle from the sink with shaking hands. Then fixed the lid, which disappeared in his pocket. He took a deep breath and held the sink with both hands.

'Aren't you supposed to do good things with all that powder?'

Timothy was grey, sinewy, dying. McLeish dropped his gaze. He couldn't look forward, dared not turn his head.

'Not going into this, not today, Timothy,' McLeish rang out in a sing-song voice.

'What are you doing to me? I'm changing. It's getting worse,' Timothy asked, leaning closer, cold breath in McLeish's ear.

McLeish grappled for his breath freshener, took a blast, faced the mirror. Timothy disappeared – silence.

He needed a refill. Once more he opened the cabinet, this time he chose the packet labelled CZ12. The stimulating mix he saved for himself. A cocktail of mood and cognitive enhancers. He took the modified spray bottle, removed the cartridge from the back, then filled the electric kettle. While it boiled, he sung to himself, an ear worm he caught on the radio, didn't know the singer, probably getting the words all wrong while fixing his personal prescription.

He had picked this up, back in the day, from a fervent student, who was always messing with a homemade chemistry kit in the halls. When the kettle clicked, he filled a bowl and dropped in the canister until it hit temperature, squeezed down the nozzle to remove excess air, ensuring there was a vacuum inside the canister, then placed it in the micro fridge.

He dissolved his prescription and waited two agonising minutes for the canister to cool, ignoring the mirror, humming inane tunes to himself to mask the silence. When he could wait no longer he grabbed the canister, upended it into his solution, and pressed the plastic nozzle to hoover his candy.

The homemade aerosol was almost complete. He licked his lips, took a butane bottle from the cabinet, filled the cartridge with gas, and squeezed it to the plastic tubular housing with the spearmint logo on.

He drove down the spray lid and took a long draw. The familiar kick hit the back of his throat and turned it numb. Senses tingled, creaks and bangs increased. Comfort took over – and relief. He could keep high in plain sight.

'Ahhhh. It's good to be the doctor,' he said, now happy to face his reflection, smoothing down his wispy hair and attending his flaky scalp. He tried the grin.

Then took the service elevator to the ground floor.

'Good evening, Miss Caulk,' he said formally.

She thought no one could see her in the alcove. 'I can help,' she attempted.

'Of course you can,' he replied, not waiting for enlightenment as he hopped up the stairs two at a time to the first floor. To the patients' wing.

'I can help all of them.'

This time only the walls heard.

Chapter 21

Mario squirmed. Getting to sleep in the works van was impossible. He just needed to ride through this for a couple of nights, smooth it over with Lola at the weekend. He had one leg on the driver's window, the other on the dash. That didn't work either. He changed the music on his phone to something ambient and slumped back, staring at the ceiling. It wasn't just the inhospitable van that was stopping him from getting some sleep – it was the large packet of marijuana burning a hole in his rucksack.

He gave in, delved deep into his bag, and pulled out the package. *Can't smoke it by myself,* he thought. Mario looked up 'Frodo' on his phone, hit that overused green button.

'Frodo, what're you doing? I guess you're needing a smoke?'

'I suppose you've opened the present,' a sleepy Frodo enquired. 'I thought you would have called sooner.'

'No, it's still here intact – which is why I'm on the streets by the way.'

'You haven't got to the bottom of it, then?'

'How hardcore do you think I am?'

'Look a bit deeper.'

Mario opened the package and peered inside, not yet surprised by the contents. 'Looks like grass to me.'

'Dig down.'

Mario put the phone down and delved into the weedy contents, the van filled with a pungent aroma. A few centimetres in and his fingers felt some cellophane wrapped round something hard. He prodded, then retrieved a pack of white pills. The grass, suddenly of less interest, spilled onto his lap. That's why the pack had felt so heavy.

He grabbed the phone. 'What the hell is this?'

'Halloween.'

'And what's that when it's at home?'

'I don't know, but I wouldn't touch it if I were you.'

'Thanks for the advice, but I don't intend to. What are you doing with it, anyway?'

'We need to talk, Maz.'

'I know – you talk, I'll listen. Holding on to a bit of dope is one thing, Frodo, but a pound of chemicals isn't something I signed up for. Oh, and by the way it carries a heavy sentence.'

'I know, mate, I know. I meant to talk last night, but I didn't get a chance, you passed out before I could get onto it.'

'This is going in the nearest bin.'

'No. I'm supposed to hand over a grand in cash on Sunday, and I don't know how to shift it.'

The line went silent as the words sank in.

'You're right. You *are* in trouble.'

Mario, however, ever curious, needed to know more.

'I'm coming over, and we're going to talk – no, *you're* going to talk. A lot.'

***

The pair sat opposite each other at Frodo's kitchen table, supping tea. Mario cradled his mug. A plastic clock on the wall ticked the seconds away loudly, accompanied by a humming fridge. A crying clown hung over Frodo.

'Best keep the noise down, you know what Mum's like.'

'Who's there now?' hollered a voice from upstairs. Frodo was soon at the doorway. He called up in a shout disguised as a whisper, 'Mario is dropping off some CDs. He's staying for a cuppa.' He pushed his hands into his baggy flannel sweatpants, waiting for the okay.

'Well, be quick. It's bedtime, and I've got a cracking headache.'

Frodo reassured her, and sauntered back, catching the table leg. Tea spilled over doilies. Mario reminded him why his nickname had stuck so well, his huge hobbit-like feet and general blundering mannerisms to boot.

The hobbit laid it on the table for Mario. 'I've done a little bit of work for a guy in London. And when I say a *little* I do mean a very little.' He went on, not waiting for a response. Mario was listening.

'This random contacts me on Messenger, right, and he seems to know a lot about me. I don't know how, but he just knew about my previous run-ins. I gave him my number and we start talking. He made out I was a bit like him and all that. Anyway, I wasn't buying any of it, but he just came out with how I could make a quick earner, sell some gear for him. I said I wasn't interested, but we gets talking a bit more about cooking up and all that,'

Frodo paused to gulp back his tea. 'I tell him, I don't know why, that my cousin works at a chemist. You know Jeff?'

'Nerdy Jeff?'

'That'll be the one. Although it's more like depressed, just murdered someone, Jeff now.'

'Bells Road.' Bells rang in Mario's head. 'My uncle was there. It almost killed him.'

'I know, Maz. I'm sorry.'

Frodo's mother interrupted with a holler from upstairs. Their anxiety was getting the better of them. Frodo promised her there would be silence, and that Mario would soon be gone.

'I wanted to explain earlier, but I don't know, I just didn't.'

Mario was crouched round his mug, warming his palms, swamped in his oversized Carhartt.

'So, what did Nerdy Jeff do?'

'This guy, Frank was his name – I don't know if it was his real name – asks if there was any Pseudoephedrine at the chemist. Don't ask me to spell it, it's hard enough to say, but I ask Jeff, and he tells me yep, defo, absolutely, and where it is. It's the raw ingredients for making crystal meth.'

'I know what it is, you lunatic. I just can't believe you would work for this guy.'

Frodo looked down at his half-empty mug. 'Cash.'

'So that was it. That's all you had to tell them, that there was this stuff for meth at the chemist?'

'And Jeff had to make sure the alarms were off, close of play Saturday. He was expecting the gear would vanish by Monday and that the chemist wouldn't even know for a few weeks. But the stupid thing is there wasn't any of this stuff there. They don't keep it at the chemist – or any chemist, for that matter. Jeff got his names in a muddle, the dopey twat.'

Frodo shook his head, continued with a shrug, palms facing the ceiling. 'There was nothing there for them, so God knows why it all went up in flames. As for Jeff, he's suicidal and ready to do a runner, if he only knew where to run to.'

They paused to reflect, listening to the beat of the clock. The fridge gurgled its merry tunes. Mario pressed on, wanting to know just how big the mess was.

'What's it got to do with this nightmare powder?' he whispered, leaning forward, elbows on table.

'Halloween, actually,' corrected Frodo.

'Well, excuse me, Mr Narcos.'

'Now this is where it gets weird.'

'And up till now it's been Mickey fuckin' Mouse.'

Frodo waited, head cocked to the side, for the yell from upstairs. None came. He restarted in a whisper.

'Well, Jeff gets a visit from this copper, CID type, and he comes on real strong. There's CCTV of Jeff switching off the alarm and Christ knows what else, but he could be up for murder, manslaughter at least.'

'How do you know he was a copper?'

'He showed him his badge. Maybe he wasn't, but how would he know about Jeff switching off the alarm?'

No answer from Mario. Just those deep brown Italian eyes, searching for more. He wiggled his monobrow for the hobbit to continue.

'He tells him that if he wants to stay clear of the filth he's to do as he's told. Then he takes Jeff's mobile number and tells him he's going to get some instructions. That was it, just like that. The copper's bent, I guess.'

Mario slurped the last of his tea, and sat back. 'Just a bit. And Jeff no doubt gets a call from Frankenstein?'

'That's right. The very same day on Monday evening he gets a call from Frank, probably the same Frank I spoke to, who tells him to go to Yarmouth sea front. When they meet up, he gives him this bag of gear and instructions.'

'The bag of gear I've got burning a hole in my rucksack like molten lead?' Mario asked, although he knew the answer.

'Halloween has never been sold on the streets anywhere.'

'Aren't we lucky.'

'He told him he needed to find some guys who wanted to make a few quid and get them to punt it out by the weekend. There are 100 pills to sell at £20 each. Cheap, if you ask me. Said he could keep half the profits.'

'And nerdy-cum-dopey Jeff the businessman says yes?' Mario sighed, rubbed his face, attacked his monobrow with his palms.

'He had no choice, so he brings it round to my house yesterday after work, asks if I can shift it for him.'

'And you bring it round to me one hour later. You're such a pal,' he said, standing to stretch.

'Well, at least I put a bit of weed in it for you,' Frodo tried. Nothing was safe in the house, there were never any secrets for long. He had a hysterical mother.

'She found my porn stash just yesterday, and that was in the shed.'

Mario had to laugh at this, but was silenced by the shrieks of Frodo's mother.

***

Mario left the house in contemplation. At least he wouldn't feel bad about smoking the grass without Frodo.

What he found most humorous was thinking what Lola would say if she knew that the package she found was not just dope.

It was a kilo of an unclassified drug called Halloween, put on the streets for the first time by a bent cop. Maybe she would have him back after that confession. He shuddered at the thought as he turned the key. The engine growled. At least he would be early for work, two days on the bounce.

He had an idea – he would see if he could stay with Uncle Eric.

Chapter 22

Sinatra crooned from the tinny speakers. She swooned around the drab room in reverie – her imaginary lover close to her side. Rose petals peppered the floor. A single picture on the wall watched her, the face of a previous lover, there had been plenty, now almost forgotten. Each year taking another bite into her memory.

A knock at the door yanked her from the past. She looked round to see McLeish, and squealed in delight. But tonight, McLeish gave her no smile – it was down to business. He had to prove that Timothy required treatment, as far as anyone knew he was simply analysing the boy. He had to know for sure the remedy worked. There would be modifications each day to find the optimum formula before Levin trialled it. Time was running out, he wouldn't have Levin for much longer.

This remedy couldn't just be a sedative or a tranquillizer, it needed to make the patient lucid and coherent, which was the basis of MR11.

According to the cook, the beauty of it was that the ill feeling that came with HAL31 would subside naturally after a few months. But the user would want an instant cure, and it would come in the form of MR11. If still not right, it would come in the form of MR12, and on. There had been eleven attempts so far, it was improving – first the HAL31, then the MR remedy.

McLeish had sampled the HAL blend. He made his recommendations, asked the cook to tweak the formula. Impressed, McLeish moved to trialling the insane, they were perfect, their screams of mental torture went unnoticed – and were fun to watch. The eyes dilated, they became euphoric, but within an hour they wished they were dead. McLeish had some close encounters himself, the occasional dab gave slight side-effects, a whisper in the ear, a cold breeze, some self-loathing. But it soon passed.

He put the latest visuals down to overuse of his nose candy, along with the stress of innovating the best medical recipe known to man. Ironically, he assured himself in front of the mirror. And that once this Halloween gig was wholesale, every hospital in the country would want the remedy – he'd get a slice for every gram BetaPharm sold. That was worth a few headaches and visual distractions, surely. Then, he was going to clean up his act. No more candy, jump on a health kick, get fit, do some classes – or go wild on a party island full of beach babes.

HAL31 was some fix, Timothy could vouch for that. McLeish congratulated his partner, some cook for sure, only thing now was a street name. Thirty-one days in October, the cook's initials of HAL used to denote the formula, it seemed fitting that the streets would know this hybrid as Halloween.

Most of the elements that made up HAL31 were nothing new. Dextroamphetamine and Lysergic Acid had been around for decades. The most interesting active ingredient was the psychoactive brew, Ayahuasca.

A South American medicine used in ceremonies among the indigenous peoples of Amazonia. In the eighteenth century, doctors explored the rain forest, obsessed with discovering the passion flower – never to return. The sixties saw beatniks gaining inspiration from the flower, writing tales of enlightenment. On to the nineties, and a reporter for a mainstream journal took a trip to the Amazon to investigate the supposed spiritual revelations from absorbing the plant. He penned how he was attacked by a six-foot goldfish.

This report inspired some to follow suit, albeit not for the same reasons. One chemist intrigued by the article took it upon himself, like many others, to investigate further. Most found the flower problematic to synthesise into a pharmaceutical, the cocoa plant offered much more profit for a lot less difficulty.

Hence, Ayahuasca was quietly forgotten by the developed world. However McLeish's partner, unlike any of the others, persisted. Found how to harness the flower, discovered the key was blending it with other pharma that complemented it. And unleashed a drug that imparted vivid hallucinations unique to each user.

Primrose sat on the edge of the bed, waiting patiently for her injection, babbling, blissfully unaware of the role she was playing. She hitched up the front of her gown, revealing a mottled veiny blue thigh to tempt the doctor. She pondered, trying to recall if he ever stayed after the medication; it was worth a try.

Besides, she loved to flirt, to play, like she used to. That much she could clearly remember. Through her youth she had always loved to hop from one lover to the next, keep them all guessing, keep that phone ringing.

The seventies was a raucous decade, leaving dancing school, latching on to a rock band as a dancer-cum-groupie for a couple of years, then on to some part-time acting. She had fun, no one could deny her that, the eighties didn't slow her down much either. She was still there in spirit.

McLeish dug in the needle. Primrose squeaked, showed a face like she was offended – he was rough today. Then she lay back, as instructed, relaxed, and answered his questions. The same questions he asked after giving a placebo, days before. This time she recalled names, addresses, facts previously hidden away. McLeish showed ear-to-ear teeth. His eyes welled, he beamed like a proud teacher. This might turn out to be some miracle cure after all. He rested his hand on her thigh. 'You've done ever so well, Miss Primrose. You deserve a treat.'

Chapter 23

Eight am. Nathan Ross, the senior investigating officer, was heading up the progress meeting on the killing of Agatha Levin. A burnt corpse and various charred rooms peppered the wall behind him. He pointed to each photo in turn, updating on the forensic and pathology reports.

'…to summarise, Agatha Levin, aged thirty-two, killed. Blunt trauma to the back of the head and crushed larynx sent her unconscious. Died from smoke inhalation at the top of the stairs, here.' He paused, stood back, slipped a hand into his side pocket, in thought for a moment, then shook a finger at the photo of Timothy Levin's bedroom. 'Entry to and from the building here. The attic space was accessed from the chemist next door, interconnecting lofts with half-height walls between.'

He stopped to smooth down his hair and took a sip of water. 'Her son was discovered unconscious, downstairs, in the hallway by Eric Haines – a friend of the family. DS Burnt, has Timothy Levin given us a description yet?'

'No, sir. I visited yesterday morning, but he was completely catatonic, and my presence only seemed to make him more withdrawn. He's started therapy, so let's hope things improve.'

'Any history there?'

'He had therapy up until a couple of years ago.'

'Should we suspect him? Of starting the fire, that is.'

'The fire started in the boy's bedroom, that much we are certain,' said Veronica. 'Evidence shows the bedside lamp sparked the fire, and because entry to the house was right above it, I think it's very unlikely to be anyone other than the perpetrators coming through the roof space.'

'Sounds like a couple of local druggies bungled it to me,' said Griffin.

Burnt cut in, 'You said that yesterday. Why so sure?' He craned forward.

Griffin sat back, looked to the charred body remains. 'A few prescriptions snatched, couldn't find anything worth taking, turned their attention to next door,' he said with a shrug.

'But why?' asked Ross. 'Was there a connection? Timothy's account will be essential. DS Burnt, I want you to visit him again, take a forensic artist and see if you can get a picture.'

'He could probably draw it himself,' said Burnt. Raised eyebrows from Ross. 'Really. You should see his drawings – they're amazing.'

'Well, if he doesn't want to speak, ask him to draw the perp for us,' said Ross, lightening the mood. 'Also, call on any offenders found on HOLMES. Griffin, use your local knowledge, there must be a snitch who will spill his guts. Put a bit of pressure on, they won't stay loyal for long.'

Burnt was still pondering over Griffin's comments when he looked at Veronica. 'Didn't forensics say the tyre marks were thick tread, new, suggesting a well-maintained vehicle?'

'Yes.'

'That doesn't suggest they were amateurs. If they were, they would most likely be on foot.'

'Good point, we must keep an open mind. What about Haines?'

Griffin shrugged again. 'Knocked out in the dark, no ID.'

Ross sighed. Witnesses would be vital.

'There was one other witness,' said Ashley. 'Mr Evans said he saw the van speeding away from the scene. It was grey and had a huge logo on the side, but he's not sure what it said. He thought it might be 'Demeanour'.'

'Well at least that's something to go on,' said Ross.

'Although Mr Evans was half cut at the time, he was making his way home from an afternoon session at the local by the sound of it.'

'Search for any business names starting with D in the area, Ashley. If they have vehicles, see if any fit the description.' Ross stood up. 'We need closure on this. We've got a manslaughter case on our hands at least, and no DNA. Constables, go and interview every person on the street, even if it's for a second time, and ask about the vehicle. Someone must have seen something. I want an update in forty-eight hours.'

Ross told everyone to bugger off. The officers made their way out of the door, all except for Burnt, who had a couple of questions of his own, for Griffin. But Griffin's phone rang. He excused himself, crept away, phone to ear, mumbling. Leaving Burnt with his thoughts.

***

'You'll be late,' said Eric.

Mario was sitting at the breakfast table, chomping on toast, the side of his mouth caked in peanut butter. He mumbled, mouth half-full, 'Well, I was early yesterday, so I guess I need to make up for it. I'll go in late today.' He winked at his uncle.

'Always the comedian, Mario.'

'You've got to keep your chin up, uncle,' Mario replied, licking the toast clean.

'Kicked out, living on the streets, owing gangsters money, enough pills in your bag to get you locked away for ten years. Yes, Mario, you've got to look on the bright side, which for you is the fragile light of a candle burning down to its wick.'

Eric hovered round the sink, fretting over the dishes.

'That's a bit solemn.'

'Not as solemn as your arse will be when it's spanked by your mother when I tell her,' he said, back to Mario, rinsing cutlery.

'Let's not be rash.' He paused with a slice of toast hovering near his mouth, eying his uncle, trying to measure how serious he was. He knew he could trust his uncle with most things, but this was on a different scale.

Eric grabbed a tea-towel, wiped his hands, sighed, and turned his attention to Madge who was bounding around the kitchen, excited at having a visitor.

'Leave that stuff with me for a start. You can't go taking it around with you. I'll bin it.'

'No. At the worst we just give it back and say we couldn't sell any.'

'Your hobbit mate does, not you. It's his problem.' He plucked out a tin of dog meat, and fixed Madge's breakfast.

'Frodo? I know, but if we can just keep it for him. His mum's bats. She checks everything he owns, both in the house and out.'

'She's got the right idea if you ask me. Okay, I'll tell you what.' He paused, tin opener in hand, Madge nibbling his ripped slippers. 'I'll hold on to it, and at the weekend we give these gentlemen the money they want and bin the powder.'

'How?'

He pulled his foot away with a yelp, Madge scurried off with his slipper to wrestle within her basket. 'Bloody dog. Just leave it with me. I'll get you the money. Now get to work before I change my mind.'

Mario finished his breakfast, burped, and swaggered to the sink. 'Fair enough, uncle. You know, I think I should be a negotiator, think I'd be good at it.'

'Christ almighty, I've heard it all now. Leave the dishes, safer, I'll do them. Get gone.'

Mario gave Madge some hugs, scooped his Carhartt from the edge of the chair, slipped it on, but paused, hovering by the door, hand on handle.

'Just one thing,' he posed.

Eric finished mushing the dark meat in Madge's bowl, threw the fork into the sink. 'Go on.'

'How come you were in that fire?'

'I was robbing a chemist and tripped over a gas canister.'

'No, seriously.'

He placed the bowl next to Madge. 'I was calling in on Agatha, she needed a hand with some stuff around the house.'

'You knew her?'

'Remember Gary?' He walked to the mantel, took a framed photo off the shelf. You'd have been about ten at the time, I guess.'

'The one killed in Iraq?' asked Mario, looking down at a younger uncle, three army-clad guys grinning for the camera, desert backdrop behind.

'That's the one – along with a few others. That was Agatha's husband.'

He tapped the face of Gary Levin, said, 'One unlucky family if you ask me,' and shook his head, clearing his throat to stop the tremor.

'So, what happened?' asked Mario.

'You need to get to work. One thing I'll mention, though, and that's the boy Timothy, Gary's son. He's in some mental hospital and it hit him bad, as you'd expect. I need to get in contact and see if I can talk to him. The staff have told me nothing. I guess they'll find him some foster parents, or something. I don't know how it'll work, but he can stay here if he wants. It might do him a bit of good, got to be better than a bloody loony bin. So just be a bit mindful around him if he's here.'

He placed the photo on the mantel. 'I just can't believe it. I saw them on Sunday afternoon, on the beach, they seemed … so happy. A few hours later, his mother was killed, Timothy's world turned upside down.'

He turned away, Mario stood helpless at the door.

'You saved his life,' he insisted.

'I guess so. Now get off to work with you and leave that pile of crap behind. We'll talk later. Oh, and keep out of trouble – for a day at least.'

Mario checked his watch, belted out a 'holy fuck is that the time', and flew.

Eric hardly heard him leave, his eyes welling, gazing into the photo, the years falling away. He stared into the twinkling eyes of the man he sent to his death.

'These things happen in conflict, Lieutenant Haines. Levin was a victim of war,' they'd told him. The report for Agatha Levin spared detail, Haines unable to tell her the full truth…

The troops were in fine tune. They slapped backs, joked, horsed as the early sun poked over the Afghan mountains, casting shadows long and lean across the desert plains, making puppets of the infantry.

Smithy asked Levin which sister he was going home to. Smithy, never too shy. Levin, always bashful, didn't have to answer. Haines cut through the banter, told them to listen up, take their orders, last patrol of the tour – no mistakes.

A simple operation, baby-sitting a couple of journos for a propaganda shoot in a nearby burnt-out village, Nakonar, strategically close to Kandahar. It was good practice for patrols, no Taliban been near the place in months, the locals not so much friendly, but passive, didn't hinder. Allied forces would take the opportunity to strengthen bonds with the Afghanis, providing supplies, and on occasion, medical help.

The morning ritual, shower in a can, kit on, fill the socks with foot powder, pop tarts and instant coffee for breakfast – then morning duties. Levin's turn to fire up the 440 KV generator, throw the switch to charge the battery back-up, and take the load off the 310 KV night generator. A constant drone for six months, gnawing away at morale.

Then, time to gear up, body armour, Kevlar, helmet, assault rifle, and as much water as possible. Eight soldiers escorted a bearded cameraman, a bespectacled translator, and a plucky, yet beefy blonde reporter that Smithy couldn't get enough of, into a John Deer Gator, and ambled away from camp as the sun started to burn through the wispy clouds.

Half-hour drive later, they piled out of the dust-smeared trucks, coughing and spitting, slugging from their canisters.

Haines stationed everyone at the outskirt of a dissembled school. He shouted orders, gave tasks, told them to stick tight. The beardy guy fumbled in his hemp day bag for the right lens, while plucky blonde girl encouraged Smithy with his pumped biceps and tats, who took the lead.

Haines connected his earpiece to his chin strap, and tuned the radio. A quick two-way with HQ, then back to barking orders. The guys were excitable, needing release – needed to get home.

Kids flanked them, giggling, hands out, asking for dollars. The translator got busy, Blondie posed questions to the kids for the camera, all responded with a nod, and returned in Pashto. The walls narrowed to an alley, which in turn opened out to a bombed-out courtyard. That's when Haines got the first command from HQ.

'Haines. Pull back immediately, please confirm.'

'Journos having a ball here, HQ. What's the rush?'

'Drone intelligence, there's been overnight activity, possibly harboured Taliban. Pull back.'

The troops were dispersed, chatting with the locals, taking in a crafty fag. Haines had let his guard down a little low, he needed to recall his troops.

Then the wailing started, from a Mitsubishi Barbarian. Two children ran to the journalist, grabbed her hand and pleaded with her to help their mother. Sweat poured down Haines's forehead, Smithy pumped his chest and advanced to the Barbarian. A mother with a baby, sitting locked in the front seat, frantic. The translator spoke in a flurry. 'She been in all night, baby got no food no water, battery flat cannot unlock door.'

'Smithy!' bawled Haines. 'Take the charge back to the vehicles, were leaving.'

'What?'

'Orders from HQ. Everyone, we're pulling back.'

'Since when have we listened to them?' He continued striding to the Barbarian. Baby screams bounced from the decaying walls. 'They need help. Hasn't been Taliban here for six months.'

'Smithy. Back to camp.'

Kids surrounded them, pleading, swamping the translator, who was struggling, pulled by the crowd. Haines was ordered to return once more. Smithy wheeled round and made back to their trucks, huffing. The journo followed.

'Haines. Back to base, immediately.'

It's always good to help, keep the peace, especially for the cameras.

'Levin, put the windscreen through, then fall back.'

Levin strode to the truck, Haines waiting, Smithy grumbling back through the alley with Blondie, Beardy swinging the camera round as he headed back, taking in the excitement.

Levin squinted to see through the sand-covered window, could just make out the mother with a crying baby in her arms, rocking, praying.

'Calm down,' he warned, 'get back.' Then motioned for her to move away from the window and turned to the translator over his shoulder, told him to explain. He was at the vehicle now, butt of his gun in the air, then the look in the mother's eyes made him stop.

'Levin, fall back,' Haines screamed, hand to ear.

It wasn't panic – it was hatred. Not crying, yelling. She reached into the folds of the baby's shawl, and grasped a detonator, locked eye to eye with Levin, spat like a banshee, and pulled the trigger. The IED was under the Barbarian, and the blast blew Levin's legs from his body. Haines and the translator were blown to the floor while clouds of sand swirled the courtyard.

HQ was yelling, the translator crying. Haines could only hear a high-pitched screech, a badly tuned radio in his ear. Then wails of pain, this time Levin. He crawled across the blood-spattered yard and grasped Levin's shaking body. His pale face stared to the sky. He was murmuring, gripping Haines's hand. Then fell limp. And then the *put-put-put* of gunfire…

Crouching over the dying man whose legs had been blown from his body was a memory that he would never erase, and one that haunted him when he slept. The hopeless attempt in trying to pacify Levin as he shook in spasms made Haines sick to the stomach every time the memory was triggered. He recalled whispering to Levin that it would be okay when he had just seconds left to live, making idle promises that had so far proved to be futile.

Eric stared into the photo, rubbed at the scar, let the tears well. Madge nestling in for a love, and Eric, giving over, crouching, and rubbing her behind the ears, began whispering something – but gave up.

Chapter 24

Burnt was greeted with the smell of disinfectant dampened by unwashed laundry. Security buzzed him through. Orderlies trotted across the foyer, he had to dodge an industrial-sized laundry bucket on wheels, the porter looking elsewhere. He skipped over to the reception desk.

'I'm looking for Doctor McLeish,' he said, holding out his badge.

'Aren't we all? He's a Scarlet Pimpernel, that one.' He eyed the nametag. Barbara Stamford: Head Nurse. She busied herself, leafing through a folder, sighing in exasperation.

'Do you ...'

'Christ, where is it?' She plucked out a page of A4 from the folder, studied it briefly, then buried it.

'I want to see ...'

'This is the filing system. Can you believe it?' She threw the folder on the desk, spat a contrived laugh, and tugged at her ponytail. She had a hard look, and was wide enough to be a shot-put champ, thought Burnt.

'Timothy ...'

The phone rang. Barbara cursed under her breath and answered as Burnt rocked on his heels. He scanned the room, picked out the student psychoanalyst rushing towards the stairwell. He called her before she could get any further, hoping he had got the name right. 'Miss ... Joy?'

She spun round, hand on banister, surprised. She looked tired, rings circled her eyes, lines beginning on her forehead; a few months in and the real world was aging her.

'Oh, hello, detective.' She swept her hand through her floppy red fringe.

'I'm looking for McLeish.' Burnt covered the foyer.

'He's in a meeting all morning,' she called, over the din of air-con, bashing doors, and whistling porters.

'Busy, is he?' Stamford hollered, 'He'll be more than busy when I get hold of him.'

Bryony gave a smile and ushered Burnt up the stairs. 'And when he gets out there'll probably be a queue for sure. We are understaffed, and he seems to be out of the office a lot at present. Everyone deals with pressure differently,' she said, nodding back to Stamford who was tipping up a box onto the counter.

'I still need a statement from Timothy Levin,' said Burnt, pulling out his notes.

'I'll take you to him. I have to say that I myself have had hardly had any time with him. There are strict instructions not to engage with Timothy within certain hours.'

'Instructions from McLeish?' asked Burnt.

'Yes. Timothy seems to sleep a lot. I haven't made any diagnosis myself, although Dr McLeish seems quite convinced about Timothy's condition.'

Burnt detected bitterness. 'Palinop ..?' he started, leafing through his notes as they bounded the stairs.

'Visual Palinopsia. That's right. It's quite rare, though I'm not sure I totally agree, but anyway, time will tell.'

Bryony trotted through the first-floor corridor nodding at passing porters. Burnt, a little breathless, skipped along behind glancing at his notes, squinting at his spidery scrawl.

She pushed through to a breakout-cum-recreational area. Timothy in the far corner was staring at the large screen TV like it was sacred. Knees to chest, palms on shins. They edged over, Burnt swerving a couple of patients who had taken to him. They pawed his black jacket, begging for attention. Bryony called them off. Burnt shuddered, the place gave him the creeps, he wanted to interview Levin away from this mayhem but couldn't get the clearance. Maybe next week.

Bryony coaxed Timothy away from a rerun of *The Jeremy Kyle Show*. The boy looked gaunt, pale.

'Have you eaten, Timothy?' asked Burnt. Timothy nodded and looked to the floor, dark hair falling over his face. Burnt felt nothing but pity. He crouched on one knee, met the boy's gaze.

'I would really like to find who started the fire at your house.'

No response. 'I can bring someone to draw the person if you can tell us what they looked like.'

Timothy shook his head and scratched at himself, searched the floor, troubled.

'He does that a lot,' Bryony whispered. 'Maybe you could draw him?' she suggested to Timothy. Timothy stopped twitching and sat back, huddled his knees.

The intercom sounded for Bryony. She sighed and made an apology, explaining there was a shortage of porters. Her services were required to cover other duties outside her remit.

'Yes, it seems you are all very busy,' *apart from McLeish*, thought Burnt. 'Can I sit with him a while?'

'Of course. Call me if you need me.'

Burnt hunted down a hard, wooden chair, and dragged it in front of Timothy with a scrape. Heads turned. He sat, sighed, gave a polite smile and leaned in, elbows on knees.

'You like Bryony?' he tried. A shrug for an answer.

'You like McLeish?'

Timothy clasped harder around his calves. 'Medicine man,' he said, looking around the floor. Burnt nodded, in empathy. They sat until his phone broke the silence. Blue smocks gathered as he took the call. It was Jackie, reminding him of his fatherly duties. He had an afternoon pencilled in as a holiday, the kids were off school, and Jackie was holding him to it.

Timothy took the opportunity to vanish, while Burnt tried to wriggle out of his family date, trying to turn his back on the patients; they were surrounding him, no staff in sight.

After some guilty persuasion and a bit of lecturing, followed by a one-sided conversation with his four-year-old who wanted to know if he'd killed anyone today – and if not, why not – he gave up, said he would soon be home.

He'd lost Timothy, but was happy to call the morning a write-off, get authorisation to shift Levin to a safe house for interview, away from this claustrophobic hell-hole. Blue smocks with long pale faces bored holes into him, started poking him in the back. Body odour engulfed him.

He started sweating, barged through, an old gent tottered and Burnt had to catch him. Some started to shout. He made it to the double doors, then facing him in the corridor there was Timothy, those big brown eyes swimming. *Everybody's* eyes were swimming. Where were the staff? Timothy thrust a folded sheet of paper into Burnt's hands.

'Him. Find *him*.'

Burnt opened his mouth to ask questions, as Timothy strode through a side door to the fire exit. A porter rammed a caddy between Burnt and the exit, the flock caught up with him. With their smell. Prodding, babbling, asking questions. They were not easy to brush off, the same sort of questions his four-year-old would ask, the sort you can't give an answer to. Why are you wearing black? What is the unluckiest day in the year? He confessed he didn't know and scurried away, was going to be sick any minute. A porter swiped him through to sanity.

Burnt descended the stairs shaking his head. He was dizzy, wiping himself down like he didn't want to catch what they had, and looking over his shoulder. He locked with Stamford at the desk as he hit the last step and she caught the look. One of repulsion.

He made it outside, guilt layered in his stomach. He slowed to an amble, took in the fresh, salty air, steadied his breathing and stopped at the Mondeo. He searched for his keys, remembering the drawing in his hand. Flicked open the sheet of A4. Stopped dead. And stared hard at a portrait of Agatha Levin's killer.

***

Myra McLintock, head of social work, sat with a stiff back to the window at the oval table. Bright sunshine poured in, outlining her with a glow. Dressed in a suit, formal as an undertaker, she declared the meeting underway.

Seated to her left was solicitor Gregory Ravel, suited, and showing cufflinks. An impartial board member with the right credentials for a position that needed a community-minded servant with a strong ethical background. It was unpaid, so expected to attract only morally minded individuals.

Next along was Harry Arthur Leeman, also delivering his services for the good of the community. A director of Zenacare, a small pharmaceutical manufacturer based in Norwich. Although the company found it difficult to compete with the large conglomerates, its distribution was worldwide and it ran at a healthy profit. He slouched, pen in hand, tapping on the desk, striped shirt untucked. He had started as a chemist after graduating, and ten years on had moved into management. Another ten years of climbing, and he found there was nowhere else to go. He had hit the ceiling. Never expecting a CEO position, if he had needed extra income he would have had to look elsewhere, and with the demands of his current, much younger girlfriend, looking elsewhere was becoming essential. His trophy chic certainly had the edge on his ex. But this was costing him and trying to get a ring on her finger had not proved easy.

Facing Myra was McLeish, pale and twitchy. In need of a hose down, a manicure, a health spa even, maybe just the attention of a good woman. Someone who could pull him up when he put the same shirt on after three days or decided to dress smart by wearing bright red braces.

The space to McLeish's left was the preoccupied head of finance, lost in his spreadsheet.

To the right of Myra was an empty chair. Myra invited the governor for health and social security to every meeting, but he attended very few, and relied on the minutes sent to him by Myra.

The first two items on the agenda held no interest for McLeish, there was nothing for him to contribute – or defend.

'Agenda item three: pharmaceutical supplies and costs,' Myra declared, narrowing her eyes through her large rims at her printout.

The accountant tapped the keys and filtered his list. The outgoing costs and inventory were projected on the far wall behind McLeish, who had no need to crane his neck – he knew the numbers.

'An increase in the supplies from BetaPharm. There hasn't been any agreement for this. Is there a good reason for the change from Zenacare?' She looked between the director of Zenacare and McLeish, anticipating tension.

'It's not changed, just adjusted.' McLeish bemoaned the need for the new supplier, alluding to the lack of funds that compelled him to take a proactive decision. 'Mrs McLintock, we still rely heavily on Zenacare, but demand has outstripped supply. BetaPharm has a more competitive edge.'

Ravel jumped in. 'Nothing wrong with that. Bringing more competition to the area and sharing the work amongst rivals is healthy.'

The accountant stirred. 'The costs are much lower.'

'Please send on the business registration number, we can check Companies House for any irregularities. How did you authorise a purchase order?'

McLeish looked up to give his rehearsed answer, he knew it was coming. But was distracted. Above Myra, McLeish glared into the sunshine at Timothy Levin, knife in hand. McLeish could see through to his bones. Sinews of muscle twitched as he poised the knife at her throat.

'Doctor?' asked Myra. Ravel searched the room, Leeman narrowed his eyes on McLeish, wanting to answer for him.

'Certainly,' called out McLeish, with a jump. He continued before Timothy could distract him, the jaw full of teeth opening and closing without sound.

'Someone had to make a decision,' he started, scratching at his neck. 'I couldn't wait for the next board meeting or we would have had a mutiny.' He forced a laugh. 'BetaPharm took the order on good will, no PO necessary. I would expect we can set up an account with them, as a preferred supplier.'

McLeish hoped to conveniently forget to send on the details. The business was registered outside the UK, and if Myra studied it thoroughly she would find it linked to McLeish and Leeman's bank accounts.

The others joined in the laughter, all except Myra. McLeish had never seen her laughing since they met. In hindsight, trying to seduce her was not his best move. But even had he been Brad Pitt he would not have broken the wall of Myra. She was not for charming.

'The governor will want to see certification of any pharmaceutical vendor for the establishment.'

'This is a fifty per cent saving,' chirped the accountant, unable to pull away from the screen.

'I shall pass on the details,' said McLeish. He felt he was going to win this one. The governor wasn't present and the accountant was on board – and Timothy had dissolved. He asked, 'Shall we put it to a democratic vote?'

McLintock insisted it was not correct procedure, that the governor was ultimately responsible.

'Well it's got my vote,' said Harry Leeman, 'and I'm the director of Zenacare. As Gregory says, it's healthy competition. I recommend a second source for supply. Who knows what could happen to Zenacare? They might go out of business tomorrow.' He laughed, knowing full well that profits were soaring. Everyone wanted drugs.

The tone lightened. Myra typed actions into the minutes for the doctor to provide details, and the meeting rumbled on, McLeish less twitchy, affording himself the occasional spray of mouth freshener.

Zenacare profited from the endless circle of treatment for the sick. Someone with cancer had chemotherapy, which made them nauseous. This required more medicine, which would mean they were usually unable to sleep, so they were prescribed sleeping tablets. But this could induce depression and hence more drugs – which would produce yet another side effect. It was a circle that the pharmaceutical industry had no intention of breaking. Zenacare, along with the other manufacturers, would happily announce they were spending millions on research to cure cancer. This was a lie – it is more profitable to spend millions on finding ancillary medication.

***

Doubt bit into Burnt's stomach. He took bigger bites with each step on the cobbles. His fists thrust into his bomber jacket, head down, eyes shining with tears. Past rows of steep bedsits with their peeling paint and chipped woodwork. Creaking, whispering – suffocating him.

Was she cheating? The doubt consumed his thoughts. The thoughts that should be filled with perps, MO, witness reports and evidence. If he could just push the doubt to one side, move it to the back of the queue, or better still, handcuff it and lock it away.

Then he could focus on being a policeman, on Levin, on cleaning up the town. Could do it without biting Ashley's head off all the time. Ashley, his only ally, loyal and committed, who knew Burnt was better than the rest, that justice was the only thing on his agenda.

Breaking glass broke the spell. He was passing an opening that gave access to the rear of the terraces. An abandoned pushchair lay in the centre of the lane strewn with weeds. A football bounced from an adjacent alley. Burnt turned, trod carefully to the ball that now rolled to a standstill at the upturned pushchair.

Two boys around eight years old came bursting from the alley, one in a muddied and faded canary yellow Norwich City shirt with the logo peeled away, the other a Man United top. They skidded to a stop, panting like dogs and eyed Burnt who stood with his foot on the ball.

'This yours?'

The one in the canary shirt nodded, then looked to the floor. Man-U shirt crossed his arms, looked to the sky.

Wind blew through the alley. The panting boys fidgeted.

'Someone's had a window smashed in. You know anything about that?'

The boys looked to each other, the stocky one in canary yellow answered. 'Weren't us. Big kids did it and ran away.' He made big eyes, looked over his shoulder, then to his pal for support, who nodded.

Burnt gave a wry smile and shook his head, toe-poked the ball to their feet. 'Well, best you get out of here before anyone tries to pin it on you.'

Raised voices from a few doors down filled the alley. Man United shirt scooped up the ball and they pelted.

Burnt turned back to the main street, his spirits raised, mind refocused. The doubt pushed to the back of the queue – the spitting demon handcuffed. He sauntered back to his car, mulling over the boy's lie – a big kid did it and ran away.

No way was the fire started by Levin.

Chapter 25

The Nelson, Southwold. Burnt and his family nestled into a spot in the snug. The pub offered corners and cubbyholes to sit at and was the Burnts' regular haunt on a family day out. His two boys argued happily while they waited for their fish and chips. Jackie leaned into Adam and thanked him for taking time out. He supped on his real ale, held her hand, glad to take the brownie points. And he had found her phone, down the back of the couch, he said.

Jackie, still unsure Norfolk was for them. He insisted it was, told her it would get easier, but she felt isolated, cut apart from friends and relatives.

A petite barmaid, hair in pigtails with a red face, approached with two enormous plates. She manoeuvred around punters who couldn't get a seat, slammed down shark and chips in front of Burnt with a brief apology, and weaved through the crowd for the remaining dinners.

The Burnt family scoffed and drank. The boys swapped stories of school, Mum organised the weekend, Dad nodded, half listening.

After, the boys turned to their father for a tale, as they always did at the dinner table. Adam pushed away his unfinished plate, littered it with his paper napkin and sighed, deflated. Beaten by the shark. He scratched his chin, thinking over which one to pull out of the vault. Some were real, most started true but had dull endings so needed editing.

Jackie straightened in her seat, aimed a raised eyebrow at Adam.

He had sometimes been too enthusiastic with the endings, to the point it gave his youngest nightmares. It was when they first moved into their house, when it was all upside down and they were living out of boxes. Only a Z-bed for the youngest till the furniture arrived. Adam gave an overzealous escaped convict in the countryside tale. Lucas slept with his mother and Adam got the Z-bed.

Adam thought better of it. 'I could tell you about my first ever case … Or we could go to the amusements.'

The vote was unanimous. They were off to the pier.

***

They strolled along the bustling walkway onto the pier, while gulls cackled for attention overhead. The kids ran on to the amusements, leaving Adam and Jackie to stroll, hand in hand, her head nestling into his shoulder, the warm breeze bringing them closer. Heads turned to eye Jackie. Middle-aged men who could have done better, wondering how Burnt had managed it.

They stopped, leant against the railings, had a little love-in, whispered a few words, took in a makeshift jazz band ad-libbing a rendition of 'Take the A-Train'. The thumping rhythm from the scruffy teenagers augmented by passing gulls overhead gathered a growing crowd.

They couldn't stay outside for long. Duty called as their children dragged them into the vintage arcade to show them what they had found.

'Look, a stamper,' screeched the eldest, pointing to a machine that let you put fifty pence into its mouth to receive a stamped penny in return. Burnt felt the need to explain that this wasn't a great deal he was getting for his money, but knew better than to be cynical at times like this, so showed the enthusiasm required by a father and handed over coins.

The kids loaded the machine and listened to the whir as the cogs crushed a penny, spitting out an old brown worthless coin that dropped into the tray. 'Again,' shouted Lucas, and again the cogs whirred round – just as they were in Adam's head. He was never 100 per cent paying attention to his kids. Right now he was thinking about fires, doctors, patients, and witnesses. Then the penny dropped.

'Feel it, Daddy. It's still hot.' But Daddy wasn't listening, he was wondering why he had been given the wrong address for a crime scene, how Griffin had got to the scene before him, and why he still hadn't found who was responsible.

'Where are you, Adam?' Jackie asked, giving him a prod in the belly. 'Come on, detective, give it up for one afternoon.'

Burnt realised he was staring into free space while the kids jumped around him in excitement.

'Who needs electrocuting?' he shouted, trying to rid himself of work.

'You do,' the kids exclaimed, running to one of their favourite consoles.

A toy generator challenged the user to withstand 1,000 volts for twenty seconds, gave great entertainment for his kids – and wife. It had become the pinnacle of the regular afternoon visits to Southwold. Although not convinced it was totally legal, Burnt would happily take on the challenge to show off his endurance skills. He grabbed the iron bars in front of Frankenstein and thumbed the red button.

Fake lightning cracked from the speakers, the booth flashed – and Burnt played the fool. He pulled unflattering faces of pain, and finally after a long twenty seconds the booth duly spat back his pound coin as reward. Which Lucas pushed back into the slot.

'Again,' he cried, and before Burnt could object, the electrocution resumed. His record was six sessions, before running out of the arcade to spew over the pier.

Luckily his phone rang, saving him from another stint. He made his apologies to the boys, they soon turned to the crazy mirrors, and Burnt wandered outside to take the call from Ashley.

'Where am I? On the seafront where ordinary people spend their afternoon off.' He squinted into the sun.

'Just thought you might want to know. Ran a check on McLeish as you suggested and got a hit. He was reported for sexual harassment nine years ago.'

'I'm surprised he could practise with a criminal record. He should be on a professional register. Can you follow up a bit more on that? And you might as well check out his family background while you're at it.'

'Anyone else?' asked Ashley.

Bunt leant on the handrail, looked out to sea. 'No, just McLeish. Oh, and I mailed you a picture ID of the perp.'

'I saw that. Did he draw it?'

'Yep. I guess we could find a job for him.'

'Ha. I'll get it circulated.'

'Okay, thanks. I'd better get back to being Frankenstein.'

'Sorry?'

'Never mind.'

Burnt hung up, fixed his gaze on a fishing boat pottering into the harbour. He had requested a HOLMES check on McLeish, not because he was a suspect but purely because the doctor gave Burnt the creeps. The information found about his misdemeanour might prove useful when trying to bargain time with Levin. He couldn't help but feel there was something more than just a bungled robbery that caused the fire, and was certain that he was sent to the wrong address, but why?

Lucas grabbed him by the hand, pulling him from his thoughts – for more torture.

Chapter 26

A dull thud, followed by a whoop of joy as the dart hit double twenty.

Graham said, 'That's all your pocket money,' then ran the back of his hand across his runny nose.

Tom looked up from his stool, shrugged. 'I've got no money.'

'Torture then.' Graham tightened his fists and made a show of his biceps, swamped in a T-shirt with 'Too Stoned to Care' on the front.

Tom gave his elder brother a meek look. Graham came at him and pinned him to the floor, was soon on top with knees on his chest, taunting him to hand over imaginary cash.

He knew there wasn't any. There was never any cash around their house for long. The minute the social security cheque came through their father was off to the supermarket, straight to the spirits section.

Since Graham woke he was animated. He bounced out of the bottom bunk, shook up Tom, gave one of his older self-assured brother speeches. Tom saw the side of Graham he admired. The sort that reminded Tom who was in charge, who had all the ideas, the one with cunning. Reminded him how much he needed him. Like when Mum buggered off. Tom, in the top bunk, crying himself to sleep, choking back the pain, fearful of where life was heading. Graham whispering from his bed, 'It's goin' to be okay, bruv. One day we gonna get lucky – I know it.'

After some grappling in between fits of giggles, they stopped. Graham, with another idea. Arm locks. A repeat, along with the array of self-defence moves from his few lessons in Aikido at the community centre.

Tom was all ears, slouched in his baggy woollen jumper and half-mast school trousers, last week of the summer holidays but nothing else to wear. His mousy cropped hair still sculptured by his pillow.

Graham posed casually, adjusted his grey floppy beanie, smiled a goofy teeth grin, said, 'Right. Pretend you've got a knife and come at me.'

Tom shrugged, padded over, fully expecting to get floored. His arm was soon on his knees yelping for submission, arm behind his back in a half-nelson.

Graham gave in, sat cross-legged for a moment, smiling at Tom who was rubbing his shoulder.

'Let's use the real thing.' He jumped to his feet, hoisted up his baggy jeans. 'Come upstairs, I'll show ya'.'

He stormed out of the shed into sunshine. A neighbour putting out her washing looked over then turned away, thinking better about any confrontation with the Hackets.

Graham bounded through the back door into the kitchen, Tom trailing. The hum of last night's tea hung in the air. Burnt sausages, the frying pan left glazed in white fat, sliced white bread going stale on the Formica, a tub of Stork left open with a knife stabbed into it. Graham scooped up a round of bread, smeared it yellow, and waltzed through the half-hinged kitchen door that had stood broken for months. It was another job in the house lined up for repair. It stood fully open on a slant, a reminder of the day Dad watched Mum walk.

Dad had put his foot through the door. She'd told him that there was no point in trying to stop her. Her new fella was a judo instructor for one, and second, had a job. No Baliol Road for her anymore, it was the upper echelons of the Magdalen Estate. Dad was fighting depression, she said he would have to fight it on his own. Said she was getting no younger, so instead of kicking him out and trying to keep custody, she severed all ties. Her children were an unwanted distraction, teenage mishaps.

The boys raced up the stairs, knocking a photo of two grinning schoolkids to an angle, missing the troublesome third step, their thuds on the uncarpeted stairs echoing in the upper rooms, reminding Dad they were in the house. Dad in his bedroom, sat round his lappy lining up another wasted bet.

Graham was on hands and knees, ferreting under his bed when Tom got to the bedroom.

'Close the door,' he ordered, and yanked out an Adidas bag, threw it to the bed. Inside, sandwiched in the folds of a borrowed but never returned judo suit were three folded blades. Graham's eyes shone.

Tom stepped back. 'Where'd you get 'em?'

'Know someone, don't I? Cost me a mountain bike.'

'You ain't got a mountain bike.'

'Well I found one.' He chose a weapon, pushed at the spring pocket blade. It glided open. He held the rubber grip and gave Tom a toothy grin. 'Isn't it cool?' he whispered.

He cast it from palm to palm, enjoying the weight of the handle. Told Tom how to open it, said this one was for hunting, the others for throwing. Then stopped. 'Let's go to the woods, set some traps, do some hunting.' He handed Tom a brown-handled folder knife. 'I'll show you how to skin rabbits.'

Hunting was the sort of excitement Tom had hoped for, the long hot summer boring, even though neither of them knew the first thing about setting traps or skinning a rabbit. They grabbed jackets, tucked away their weapons, and changed to stealth mode, creeping out of the back door, mounting their bikes – adrenalin bubbling in their stomachs.

The pair, now buzzing, raced through the streets, jumping kerbs, swerving mums in prams, empowered at holding a secret in their pockets.

Chapter 27

Doorway to alcove, passage to dorm, this was Caulk's skulking ground. Eyeing every patient, ensuring all guests received the right attention.

She was essential to the day-to-day running of the hospital and would soon be able to hold a proper job. The doctor had told her so, had assured her that if she stayed out of trouble, tried her best in the assessments, she would soon be working for him. Just had to avoid the orderlies – they didn't understand.

She barged in on Miss Primrose. 'Is there anything you need? Are you sure you haven't forgotten anything? I know you can be very forgetful.' She snooped the room, looked Primrose up and down, practicing her nurse-like manner.

'Yes, I know. The doctor was here earlier, and I feel fine, so I must have taken everything.'

Primrose sat perched on the edge of her bed, blathering about the doctor. She was never sure who visited when, the hours merged into months.

Julie bit her nails, unable to stay in one spot. She paused only to catch every noise – in case she had missed something. She claimed to hear every scrape and clang in the building. She rarely slept, was too busy trying to hear if everyone else was asleep.

Whenever possible she would avoid her medication, not sure why, it just felt wrong – like she had been ill since taking drugs, wanted to know what life was like without. So, she pretended to swallow the pills or vomited them afterwards. Felt better for it, more tuned, excited.

Her eyes widened – a white coat hung up on the back of the door. This was the opportunity she had been waiting for. 'The doctor's coat.'

'Yes, he's always doing that, he's a bit forgetful. I'll look after it for him until he comes back.'

Caulk dashed over and grabbed the coat before Primrose could move.

'No, I'll take it to him,' she said, filling it.

She brushed down her new garment, admired herself in the stainless-steel safety mirror, unperturbed by her greasy hair and stray teeth that were too late for a brace. Without another word, she left.

As soon as she was out of the door she caught herself, and moved into covert mode, eyeing the human traffic in the corridor. Before she could change course, two orderlies approached – but passed by with a snigger.

They knew the doctor would give Caulk privileges by letting her wear his coat on occasion, so thought nothing of it. It was common to see her sneaking around in her fantasy world. Caulk was harmless, and good for comedy value, especially with new guests. She certainly livened up the place for the staff who wagered bets on who she would next try to cure. Her infatuation would last about a week before she moved on to someone else. This week, all bets were on Timothy.

Caulk dug her hands into her pockets, stiffened her back and pulled her shoulders to her ears. She glared at her patients, resembling a hawk as she covered the corridor. It was then she received her second surprise of the day. The doctor's swipe card. She didn't need to remove it to know what it was and what it could unlock. She rolled it over in her right palm, keeping her prize hidden. Eyes like saucers, she glanced over her shoulder, and doubled her step to the basement.

***

'Went better than expected,' McLeish said. Took a sip of Pepsi, fingering at an opened bag of crisps on his lap.

'It was always going to be easy as long as the governor wasn't there, we had his apologies up front, so we knew the only fly in the wine was the old social jerker. She was always going to dig her heels in, but the number cruncher was never going to see any further than the bank account.'

Leeman put down his pint of mild. 'Come to think of it, where's Dirty Dick?'

'Don't call him that,' Ravel nipped, holding mineral water to his lips. 'He's cleaning up after us, that's for sure. Without him our plan would be going nowhere.' He sat with a straight back, he was clean-shaven, groomed.

'Calm down, he's getting his cut.'

The devil appeared. Ravel went to the bar to get the fourth member something fizzy but clean to drink. When he returned, Leeman got straight to the point.

'So, Detective Griffin, do we have a supply chain for our new product?'

'Don't call me by that name,' Griffin hissed, looking uneasily around the empty alcove.

A few regulars, mainly pensioners, swapped stories at the bar. The lunchtime drinkers had plenty to tell and were just getting started. Sunlight glinted through the single window, giving a few rays of natural light on what was usually a dark alehouse. The barman had the duty of being a listener, he'd heard the stories before but never complained. Safe FM played out the background for the fragmented group.

'Settle down, no one can hear, that's why we choose this place.'

'I don't like coming here, there are other ways.'

'But this one doesn't leave a trail,' insisted the director of Zenacare.

They knew Leeman was right, any other communication would compromise their security. Verbal, face to face, was the only way to make decisions and plans.

Griffin changed the subject. 'What the hell happened on Sunday night?' He fixed McLeish, didn't wait for a response. 'You know what I had to do to give them time to get out?' He whispered just loud enough for the group to hear. 'What on earth were they doing there?'

'Beats me,' replied the doctor. 'They're criminals, you know, they don't always do as they should,' he said, crunching on cheese and onion. 'You should know that better than anyone.'

'It was good work, Simon, and we're all very thankful,' said Gregory. 'You took a big risk. We just need to keep that pair in line. Have you had a word Alex?'

'Yes. I've been guaranteed it won't happen again.' He tipped his head back and poured the upturned packet down the hatch.

'Do we still need them?' asked Griffin. 'I had to use my boy at the telephone exchange to dig us out.'

Griffin had a dirty helper on his side who worked for a telecom giant. The giant had recently acquired Airwave communications, now used by Norfolk police. Ideal. Griffin was investigating a pornography ring when he had discovered an employee with a chequered past. The spot check revealed that he had enough indecent material to give him a record, but instead of nailing him, Griffin had decided to keep him in his pocket. He had a collection of small-timers at hand. If he uncovered anyone with a useful day job, rather than making an arrest he would keep them in his grasp – they might come in handy.

'For now, certainly,' assured Leeman. 'When it's time to clean up the town they can be your very first call,' he continued, and after draining his pint gave Griffin a wink, 'as payback for your hard work.' He eased back, licked the foam from his lips, belly pushing at the button on his stressed striped shirt.

Griffin said, 'I look forward to it. It's just there are a lot more like them.' He craned his neck to eye the locals at the bar.

Leeman moved on. 'There's something else I want to talk about. I don't want anyone else turning up at my workplace picking up deliveries – we need a lab.' He tapped at the table with his index. 'This Sunday is the last pickup. There are twenty kilos ready, and that will last a long time. Until then we need to case out a new spot. The lockup will need to go as well, once we find a new place we'll produce and pack it all there.'

Everyone nodded their heads. Much as it was a democracy, Leeman was calling the shots.

'We should change location every six months,' added Ravel.

'Do we trust these guys to collect and deliver the cash?' asked Griffin.

'Don't worry, we've got enough on them to keep them in our pockets for a good while, they can't go anywhere. This town is small fry. I've lined up some big hitters. We'll be wholesale and leave the distribution to someone else. We just need to prove that it works.'

The doctor coughed into his Pepsi. 'Oh, it works all right.'

'Well, I think we're all agreed. We'll see where we are after this weekend, and how it's all gone down. If we've found the new Ecstasy, there are twenty kilos lined up for wholesale, and we're in business.'

McLeish thought on the hidden agenda between him and Leeman. Endeavour was delivering supplies that day on behalf of BetaPharm. Scooped from Zenacare, sold legitimately to the hospital.

The pack of wolves sat chewing the fat a while, then Harry's blazer banged out 'Born in the USA'. He floundered in the side pocket, 'Hello, Pooch.'

The others shifted uneasily in their seats, digging out their phones, making themselves busy, Leeman exchanging love messages as he clambered from the table. They had sat through this before, trying to make conversation, cover up Harry's gushing, his personality changing whenever he spoke to 'Pooch'.

Harry stepped out of earshot, phone pressed to ear, and listened to her requests. Jennifer wanted a wardrobe upgrade. She had asked for a card of her own. He hadn't gone that far, so was ever present as the debt racked up, trying to keep the young girl on the hook. It was becoming a battle but hoped it would all work out if he could find a suitable point to pop the question. Once they had settled down he could draw the purse strings. Nevertheless, he was enjoying the attention. Also, she had come in very useful for his latest business adventure – she was the director of Endeavour. Not that she had to do much, just shuffle some money around and pick up the phone occasionally to organise a delivery once or twice a week. Blissfully unaware of her sugar daddy's plans, she was the perfect front for the scheme.

Harry hung up, shuffled back to the table with a pained expression. 'Well I'm afraid I'm going to have to make my excuses, duties are calling me.' He grabbed his blazer. 'Think we're all done here anyway.'

They agreed, set a date for the next pack meeting, and left one at a time. Alternating their exits through the front and rear doors.

Chapter 28

Griffin strolled to the promenade, crossing the road to his black four-wheel-drive pride and joy. He clicked the fob, pacing his stride so that a few teenagers could acknowledge him, and ogle the vehicle. No pool car for Griffin, style over cost every time.

Once seated, he checked for messages. Nobody required his immediate attention so he could indulge himself for the rest of the shift. He was in that mood that came round every few weeks, sooner recently. Griffin was in control – of the streets. Rule one in becoming a police hero. If you want to fix problems in the town then create them first, in your own time and in your own way. The key to career progression.

There was only one person to impress – Ross. Once he was DI, he would slowly make Ross look inept.

Griffin had his ducks lined up, he knew every person's weak spot, those that mattered, at least. Right now, he needed to put Burnt out of the picture. He would be promoted in a matter of months, and then he could move on to undermining Ross. His moment of fame was coming.

Halloween would flood the streets, then he would clean up and the two courier drivers for Endeavour would see his smoking gun. He had taken every opportunity to take pistol practice at the shooting range, and the need to make it real was becoming desperate. He had a compulsive urge to blast someone away for real, no more cardboard cut-outs, why else would he become a police officer? Needed to keep it legal though.

Once Halloween had proved itself he would move it out of town and keep Norfolk clean. Griffin had a master plan, and no one would be able to stop his promotion through the ranks, he would be relied on too heavily.

If anyone pushed him aside, he would supply a dealer with a couple of kilos of Halloween, then turn to his superiors, say that this is what happened when no one listened to him.

Griffin cruised the streets, inspired. This was proactive policing. You needed to know every crook around the place, to do that you aid them, that way you control them.

Ross, with his ever composed and ordered routine, used archaic policing methods. The modern officer needed to take the initiative, the force needed to see the bigger picture.

Burnt. A joke, with his so-called experience of real city gangs. Naive and easy to trip up – especially the last stunt. Got his boy in telecoms to hack the phone of a local chump on the sex offenders register, then used it to send phoney text messages to Burnt's wife. Burnt took the bait in one gulp, flew off the handle by all accounts. Griffin called in on the chump, gave his good cop act, said he might be able to help him make a complaint. Burnt wouldn't be around for long.

Griffin was in one of his tyrannical moods. Should he take it out on his obedient doormat of a girlfriend? Should he drive to Norwich and pick up a random and give her a beating? Maybe later, but first he would pay a visit to Kingfisher boxing club and catch up with Finny.

Finny had previous, so didn't have the required paperwork to work with juveniles, but people who knew Finny appreciated the fifty-year-old's intentions were genuine. He guided the kids, ensure they kept on the right path.

The manager turned a blind eye to the lack of paperwork, there were enough registered coaches to keep the authorities content, so Finny could help – supervised, of course. His enthusiasm was boundless, and the unpaid job was as much a solace for Finny as it was a rock for the youngsters.

This was where Griffin took the initiative. He used his cunning, creating an opportunity to put the coach in his pocket.

It was easy. He paid a twenty-five-year-old loose cannon called Clair to spend the night with Finny and make sure he felt special. Poor Finny was over the moon. Only three months out of nick and he had pulled a corker. She truly loved him – for the night.

Next day Griffin called round to Finny's bedsit, said he was following up on a rape allegation from Clair. Took a DNA swab, and from that day on Finny was in Griffin's pocket. At first Finny heard nothing, until Griffin showed up a couple of months later at Kingfishers. From then on it had been fun, fun, fun – just like now when he needed to let off steam.

Three-storey, bay-windowed holiday rents lined Prince's Road, plaques boasting a Victorian history. Repointed, salvaged and proudly restored, moderately trimmed with hanging baskets.

Two minutes' drive deeper into town and terraces jutted onto the street, slim and pointed. A broken drainpipe dripped onto the path, the trickle lapped by a cat that stopped to fix its glare at Griffin crawling past.

Griffin, who knew the locals, knew their history, knew where the old man had bolted to, who he had shacked up with and what he had left behind. He purred to himself; the kids on this street were too young to recruit, but give them a few years and they would need him.

***

The smell of stale sweat greeted the DS as he sauntered into the boxing club. It would be another half hour before the kids turned up for their lessons, only those training for a pro fight would be punching the bags at this time.

A semi-professional, the Baron, pounded away at a thick padded Lonsdale puncher. Griffin's target, Finny, held the punch bag firm. The owner, Albert, was mopping the floor.

Griffin caught their attention. The Baron stopped. They turned towards the DS with a look that thrilled Griffin. It was a look not quite of scorn, but one you give when you revere someone – and when you are not sure what to expect.

Griffin nodded towards the ring, and Finny, who knew the drill, took two pairs of eight-ounce sparring gloves off the shelf. He handed a pair to Griffin who exchanged cold pleasantries while taking off his shirt and tie.

There was little point in Finny wearing hand protection. He wasn't going to make contact with Griffin. Finny was the dummy, and Griffin could improve his boxing skills.

Griffin rolled his head, loosened his arms, shadowed a couple of jabs. Finny, nose across his face from years as a punch-bag and few teeth left, slipped in a gum shield, pushed up his fists and ambled around the ring. The Baron looked on in frustration.

Albert swept his hand over his bald head, turned to the Baron, told him to get changed, but the Baron wouldn't budge, stood firm. Looked on helplessly.

Griffin started to duck and weave as Finny threw some telegraphed, lightweight punches. Much lighter than the DS, who had the longer reach and wide angular frame, this was a mismatch on more than one level. Griffin blocked and moved, finally unleashing his first jab. Finny swerved. Then he launched a second, this one blocked, which frustrated Griffin, a third skimmed the top of Finny's scalp. Griffin paused, peered over his mitts – Finny should not be blocking.

Finny dropped his guard slightly, and Griffin came in with a wide right hook that smashed against the side of his face. Then a stream of jabs followed, another haymaker, each one smashing into Finny's hardened face.

The pummelling continued – a final uppercut cracked the veteran under the chin. Blood and spit flew into the air, flecks landed on Griffin's white vest.

'Enough,' shouted Albert, dropping his mop. 'That's enough.'

Finny grounded, Griffin stood over, panting, waiting to dish out more. Feeling the power. Finny looked up from the canvas, shook his head.

Griffin moved away, disappointed. He slipped off his gloves, pulled his T-shirt off the ropes. Not a tremor in his fingers as he buttoned up his shirt.

Finny asked, through bloodied mouth, 'Bad day at the office?'

'Quite the opposite,' replied Griffin, stepping through the ropes. He walked towards the door, ignoring the holes drilled into him from the Baron, who asked, 'Surely he's paid his dues by now?'

'Throw in the towel any time you want,' replied Griffin over his shoulder.

'Just remember, his DNA was all over that bitch. I can come around with a warrant just like that.' He clicked his fingers in the air, and strolled out of the club.

Chapter 29

Caulk raked through the medicine cabinet. Held up a bag above her head, captivated at the light catching the crystals.

She carefully opened the zipper and peered inside. The bag was label CZ12. Julie moved her head out of the light to get a better look at the powder. Two more packages were in the cabinet, had a slightly yellow glint under the light. They were labelled HAL31.

Caulk scanned the remainder of the medicine cabinet. A steel label drew her attention, sitting in between a packet of syringes and a butane gas canister. She picked it out, rubbed her fingers across the golden embossed letters. Halloween. She placed it in one of the yellowish tinged bags of powder, a good match.

She placed all three packages in her white coat, then patted the pockets in satisfaction. She now had what she needed to treat her patients – and didn't need the doctor anymore. With an air of self-righteous confidence, she left with one package of CZ12 in her left pocket and two packets of HAL31 in her right. Or bliss on the left and double misery on the right. Caulk was the most dangerous person in Great Yarmouth.

***

Burnt was sweating away in front of his monitor, head-locked with HOLMES, filtering through scores of offenders. He swore at the machine and waited for the latest search to refresh on the screen.

Ashley entered with two mugs of fresh coffee. Burnt muttered a grunt of appreciation, welcoming the interruption.

Ashley, keen to give the news said, 'Something came back from IT. Could be it was to do with the dubious message you received from control.' He let it hang, handed Burnt his mug, had his attention.

'There's been a few hacks recently. Someone, somewhere is logging into HOLMES.' He nodded at the screen, took in the caffeine.

'This came from Gaz in IT, but even he shouldn't know this. It's being kept quiet, no way will anyone admit this, not officially, so we need to keep it to ourselves.' He sat, waiting for the tirade of questions.

Burnt spilled coffee over the keyboard, wiped his hands down his sides, and began pacing the room. 'They *have* to admit it. If there has been a compromise to the IT security, it needs fixing.'

He stopped, changed direction. 'The right security has to be in place, hackers need keeping out. This is a major flaw, anyone could be getting in.'

Ashley unwrapped a Nutribar. 'That's just it,' he said, crossing his legs and taking a bite. 'It wasn't from outside, it was someone logged on internally. The log-in credentials are unknown to IT. It appears to be someone who works here, but without HOLMES's authorisation. That's why it won't go any further. It's not worth the chance of that leaking. IT have informed the gods, but other than that we're the only ones who know, and that's off the radar – and certainly if we want any more tips from IT. And before you ask, yes, he did tell me over a game of GTA.'

'Logged on internally, you say?'

'Well, they could have been out of the building, but logged into the system through VPN, in which case it would appear they were inside.'

'Surely there's tracking for that? You said yourself everything gets recorded.'

'Not if someone logs in with a masked IP address. Plenty of websites offer this service.'

Burnt sighed, accepting the answer although not happy with it.

'There's one other thing.'

'Oh?'

'Well, go back to Sunday night and the rogue call. Let's say it was a genuine hoax call from an Airwave device, and the log for it was deleted from the server, hacked.'

'It was genuine,' insisted Burnt.

Ashley continued. 'There were numerous calls on Sunday giving the address of the fire. We need a list of numbers for all calls made, not just 999, but to anywhere. It's some undertaking, I know.'

'It is, but the chances of the perps having an Airwave device as a back-up when doing a chemist is unlikely.'

'That's right, maybe *they* made a call.'

'To someone with an Airwave device,' concluded Burnt.

They sat silent for a moment. 'We're not supposed to be snooping around trying to find a traitor. We need authority to get that information. We need to justify it and saying it's to investigate corruption within Norfolk police isn't going to do us any favours.'

'I know,' said Ashley, frowning over his coffee. 'It could be a stolen device.'

'Maybe. But we don't tell Ross that,' said Burnt almost in a whisper. 'We say it's to trace all 999 calls to link us to the vehicle we are trying to trace. We're looking for the perpetrator's phone number, used on or after the incident, which is sort of the truth.'

'It's exactly what we want,' said Ashley. 'We'll need help on this. There will be thousands of numbers if we're checking every network.'

'No. We'll do it ourselves,' insisted Burnt. Anyone could knobble the data, and there were few he could trust.

'We just need the numbers over a ten-minute window. I'll get the paperwork together for authorisation.

'Christ,' he said, looking at his watch. Four-thirty pm. 'I'll need to be quick, or this will slip into next week.' He plonked the cup down, spilling more coffee across the table. 'You carry on with HOLMES, try to get something on the vehicle. Maybe we could tie a number to a van driver.'

He grabbed his jacket off the back of the chair and scuttled out of the room.

Chapter 30

A lake isolated Timothy from his mother. She gave a long slow wave from the shore. He guessed she was smiling. Why so happy? He wanted to be with her and would be but for the expanse of water he feared to cross.

He cupped his ear listening for her call, but noises of the living drowned the sounds that echoed back. He tried to ignore the whiny, swinging doors, the occasional scream of a patient and service trolleys rattling past his room.

He felt reality slip away as he regressed into his comfort zone, something he had become skilled at – the sounds of the living receded. He sank through his bed.

Timothy stepped into the water. There was no sensation, no cold, no wetness – only fear. He couldn't swim, but saw no other way to reach her. She froze as he ventured into the lake. Shook her head.

Timothy scanned. No roads or footbridges, and behind, there was only empty grey. He shivered, turned back to the water and waded in.

The lake had an oily silver surface. Black veins rippled around his body with each step. He pushed on.

There was no alternative, he wanted his mother. He ignored her warnings and trod deeper into the silver lake.

She began screaming. No sound, but he could see from the way she threw her arms around in the air that she was alarmed. He could just make out the look of distress in her eyes. She had the same look when they ventured to Torredon in the Highlands and lost their way.

The same distress as he teetered on the ridge, enthused by the challenge as the wind eddied around them. But his mother, scared and protective, saw only danger and screamed at him to climb down. He ignored her pleas then, and would ignore it now.

The water lapped at his chin – his mother disappeared. He tried to swim, he flailed, and lashed out on top of the water. The movements were fitful, fear replaced his courage.

He continued splashing but the silver gripped him. He rested his arms, let the water pull him along. He was floating, bobbing on the surface. Then made a smooth movement with one arm and glided across the top of the water. He tried his other arm, again he covered distance with little effort. He had learnt to swim. And it was euphoric.

He stopped to tread water, and spotted his mother. She stood with a look of disbelief on her face – of pride. He swam towards her, he was over half way across the lake, each effortless stroke pushed him closer.

He was enjoying his newfound skill, building his speed with each stroke, carving the water open.

At the shore he stood knee deep in the water and swept his hair back. Smiled to the shore, expecting his mother to run into the lake and welcome him with hugs. She was gone.

He scanned the shoreline, but he was alone once more. Then turned around to face the beach he had left behind, and there was his mother, standing, clutching herself looking helpless, sad – alone.

Chapter 31

Timothy sat upright, clammy, drained. But relieved it was daylight. He smashed his fists into the mattress – didn't know who to trust but knew what he must do to find peace. He couldn't lie here being part of some madman's scheme. He had no idea what the doctor was planning to do to him, he had to get away.

He lifted the covers, jumped out of bed and gulped a pint of water. Still fully clothed, he squeezed on his pumps.

The medication was getting worse. He ignored the spiders pouring through the holes in the wall, shook his head, and they scurried away. Unsure how long he had been in the hospital but guessed he had endured around two to three days of toxic injections, which left him staring at the walls. Found his watch. 5pm.

He moved to the window and looked down to the car park, planning an escape route. Could he walk straight through the front door? Would the kind lady help him? He felt the card in this hoodie pocket and pulled it out. Bryony Joy. No, she was one of them.

He watched a few of the staff move between the building and cars, was about to turn away when someone caught his eye. Someone in grey overalls, carrying boxes from a van to the hospital. Black straggly hair, pouty face, bulging eyes. He stood in shock as the certainty weighed down on him. He needed a closer look.

Timothy opened the door slowly, peering through the crack.

Two eyes stared back. Caulk barged in.

'Who've you been talking to? If you talk to the walls like that, you'll be here forever. I know. I see them come, I see them go, I see it all,' she continued, making wide eyes around the room.

Timothy backed away. 'I need to get to the car park.'

'I'll take you there.' She grabbed Timothy's hand, yanked him into the corridor. 'You're on fire.'

'Medication.'

She whispered, 'I don't take mine.'

He realised she was wearing a doctor's coat. 'I know more than they do, that's why I've got the coat on.'

Like a shepherd, she guided Timothy through the hall, down a set of stairs.

Timothy rounded the landing, looked down to the ground floor, and froze. He saw the delivery man stop at the entrance to the car park to light a cigarette. His face was unmistakeable. Timothy instinctively crouched behind the hand rail on the landing, then peeked to take another look. Ronnie was contently puffing away, oblivious that the son of the woman he'd killed four days earlier was spying on him.

Timothy stumbled backwards, tripped up the stairs, ran down the corridor to his room, and slammed the door.

Julie followed in a hurry, asking what was wrong, trying not to shout, not to run. She wanted to keep the coat on.

Timothy was at the easel when she came in, frantic, tears welling. She questioned him, got no response, then left him to his drawing, to find the man that had scared him so much.

He carried on, not letting the demons leave the canvas, allowing the pain to flood in around him, the sweat building up as the images jumped around on the page. Rodents scurried up the easel and nibbled at the pencil.

Julie watched the man in overalls take a signature then stroll to his van. She narrowed her eyes, rubbed the packages in her coat pocket. She had work to do. She tapped the pockets of the white coat, checked the swipe card was still in the breast pocket, and skulked back to Timothy's room, keeping out of sight whenever possible to avoid the staff – and McLeish.

Timothy watched the van disappear from the courtyard, bit his lips, chewed on his gums, clawed at his arms. He felt filthy, violated.

'When are they here next?' he demanded as Caulk hurried into the room.'

'Sunday morning. Why, who are they.'

'How do I get out of here?'

'I can leave whenever I want, they don't question me. But harder for you.' She nodded at his blue smock.

Timothy put the card back in his pocket. 'Take me with you. I need to get out of here.'

She came close and whispered, 'OK. We need to time it right.'

'We get out, I'll tell you who they are.'

He followed his leader once more to the closed doors at the rear entrance. They waited patiently in the alcove, eyeing the security booth. They watched on as the guard received a phone call and left his post.

'Now.' They scurried to the exit. Julie pulled out the swipe card and slid it through the slot. The click of freedom.

The guard had been busy locking up the basement after the last delivery and had only just sat down to finish his muffin. Before he could get himself comfortable the duty nurse asked him for the delivery notes and paperwork for the incoming goods, which he submitted, albeit muttering to himself that it wasn't his job – anything that involved him getting off his seat wasn't his job. He got back and collapsed into his swivel-chair, saw the back of two heads leaving the premises. One in a white coat holding the hand of her patient in a blue smock. Someone must have signed the paperwork. He wasn't overly worried, he was off shift in an hour.

Chapter 32

A chill cut across the shoreline. The darkness starting to consume the red twilight horizon. With no money in his pockets and a limited grasp of his location, Timothy wandered along the beach, the tide grabbing at his ankles. The blue smock was now ditched, and the hospital bracelet hidden. He could hear screams overhead, looked up and saw creatures circling and preying on him, waiting to swoop – to tear at his flesh. But he was soon consumed by the grainy sand between his feet and swirling patterns made by the claws of the sea.

He felt some luck on his side today, he'd escaped the prison and eluded the strange goblin in the white coat at a convenient crossroads. Timothy had made no excuses but moved on quickly, leaving Caulk reasoning with strangers.

A pale, curved object jutted from the sand. He dropped to his knees to check it out, expecting it to disappear like a mirage. It was a bowed bone with a sharp point and a thick handle-shaped stem. He wiped the sand away, rubbed the grainy markings on the side. Clutched it for protection. The preying vultures retreated so he thrust it into the side pocket of his cargos and ventured on.

He found respite under the pier – secluded and out of sight. He sat with his back up against the stone wall, staring out to sea and consigning himself to the visual display that came with nightfall. Better to sleep here than in that prison. He stared into the confusion in front of him, trying to pick out the spectacle from the real world.

Rays of light danced along the horizon, spelled out his name then morphed to swastikas that rotated and exploded, giving way to red clouds.

He closed his eyes, his body sank into the sand and turned numb. His arms stretched out beside him and grew longer, making their way to sea. They stiffened, broke into pieces like a hollow clay vessel to a hammer. His insides were seeping into the sand, tormentors took turns to swoop below the pier and peck at his carcass.

***

He had no idea how long he had been there. He hauled himself up, stretched his leaden limbs, rubbed his face. Then searched out the whalebone, pulled his hoodie over his head and shifted to the flashing neon of cheap entertainment.

He trotted onto the main drag, ignored the staring hags with shark eyes. And breathed in deep fried batter that turned his stomach as he moved past charades of fake tavernas, honest deep fry joints, slot machines and noisy arcades.

Beats kicked out from above his head, inviting all strays through a cave-like opening guarded by two crocodiles in tuxedos. Waifs and urchins queued, the mantra of the beating drums beckoned. Timothy spotted the goblin in the white coat talking to the crocodiles, swapping something to gain entrance to the hidden theatre. The windows above showed puppets on strings jangling and twisting in a trance. He pushed on.

Rows of flashing machines blinded him, electronic voices deafened him, rows of empty rooms gurgling their inane noises, miserable people trapped behind glass cages around piles of brown coins. He made for town, away from the promenade, up Regent Street leaving the noise behind.

From there, Haven Bridge to South Town Road, the long quiet causeway, would take him away. Home.

Windows of multi-coloured seaside rock beamed from behind the glass, seaside tat of hats and T-shirts. Then he was in town.

A few scarecrows on the sidewalks asked for money. One held on to a traffic cone trying to convince onlookers that it was his musical instrument. Bile poured out of his mouth, his face melted into the sidewalk.

After another 100 yards a scarecrow babbled to himself about the dichotomy of the elite and the unfortunate. The bearded beggar's dirty mouth was spitting as he gave a speech on how the wealth in the world was owned by so few. He named each, along with the value of their estates, and what they could buy for the less privileged. The monologue was the most meaningful words Timothy had heard for some time. The elderly tramp tipped his hat in recognition of the young boy's interest and introduced himself as Gordon. He straightened his filthy tie, ran his hands down his lapels as he engaged with his small audience. Others passed by, scowled or mocked. Timothy had no pennies to pass on to the beggar and told him so. That upset Gordon who decided to deliver his speeches elsewhere. He picked up his vase of money, grumbled at the boy, turned and floated away.

Timothy nipped through a snicket that brought him out to a car park that faced another drinking den. He glanced at the sign above. *The Oakwoods.*

A pack of wolves spewed out of the pub onto the road, mounted their motorcycles, growling and barking at each other. The words 'Outcasts' proudly brandished on their backs, partly covered by their hairy manes. They started their engines, burned into the night.

Chapter 33

'Nice outfit,' Graham said, more to his friends than to the strange looker in the doctor's coat. They were loitering at the crossroads next to the Albion, skilling on their bikes, outdoing each other.

'I'm looking for my patients,' she muttered. This was new territory for her.

The three swapped puzzled looks.

Graham paused trying to beat his bar spin personal best. 'And what do you want them for?'

'To give them their medicine.'

'What medicine?'

Caulk glanced over her shoulder then opened the pocket of her coat, just enough to show the boy a package of white powder. Graham Hacket scanned the vicinity. It was the jackpot.

'I can help you. I know some sick people,' he said, eying an opportunity that would probably never come his way again.

His younger brother, still none the wiser, paid little attention to what was going down. He was more interested in bunny-hopping his bike, trying to beat his last highest score. Drew Trench sat straddling his BMX, stuffing his face with chips, equally oblivious to what was progressing.

Graham told his two subordinates to sit tight while he did some business. The word 'business' made them stand to attention. It sounded important so they stood by their bikes, trying with all their efforts to look business-like.

Graham escorted Caulk into the Albion, stressed it was best she first went to the ladies' toilet where she should wait, and that he would go to the lounge and find the patients who would be waiting for medication. Asked her how much it was, she said for free – he followed her.

'In here,' he said, pointing to the cubicle. She dutifully walked in, Graham followed, locking the door behind them. They were almost face to face, little room to move.

'It needs packaging up, so you can dish it out in doses – in wrappers,' explained Graham. Caulk nodded, took one of the white bags out of her pockets expecting the boy to create a miracle with the powder.

Hacket reckoned this moment was the best chance he would get. He grabbed the pack out of Caulk's hand, but she immediately responded, trying to seize it back. She never noticed the upper cut from Graham's left fist until it was too late. It connected underneath her jaw and she bounced back, cracking her head on the cubicle. He stuffed the packet into his baggy jeans and pushed her to the corner under the cistern, pulling his knife to keep her at a distance as he fumbled with the cubicle lock. She instinctively put her hand into her left pocket to protect the remaining medicine. Graham, expecting her to pull a blade, poked the knife at her face, piercing her cheek. She yelped. The shock made her clench her fist, her fingernails dug into the packet of CZ12 in her left pocket. Graham bounded out of the toilet with a clatter making the plastic-framed cubicle shudder, and scarpered onto the streets.

Julie rubbed her face, looked down at her hands. She licked a trickle of blood off her fingers, along with the powder embedded under her fingernails. Her tongue numbed. She felt in her right hand pocket, relieved that she still had two packets, one of each type. She knew she had to be more careful from now on. She would find the thief and deal with him later. For now, she took on board the small amount of advice the teenager had given her – she needed to create doses for her patients. She would start with the torn packet.

Caulk desperately wanted to see the effect the medication would have on other people, and not the ones in the hospital. People in hospital never got better. The more drugs McLeish gave them, the sicker they got.

She stumbled out of the door, washed her face and stared at herself in the mirror. It was only a small cut, she told herself – one of the hazards of being a doctor.

She straightened up and looked at her reflection. Following many years of angst and blindness, she suddenly saw clarity in her image. The small amount of the powder she'd ingested stopped time for a moment, long enough for her to reflect on her life and to realise that years of mental agony had paid the price on her sallow face.

Her eyes welled up as she recalled her past – the lie she had lived with for years. The mirror, however, wasn't lying, it reflected the truth. The medication she had recently managed to avoid had started to clear her mind, which was why the CZ12, McLeish's personal prescription, was working so well.

Deep down she knew she wasn't mentally ill, not in the way the doctors had told her, not in the way they had diagnosed her. She had issues for sure, had lost her child which left its mark, but not in the way she'd led them to believe. She had feigned her condition.

Caulk had found her husband crouched over the baby, the baby she loved and tried to nurture in its short life. But she loved her husband just as much, and when she found what he had done in that one instant of madness, she felt duty bound to defend him.

They pleaded ignorance and not child abuse, but the bruises were plain to see, and her husband persuaded her to stand up for him and take the blame. With his criminal record he would never see daylight again, whereas she would never serve the same as him in prison and she could feign mental illness. Not to plead it, her husband was quick to point out, but to act it.

She quietly agreed, agonising over how immoral it was, which in turn sent her into a downward spiral from which she would never return. The doctors found some rare syndrome to attach to her personality and soon acting wasn't necessary. Then, coupled with additional medication, she became a self-fulfilling prophecy.

Once diagnosed she cracked from the inside and imploded, infrequent lucidity replaced by anxiety and mood swings – which meant more drugs to rescue her.

In a final but crucial twist of the knife, her husband had pleaded physical abuse, showed his body of self-inflicted scars and reddened face of self-torture to the courts, which condemned the sick woman to a lifetime of psychiatry. He fled with an ex.

She had been a fool and knew it, but the charade had gone on for so long that it became too late to confess. Over the years Caulk had tried to hide it from herself. She didn't have to hide from anyone else – no one would ever believe her again.

She decided any help she could give to the needy, albeit completely misguided, such as getting a boy out of hospital who quite clearly shouldn't be there, was her duty.

The few crystals had taken hold of her, a warm glow of comfort had spread through her body. Everyone deserved this feeling of well-being. Why did she not feel this good in hospital?

She was snapped out of her thoughts when she realised she wasn't the only one staring into the mirror. She had company, a chatty brunette in high heels giving it big with the lipstick and motor-mouthing away to the patient-cum-doctor.

'Are you alright, darlin'? Is it a murder mystery tonight? I dunno what people get up to these days.'

She picked out a brush and adjusted her locks. 'I just need a few gins,' she said, giggling. 'It's a great diet, I've lost three days already.'

She laughed out loud, cracked open a small mixer can of gin and tonic, said her name was Sophie, told how she was in a spot of bother. Two boyfriends in the same bar at the same time. Caulk waited, listening.

Loving all the attention, Sophie didn't notice Caulk lace her can on the edge of the sink.

When there was a gap in the one-way conversation, Julie asked, 'Do you have any scissors?' The young brunette paused to shoot her a quizzical look, realised it was probably not a murder mystery night, and that this woman was completely bats.

'Sure. I've got everything in here.'

She emptied her bag onto the counter. 'Fags, Anadin, hairspray, bit of tutty paper just in case you get caught short, Rohypnol – in case they say no, ha-ha, make-up – loads of that.'

She once more laughed fanatically. 'Guess what? You keep 'em, love, and God bless ya.' She handed over a pair of minute plastic-handled nail scissors, then tidied her bag, adjusted her hair, and strode out of the ladies' room glugging back her can and throwing it into the bin as she left, belching in another fit of giggles while tripping over her heels.

Julie smiled for the first time in a long time and lifted some flyers from the edge of the sink, of a hypnotist playing at the Albion, and locked herself away in a cubicle. She got to work, cut up small paper wraps, making squares between the hypnotist's eyes and teeth. She measured out unequal samples of McLeish's candy and placed them in their bespoke packages.

Chapter 34

The large utility vehicle crept quietly along the suburban road. The blacked-out windows were giving nothing away. This was the classier end of Norwich.

It was safe for some of the needier to make ends meet, and do so without feeling threatened. Donna was a regular in this part of the town, could see the punters coming a mile off. Watch them cruise up, pass once, then return at a slower pace. Then stop and tell her to get in. Occasionally they would drive off, asking no more questions – she guessed the price was too high. Donna's prices fluctuated depending on the demand. Her twenty-five-year-old body stood out against her competitors, if she was doing well the prices went up.

Lately, however, more busts in the area meant a tighter and smaller circle to canvass. But her two youngsters, presently curled up at home in bed, needed feeding.

Two kids with two different partners and a drug habit she had recently managed to kick had left Donna with little on her plate. Determined to give her children more than she'd grown up with she took to the streets, promising herself that it was only for a few more weeks.

She'd fled from home at a tender age and made her way down south, seeing London as the city of opportunity to rid herself from Newcastle and her perverse stepfather, her mother beyond caring.

But she'd met a guy from the east coast who talked her up and let her down when she was three months gone. With dignity, she took small job after small job, refusing to go back home and admit she had made a mistake, but after the baby arrived the burden became too much. She spiralled, found another partner who dropped her as quickly as the last. Two children now, and alone – with a habit.

She had learnt to survive and use the system to her benefit. The taxpayer paid the rent, and she made extra by using her body in the only erotic nightclub in the city. She kicked the drugs and knuckled down to being a parent. When on the streets a colleague looked after the children, and she returned the favour, both making it work for themselves. And she enjoyed the daytime with her small family, proud not to rely on a man, but taking money from them all the same.

But a little greed set in, a fellow dancer told her about the money she could earn if she put in a few extra hours. At first it was just going back to a rich punter's after work, but that led to the streets where she called her price. When she showed punters her figure they couldn't resist. Slim legs, lean shape – fresh face.

It went well for a year or so, kept telling herself that it was only a few more weeks till she found a proper job. She had started a college course in computer science while the kids were at playgroup. Once the course was behind her she hoped to move on. This ambition, however, turned out to be short-lived. An older, sly colleague with less time left to serve in the game whispered some hollow lies to her manager at the club. She was jobless overnight.

Her savings wilted, unforeseen debts arrived at the wrong time, the streets became her only hope. She knew she would have to find another partner, but with Donna's own baggage finding the right person would be a struggle. She hoped the day would never come that she would need to tell her kids the truth. For now, Mummy was out dancing.

It was safe in Norwich, and she was careful. She carried a blade, some spray, and an alarm – none needed so far.

The vehicle crept alongside and slowed. She couldn't see through the blackened glass but knew there would be one male in there, probably mid-forties, checking her out. She slipped her mac open revealing a low-cut dress a little too tight, her pert breasts baiting the invisible shopper. She would make this expensive, he could afford it, he had a new Range Rover. But it picked up pace and cruised past.

Inside, he scanned the area. In a black windcheater with the collar pulled up around his ears, and a grey beanie pulled down almost to the lobes. The windows offered protection, but he knew that with CCTV anywhere and everywhere, as soon as he pulled down a window or stopped to refill the car he could be recognised. The plates were false, he changed them whenever he was on such an outing. He started to sweat, turned the air conditioning up full.

He coasted past a couple of forty-somethings, saw the hollow eyes and haggard addict faces, so cruised on. On to another candidate, he slowed, checked her out, she flashed her wares, his heart raced. It was her.

He'd had her before. He clenched at the wheel, pausing briefly to consider it, but drove on, sweat forming on his face.

At the next street he turned and thought again. *Would she remember?* That time he'd been in a different car. He looped the block and crawled up alongside, slowed to a standstill and opened the window.

Chapter 35

Hands in pockets, head back, Julie marched onto the main drag of Yarmouth seafront, showing a wry smile to those that stared her down. She stopped partygoers to offer her wares – only to those she considered needy. She questioned each patient, and if their response satisfied her, they got a wrap. Taking no money made her popular.

The small particles she'd inadvertently taken woke the sleepy corners of her mind. She was blissfully unaware of how close she had come to having a nightmare; with the pack of magic powder in one pocket and the doom potion in the other it could have been different. She had packaged up the CZ12 mix into wraps and left the remaining HAL31 package untouched in her side pocket.

Graham Hacket had taken half of the doom, which would be better known as Halloween once McLeish and his fellow cronies had started to sell on the streets. Until now, it had only been used at St Nicholas Hospital.

The hard work carried out for them by Hacket and Caulk had begun earlier than the associates had expected, but they would be none the wiser, which was just as well as they would see none of the profits for tonight's endeavours – it was more like a loss leader. Ironically, one of the most mentally unstable women on the east coast had delivered it. The youngsters wouldn't care, they were having a ball.

One very satisfied customer was Sophie, Julie's first customer at the Albion. The penny would drop in the bimbo's empty head around three am when she was straddling one of her boyfriends for the second time that morning and pieced together the point she started to feel like the goddess of love. The only problem Sophie would have, other than to find the pseudo doctor to thank, was to determine which one made her pregnant.

Julie meandered on, occasionally stopping to help the needy. She had improved her patter, learnt quickly. 'Wanna feel on top of the world?' she would ask.

She approached Tiffany's, the biggest club on the strip. Not as busy as previous years, but youngsters still needed somewhere, and for those with not enough money in their pockets to pay for drinks, it was a meeting point and pick up area.

Tonight was a good night for an opportunist, free powder was on the streets. Julie approached the doorman who took her to one side to frisk her. She was half way through explaining her duties when she spotted Timothy idling past. She needed to catch up – he was the boy she was trying to protect. Somehow, he had given her the slip.

The bouncers were suddenly interested in her story, always happy to punt anything extra out on the side, although they would be charging for it, so attempted to do business.

Her duties changed in a moment, Caulk did not care for any questions, so handed over the remaining wraps and left the few followers that had gathered around her as quickly as she had met them. Her focus lay elsewhere – she trailed her charge.

This brief interaction with the real world enriched many young minds. 'You're what this town needs,' a young space cadet told her, 'a real doctor.' But no sooner had the doctor made her presence known, than she vanished in between the enthusiastic crowd, eyes focused on one person.

***

The three teenagers coasted in and about each other on their bikes. They cut across Deneside Road, swerved down an alley between a bistro and a pet shop. With the first step of the business completed, Hacket plotted his next move. He needed a buyer, someone who would deal wholesale. He spoon-fed the story to Tom and Drew when they quizzed him. He was bursting to tell them, but waited till they asked, tried to keep it cool. But he was pumped, this was one big break.

'We need to find Spike,' he shouted over his shoulder as they weaved around each other. 'He can sell it for us.'

Drew, out of breath, struggling with the pace. 'Sell what?'

'Mandy.'

'What?'

'Marchin' powder.'

'Eh?'

'Disco biscuits, bouncing burgers, ya know.'

'What ya talkin' about?'

'Drugs.'

Drew skidded to a stop. 'I don't want anything to do with that. You bought drugs from that madwoman?'

Graham braked, taking the opportunity to nosey his bike and pump a couple of hops. 'Yeah, of course, and now I'm selling on for a profit,' Graham explained. 'It's called business – I'm going into the drug business,' he said, pushing out his chin.

'You ain't got any money,' posed Tom, scared of the answer.

'It's on loan, innit.'

Tom straddled his bike, baggy jumper swamping him, still wearing his half-mast school trousers and scuffed black Velcro shoes. He searched Graham for a clue as to where this was heading. He didn't like it when Graham got this excited, it usually ended badly. 'Where you gonna sell it?' He asked, his voice faltering.

'The Oakwoods. Everyone goes there to score, and I'm selling wholesale,' he explained, pulling away once more, fully expecting them to follow. 'I just need to find Spike, I bet he's in the Oakwoods,' he called over his shoulder.

With a plan made, the trio continued; Graham stoked, Tom expecting the worst, Drew trailing.

Graham instructed the pair to wait, keep a look out. They didn't ask what they were looking for or what to do when it happened, but rested, perched on their bikes on the pavement outside the Oakwoods while the elder Hacket marched into the lion's den with enough powder in his pocket to send the whole pub to the moon.

Drew grumbled quietly, Tom kept shtum.

They spotted a hoodie walking towards them. Drew recognised him. He piped up. 'Loony Levin. What's he doin' here?' The screwy kid from school. This gave Drew the opportunity to prove himself to Tom who, with Graham out of the frame, now became the leader, something Drew wasn't happy about.

'Timothy,' shouted Drew, blocking his path on the pavement outside the pub. 'What are you doing out so late at night?' He didn't wait for an answer. 'Does your mum know you're out on your own?' he added, gaining courage.

Timothy tightened his grip on the whalebone in his pocket. At school he would ignore Drew, and out of school he was too fast for him.

'Why haven't you been at school?' He knew the answer, what happened last week was public knowledge and they were the first to see Timothy since the catastrophe. Timothy tried to edge past them. Drew pushed his forks in his way. 'Not so fast, Timothy.'

The doors of the pub burst open, and a herd of bikers poured out, roaring at each other. Each one brandished with the same stamp on their back – Outcasts. The three boys watched them start their engines and tear away.

***

Caulk peered out from the dimly-lit department store fire exit that overlooked the car park in front of the Oakwoods, fixated on her patient. He was in danger, she waited for them to make a move. She kept hidden – surprise would be key.

***

Graham Hacket skulked out onto the street, rubbing at his ribs. Timothy took the opportunity to slope.

Graham leant over, hands on knees hiding his face, breathing out and faltering into a whimper. Which turned to rage.

It was easy pickings for the outcasts, one of the gang had given him the same medicine he had doled out to Julie Caulk an hour earlier. Spike had introduced them, they went to the gents to do business, and Graham was served up to a bigger predator. The outcasts couldn't believe their luck – a shiny half-pound of powder. One of them had a little dab but was unable to determine what it was. But he found inside a small metallic label with the word 'Halloween' imprinted neatly across it. Hacket missed this detail, which is why he pretended the ingredients were MDMA. A good enough guess he thought, Mandy was the high everyone talked about at school.

After testing a small amount and coming to the satisfactory conclusion he was stinging them, they worked him over and took his sweeties.

Graham turned on Drew with eyes filled with venom, and pushed him off his bike. 'Why the fuck didn't you stop them? Scared?'

Drew stood up, confused, with no recourse other than to point to Timothy.

'He was in our way.'

With his newly found business empire opened and swallowed whole all within the same evening, Graham searched for a target. There was an easy one skulking away, the screwy kid from school who couldn't fight.

Timothy, sensing danger, started to trot down the side of the pub towards Haven Bridge. They took to their bikes and set after the gazelle. That was what his mother called him, his likeness to a gazelle when he ran. He never showed this ability in sports events, his competitive edge dampened, but when the need arose he could run for long distances and faster than most. He emerged from the alley onto the quay. Haven Bridge loomed on the opposite side of the road.

Caulk dashed across the car park. She knew the tallest had a knife, so would need to take him first.

Timothy picked up the pace, leaping across the road. He heard horns blaring behind him as the other three jammed on their brakes at the crossing. The interruption poured more petrol on the fire – Graham smelt blood.

Chapter 36

'How much for an hour?'

'Two hundred,' she said, probably a bit too quickly. 'Get in.'

Which she did and closed the door, wishing she had made the price higher. The driver eased away from the kerb while she unbuttoned her mac, her perfume filling the car.

She got her first real look at the man behind the wheel; he looked familiar. 'Where are we goin'?'

'Not far, to the woods,' he replied, and turned up Safe FM to cover the silence. Tina Turner keeping them company.

After making it through a few sets of lights they were soon away from the well-lit streets. Donna leafed through her bag, grasped at the cold comfort of the rape spray in her clammy palms. She searched out her phone, checked for messages, and sent a couple of her own. The usual practice with the girls – just in case.

They pulled into a small car park that backed onto a nature trail. He locked the doors, eased his seat back and swept off the beanie. Then turned to Donna and gave his practised, twisted grin.

She clutched her bag. 'Oh God, not you again.'

McLeish frowned. 'It won't be like last time.'

'I should hope not. I was sick for days. What was that stuff?'

'Never mind, this time I've got something better.'

He leant across her, opened the dash and pulled out a sunglasses case, then flipped it to reveal a loaded syringe. Light glinted off the dull yellow liquid.

'I assure you it won't hurt a bit.'

Donna squirmed, McLeish fumbled with his coat. She had time to send another quick text to a friend before confronting the injection.

'I can't. What if I get hooked again? I've not long kicked it.' She showed McLeish a creased face.

McLeish tapped the steering wheel. He knew there was only one bargaining tool with someone like her – and needed a beta-test for MR11.

He gave a cold stare. 'Three hundred pounds.'

She paused to reflect on her two little mites wrapped up snug at home. The money could go far.

McLeish explained it was only to help her relax, that it added to his fun. The reality was, it excited him. Women and relationships had eluded Alex McLeish his whole life, this would be his only sexual pleasure. He had diagnosed himself as having a psychosexual disorder, which rendered him free from guilt. His excitement grew, he released his belt and looked over, wallet in hand.

'Will I be ill?' she asked.

'No,' he lied, handing over the wad of cash. Donna took it, sighing. Tucked it into a zipped compartment in her handbag, irritated at her lack of self-will.

McLeish squeezed the plunger, MR11 dribbled over his gloves. He nodded over his shoulder. 'Get in the back.'

Chapter 37

Timothy dashed across the bridge, pausing at the apex to look behind. Still on his tail, trails of colour blaring from their mouths.

He peered over the granite rail, wondered if the easy option was the best option. Confrontation was not in Timothy's DNA. Like a stalked deer he raced away for a second time, and diverted to the old town, terraced streets and alleys where he could lose them.

Timothy slipped as he edged the corner to Steam Mill Lane and smashed to the ground. He sat up, dazed, and by the time he had got to his feet the trio had gained on him. He scrambled on, losing his direction and turned into a dead end. Found himself wedged between iron gates of a business unit and the water's edge. He turned to face up – time to fight. But couldn't look at their faces for long. The wind played tricks with his ears, lights spun webs in front of his eyes. Their faces looked melted, kept changing, morphing and reshaping. It made him sick, he looked to the floor once more.

I run too much. But how do I fight?

It was something he had only ever seen on TV, or heard tales about in school. He gripped the whalebone hidden deep in his cargos.

'What's he playin' with?' snorted Drew.

Unable to answer, to look them in the eye, Timothy searched the rubble around his feet. He couldn't bear to face anyone since the injections started almost a week ago. Their faces would melt or pixelate. Some would grow hair, others lose it till they were bald, the face slowly morphing to a creature. He could never hold their look for long, it made his stomach churn over. It had grown worse each day, the bending sounds that emerged from the holes in their heads adding to the ordeal.

Graham demanded he turn out his pockets.

Timothy let go of the bone. Looked up, searching for the right words.

'It's a whalebone.'

The moment the words tumbled out of his mouth he knew he would regret them. Derisory laughter from Drew and Graham as he slumped against the gates behind him.

'Let's leave it,' pleaded Tom, scanning the road above them, car beams flashing across their faces below the bridge. 'What good is it gonna do?'

'Shut it. I want to see this whalebone. Show me.'

Their laughter had bought Timothy a bit more time, but he had little option other than to try and fight – or jump. The pack edged closer, circling the gazelle.

***

'Wake up. Wake up.' McLeish shook the prostitute violently.

He tried again. 'Wake up, you dumb bitch.' Hoping an insult would help. He was thinking fast. She must be allergic to one of the components, hadn't thought to ask her about that. Thought little about this eventuality. This could put the trial back months.

He was still lying on top of her in the back seat, trousers in the footwell.

He kicked at the front seat, punched the ceiling. Elbowed Donna once more.

Froth seeped from the side of her mouth, her eyes rolled into the back of her head.

'You stupid fucking bitch,' he screamed.

Then the spasms started. The body jumped in chaotic fits. Should have brought smelling salts, should have discussed her medical condition, should have, should have, bloody should have …

McLeish writhed around on top of her, banging his head on the roof as he pushed his milk-bottle legs into his trousers. The doors were locked, keys in the ignition, so he clambered over the fitting body and hopped out into the cold, zipping himself, then back in for his loafers.

At the rear door he dragged Donna by her feet, her head bouncing on the frame to the ground. Then across the grass verge, moaning about her weight, pausing as lights flashed past. His shirt open, stained cotton vest underneath, he stood holding her legs, mouth agape, waiting for the beams to recede.

Once more it went dark, he rolled her into the recovery position and checked for a pulse. Still breathing.

Her coat lay next to her, caught in her arms as she was dragged over the carpark. He threw it over her, then held his breath as lights flooded them both briefly for a second time. Same car? McLeish looked helpless, crouched over the body. He exhaled as the car vanished. He then raced to his Range Rover and grabbed Donna's bag, catching the handle on the gear stick, swearing some more as the contents poured into the cavity. He scooped up her belongings, smashing his head on the door frame, then dashed back to Donna. Took out her phone and hit 999, gave the location, said he found someone who had had a fit, then hung up. Then threw the phone back in the bag and left it by her side.

McLeish knew his DNA would be all over her. If she woke up, would she be able to identify him? He considered this for a moment; could he take a life in cold blood? Did she matter to anyone? Doing what she did, surely no one cared. The police wouldn't waste too much time on her. How could he do it?

Bright lights from a passer-by, this time the car slowed to a halt just past the turning. McLeish had no more time.

The car reversed. McLeish dashed to the Range Rover, tripped, and went face down into the gravel. He stood up and was about to clamber into the driver's seat when the new arrivals pulled up. They wound down the window in time to see McLeish peering over the roof of his car, dripping with sweat.

A fat head filled the window frame. An excited, spotty female in the passenger seat poked her nose over her partner's shoulder. The pair grinned like lunatics.

'Hi, I'm Kevin – a bit of doggin' goin' down is there?'

'Help yourself,' replied McLeish. He jumped into the driver's seat, slammed the door shut, and wheel-spun an oversized doughnut on exit.

It was a well-known local site for the lewd. Any other night this might have been of interest to him. Some who came here would probably have welcomed his ideas, but tonight he just had to get out of Dodge.

Kevin and his spouse swapped open-mouthed looks, then rested their eyes on the abandoned body lying on the cool grass.

***

The pack crept closer. Timothy looked from one to the other – then over their shoulders.

A figure in a white doctor's coat approached. Two of the boys ignored Timothy's stares, but Tom followed his gaze to see Caulk with Graham's BMX above her head. He had time to move, but his elder brother didn't. Graham heard a roar, turned, just in time for the frame to smash into his front teeth. Graham's lip burst open and he tumbled to the gravel.

Caulk picked up the next bike she saw at her feet, walked to the river wall and hurled it into the Yare. Still growling, she pushed up her sleeves and stomped back, going for her inside pocket, making out she had a blade.

Tom scooped up his BMX, jumped on and fled. Drew scurried behind like a scared piglet, his bottom lip curling. After a safe distance he screamed, 'psycho bitch.'

Graham was dazed, his face throbbed. He shook his head, stood up and faced the pair. She had changed, become charged, empowered – determined. The knife in his pocket was not feeling that reassuring. He turned towards Timothy who guarded his own weapon. The three stood, hands on weapons, scowling at each other while headlights danced across their faces. Graham was cornered. Blood wept down his chin, his anger blunted with pain. He dodged Caulk, dragged his BMX out of her reach and dashed.

By now Drew was pillion on Tom's bike, which slowed them to a crawl. Graham caught up, berating them alongside, blood spurting from his mouth. Tom kept his head down and pushed into his pedals. It would be a long time before he would hear the end of it.

***

'Thanks,' said Timothy.

'You need to watch them. They will be back, people like that never let you go.'

He nodded, she was right. The confrontation was postponed, not finished.

She smiled, the adrenalin easing away. 'We need to get back to the hospital. The fun's over for one night.'

They walked towards the bridge, and at the turning Timothy slowed to a halt. 'I can't go back there.'

'I will look after you,' Julie started.

'I know, but I have to go where I can think, until my head is clear.'

'Home?'

'Yes,' he conceded. In the short time he had known Julie Caulk, Timothy had confided more than he had intended. He needed to see his home, even if it was just a burnt-out shell, it was the closest he could get to his mother.

'You want me to come with you?'

'No, I need to be alone.'

Caulk paused to consider. 'Let's meet tomorrow.' Chose her words. 'To help you catch your mother's killers.'

Timothy stepped back. It was all he had thought about, but hearing it felt raw.

'Okay. The embankment I told you about. Let's meet there.'

'Midday, I'll be there.'

She dug her hands into her pockets, nodded goodbye and marched over the bridge, the strange looks of drunken passers-by bouncing off her.

Timothy felt a pang of guilt at parting with the woman who had helped him to escape from the hospital and overcome a beating. But he needed solitude, to force the dancing colours of the midnight sky to the back of his mind. Needed to stay away from that doctor.

Chapter 38

The cracks in the ground talk to me. They widen, turning into mouths, telling me where to go, what roads to take, what to avoid. Can I believe them? Should I follow them?

The long strait of Southtown Road connects Gorleston-on-Sea to Great Yarmouth. Timothy took a route through the back of the industrial business units, slipping between the freight and cargo companies to avoid the main road. To navigate around the security fences, he jumped onto the metre-high wall that lined the harbour, trying not to look down – he couldn't swim. The occasional security light surprised him, he felt he was the centre of a manhunt and the jaundice yellow spotlight was chasing him out of town.

He emerged onto a wide dock that harboured Norwegian cargo ships. He considered stowing away, it would be the easiest option if he could pull it off. But more running would not help him find his mother's killer.

He wandered along, fists tucked into his hoodie, reasoning how to do it, how to get back to the hospital unnoticed, or track down the van the killer had used. He remembered seeing the guy in overalls, smoking a cigarette calmly by the vehicle, blowing smoke into the air in the carefree fashion of someone who would never take responsibility for his actions.

Timothy needed to find a way to make him accountable – could he go to the police? No, turning up at the police doorstep, high on drugs, when he had just escaped from hospital was not the answer. He needed a few hours to recoup. Tomorrow he hoped the mind games would be over.

Skulking between alleyways, trotting across the roads, he made it to the entrance of the embankment like a fox to its den.

The long, snaking disused rail link offered solitude while he walked. The moon poured its silver over the gorge, lighting Timothy's path between the shrubs and greenery. It wouldn't be far now, he told himself and then rested under a bridge to slump against the brickwork.

I know every inch of this place. I hide down here most days. After school, usually, when I need to run away. I know I'm always running, I just need to be alone, especially now.

The grasses are whispering in my ear, creeping up behind me and murmuring softly to me. I can hear the gentle voices echoing around the dune, telling me things, telling me what I should do. Sometimes good, sometimes bad.

'Go home, Timothy. Go home.'

***

A cat greeted Timothy with a screech as he crept into the back yard of his terraced house. It scampered off, leaving only the background hum of distant traffic hanging in the air. A security light from the adjacent chemist gave enough radiance for Timothy to find the back door. He prised away the weakly-boarded barricade, crept through the gap that resembled an oversized cat flap, and stood in his old home. He knuckled his eyes to push back the tears that replaced his fear.

Be firm, man up, use your wits – think.

He opened the nearest cupboard, set about trying to find a torch. He scrambled on his knees, searching under the sink and rifling through drawers, trying to remember where they had kept emergency matches, candles and torches.

In the third drawer down next to the oven he found a camping lantern and a head torch. Only the lantern contained live batteries. He got to his feet, held it out in front of him, and walked through the shell of his old home.

Yellow marker tape crossed the entrance to the living room. He ducked underneath and stopped to observe the forensic spray-painted circle on the knee-height table where his dinner plate had sat only a few days ago.

He wanted to get back there, to when he was happy, sitting watching TV while his mother slept after a fun day on the beach. He gulped back the lump in his throat, wiped his eyes and stomped to the hall where he hoped he could be closer to his mother. With each footstep on the broken staircase, like a nail banged into the back of his head, he saw his mother looking down to him, crying. And her killer, standing behind – smiling.

Sitting on the burnt-out mattress in his mother's bedroom gave him little comfort. Not sure of what he was waiting for, or what sign he hoped she would give him, he retrieved the whalebone from his pocket and held it to the light of the lantern. Mesmerised by the swirls and patterns etched across it, he turned it over in his hands and once more felt grief grip his chest. This time he let the tears fall and he cried out loud.

Suddenly, it seemed clear. He rolled up his sleeves, a great urge to meet his mother overcame him. He sliced at his forearms. First gently, and then with wilder strokes as the anger consumed him.

Turning his wrists into the light, he jabbed at his veins. A large face pushed out from the wall. It yelled and pleaded in vain, trying to escape, tormented by the sight in front of her, yelling at her boy to stop – trying to make him listen.

Timothy dropped the bone, looked to the wall, let the blood trickle down his arms. He sank into the mattress and closed his eyes.

Chapter 39

Saturday 29 August 2015

The early morning sun spread its light and burned through the thin layer of fog that drifted from the coast onto the tired town that yawned itself awake with a creak. The murmuring of vehicles scuttling through the streets filled the air. Net curtains twitched, bins were emptied, and cats let in from the cold. Morning damp clung to Great Yarmouth.

He stood poised by the church, too scared to enter, but unable to turn away. Couldn't bear the torment anymore so pushed open the huge doors, peered inside.

The wood echoed with a creak. He slipped in and pushed the doors closed, hoping to drown out the sounds from the street, to erase the constant noise of scraping steel in his head. He backed against the wall, praying he would be safe. Stumbled through the vestibule to the nave of the building and knelt on the stone floor. Closed his eyes and began to recite any prayers he could remember in a whisper. He started with the Lord's Prayer, hands clasped together hoping that the more he spoke, the quicker the relief.

He faltered after a few lines, so moved on to a new prayer, Christ be with me. This time stuttering after the first verse. He had not been in a church since childhood, had paid little attention to the hymns and protocol, such outings a monotonous task.

Trying to persevere with the worship, he started to speak louder, apologising to God directly, at various moments bursting into tears. He was losing concentration. Gargoyles sculptured out of stone in the alcoves of the church taunted him. White noise blared out of their mouths like a poorly tuned radio.

Priest Stanley stood busying himself, preparing the holy table in the sanctuary and aligning the floral arrangements for the morning's service. He was not expecting visitors this early, had only just opened the church. Was unaware the worshipper had hidden outside for hours, waiting for an opportunity to come and hide.

Surprised by the size and appearance of the bearded man, the priest felt his stomach as he looked over at the stranger. Hoping to sort out the problem with a calm chat he stopped with the floral arrangements and padded down the centre of the isle. Bible in hand for support.

'We don't normally have supplicants this early.' He felt the quiver in his voice betray him.

The man immediately turned to him and pulled at his black cassock. His beard was matted, pupils dilated, he hummed of patchouli oil. 'Help me, Father. I'm going insane. I need help.' He spat as he pleaded. 'I have nightmares when I'm awake. Everything is screaming at me, there are noises in my ears.' He gripped the priest.

'Steady down, now.' Held the Bible up out of the way, saw the word 'Outcasts' stamped across the man's back. On occasion, bikers had turned up to the occasional wedding or funeral, but none that he could remember to worship, and never in this state.

The biker stood, tottered back, scattered the pews as he fell. 'Keep away, keep away from me.' He crawled to the nearest alcove, crouched down and pulled his knees to his chest. Backed to the stone wall, he drew his arms across his face to block out the demons that poured out of the gargoyles' mouths.

'Never again,' he muttered, 'I promise, never again.' Over and over while he rocked.

The priest could only do one thing. He pulled out his mobile phone from under his cassock and dialled the local police station.

***

'What the hell is going on today?'

Ross had just put the phone down on the duty sergeant. He confronted the small gathering of officers assembled for today's brief.

'Christ almighty. We've got every gook on the street handing himself into the nearest nick. Hairy-arsed bikers wandering into churches and confessing everything they've done in the last ten years, and the weekend's only just started. Look, I know we're overloaded, but I want these guys interviewed, and if there's something bigger going on, I want to get to the bottom of it. It sounds like the whole town's gone pill-popping mad.'

He paced around the table, his normally slick black fringe hanging over his face. Lines creased his eyes, his hand shook as he mopped his hair into place.

'Higgins, Ashley, all of you, go and question every NED we have in the cells. Get some answers.'

Chapter 40

McLeish entered his office in a frenzy, white coat rolled up under his arm. The security guard had returned it to him at reception, said a patient had handed it in.

He dumped it on the desk, drew the blinds and sat on the edge of his chair. Ran his fingers through his hair, muttering to himself to calm down. Hadn't slept all night. He tapped the power button on his laptop and chewed on his nails as the fan whirred into life. He hissed at it to hurry up.

He had changed his car plates, then spent most of the night dousing the interior, wiping it clean of DNA. If asked, he would say he'd noticed the girl when driving past, tried to help her, then panicked and left. He wanted to check HOLMES, see if he'd showed up on any searches within the last few hours. He logged on, agonised with his password and bashed the desk while his PC redirected him to a router outside the country.

Then he pressed playback on his work phone and snapped at the messages as they rolled in. He jumped up and paced the room, listening to his colleague's questions. They needed his guidance. He hung his coat on the hanger, tutting at the creased streaks of dirt that underlined how slack he'd been getting. Then checked the pockets before sending it to laundry and discovered his security pass – so that's where he'd left it. He'd had to sign out for a duplicate at security two days previously. The other pocket had a pack of powder. Christ, he was getting very sloppy. If there was one thing he needed right now, it was a pick-me-up. He needed a hit for sure. What was he doing carrying CZ12 around the hospital?

He emptied the pack in a heap on the table as Professor Thomas babbled about his latest publication. McLeish skipped to the next message, he couldn't deal with that conversation right now.

He had been far too careless. Promised himself he would clean up his act, right after this hit. He had no time to load the gas cartridge but knew a blast of the crystals would help power him through this mess, help with the phone calls that were piling up. He always conversed better, thought more clearly, could deal with trouble when full of candy. He double-locked the door then scraped out a line from the mound on the desk, crudely chopping at the crystals with his security pass, growling at the stubborn rocks that jumped away. The fragments teased him. He had best make it a big line.

McLeish hadn't noticed the subtle tinge of yellow to the powder. If he had, he would have seen that it was not his comfort drug, but Halloween.

Leeman's voice was on the next message: 'Where the hell are you, man? For Christ's sake pick up.' McLeish hadn't been answering his mobile or reading mail, he had switched his phone off all night.

McLeish rolled a twenty and breathed out deeply in preparation to take in the running track on his desk.

***

'Timothy Levin.'

'I'm afraid it's not visiting hours.'

'Well then, I want to see the head of staff, or whoever is in charge of this place.'

'I'll try to contact him, but it's still very early.'

The sloth-like security guard placed his breakfast on a pile of paperwork, propelled his wheelie chair from the glass screen that separated him and Eric, and manoeuvred himself over to the phone with as little effort as possible. His blubbery belly caught the papers and with it his early morning hot cross bun. He muttered under his breath and picked up the phone. 'Dr McLeish? I have an Eric Haines in reception for you.'

The guard frowned at Eric. 'I'm sorry I didn't quite catch that,' he said scratching the back of his head, making large eyes and pulling the phone from his ear in wonder. 'Maybe it's better I talk to Miss Joy?'

The laughter at the other end of the phone confirmed he should hang up and pretend the call had never happened.

'Someone's had a good night,' he muttered to himself, shaking his head.

'Sorry?' asked Eric, drilling holes.

'He's busy, sir. I'll try another doctor.' He glanced at his watch, hoping that the next half hour would roll on quickly so that he could swap shifts.

Better luck with Bryony, two minutes and she was at reception with a friendly smile and extended hand. Eric's anger melted. She led him to the lobby, keen to discuss Timothy Levin.

'I wish I'd spoken to you sooner, Mr Haines. I didn't know Timothy had a relative.'

Eric searched the lobby, hoping Timothy would show his face. 'Please, call me Eric. I'm not his real uncle, but I knew his mother well, and his father who was killed in the army.' Eric scratched at his neck. Bryony at her wrist.

'Oh yes. He was on duty in Iraq, wasn't it?'

'Afghanistan. I was on tour with him. I've always tried to help, felt it at an obligation, really, to the pair of them. There's no other family as far as I'm aware, apart from Agatha's sister,' he said with a shrug.

'Really? I haven't seen that in any of the notes.'

'I thought that might be the case. Timothy has an aunt, but from what I could gather from Gary the sisters didn't talk to each other – although that was years ago. There was a dispute, what it was about I don't know.'

Eric sighed, held out his lank arms with upturned palms. 'That's the reason I phoned, maybe you should try to contact her. I've tried to speak to Dr McLeish on several occasions, he is in charge, right?'

'Yes.'

'He refused to let me see Timothy, hasn't been in touch since.' Eric placed his elbows on his knees, leaned towards Bryony, searching for an answer.

Bryony squirmed. She was going to find it difficult to support her superior, was fast losing any respect for the man. There was no reason to refuse access to anyone who was close to patients unless they posed a threat.

'I would like to meet the doctor, but I want to see Timothy first.'

'Of course. I'll see to that.' There was one thing she needed to know. 'Did you tell Dr McLeish that Timothy's mother had a sister?'

'I did. I could only provide a first name, Fiona. I'm not sure of her surname, and I'm afraid I don't know where she lives.'

'Thank you, that's very helpful, and I hope we can find out more.' Bryony, embarrassed, wondered why this wasn't in the case notes. She wanted to see McLeish as much as Eric.

'Well, let's find Timothy,' she said, a bit too sharply. And considered how she might approach McLeish without strangling him.

Chapter 41

*H*e's creepy, he's leachy, he smells of wee …
Go away creepy, get away from me.
The tune echoed from the computer. The monitor displayed children laughing and dancing around the boy with the ginger hair. The doctor watched his childhood replayed in front of him, crying to himself as his schoolmates bullied and ridiculed him. He moved the mouse and logged into the database. The scene dissolved, HOLMES loaded and accepted his details. He typed in his name and scanned for recent searches as Sherlock turned to tut at him and wag his finger. A pig in a police helmet sang to him. '*We're coming for you, creepy, we're coming for you.*'

His mobile rang on the desktop, the name Harry Leeman illuminating on the screen. He burst out laughing as it jumped up and danced on the table.

The parading phone stopped and lay down dead. Then his work phone jumped out of its cradle, screaming, 'Answer me.'

He jabbed at the speakerphone and yelped, 'Yes?'

'About bloody time, man, where have you been?'

The words echoed as he watched the pig morph into a prostitute with fangs. He giggled down the phone. 'I've tripped,' he said.

Now it was the pig's turn to wear the fangs.

'What?'

'I've tripped, and I can't pick myself up.'

'Have you been using?'

'I prefer trialling. Ha, ha, ha.'

'Jesus, man. You know what's in that stuff? It's weeks before that gear'll be out of your system, you fool.'

'Mistakes happen.'

He cringed as the prostitute aged in front of him. Her skin sagged and started to fall off her bones. She peeped out at the doctor and pleaded for him to help her. He began whimpering.

'Alex? Alex? You're breaking up.'

Harry Leeman stood in the shed at the bottom of his garden. It was the best way to ensure he was out of earshot from his partner, but the worst place for a decent phone signal.

'Breaking up? Yes, I am. Well, we all do in the end, I suppose.'

The screen displayed an image of a grave. The prostitute slipped into it, hands clawing into the soil trying to stay above ground, mouthing pleas for help to McLeish.

'Oh God. I'm broken.'

'You idiot. We are at the crux of the plan, the part where you need to deliver. This is where you fix all the broken souls in the town, you moron. Remember the drill? Oh, you need to stop the bad trip from the naughty new drug? Well your luck's in, Mr Mayor of the town, I've got just the thing, it's called MR11 – but you can call it miracle remedy. Oh, by the way you can only get it from BetaPharm. Funny, that. Just a bloody shame I'm too freaked out on my crazy cloud to help.'

Leeman paused to take a breath, angry at giving so much away over a phone network.

'Listen, take as much of the MR11 as you can for relief, and leave the place. Go missing, do one, just get out of the hospital for a while. Stress, depression, whatever, say someone kidnapped you – I don't know, and I don't care, but don't buckle on me now.'

Leeman gave McLeish the giggles once more. A black land cruiser with flat tyres plodded across the screen. The unhappy driver turned to face the doctor and the ashen face started to melt.

'I'll have a word with Griffin and see if he can pull some strings.' Leeman hung up.

McLeish howled with laughter, then whimpered as the monitor reflected his body as a puppet. Timothy Levin stood above him, peering down with a grin, pulling the strings attached to his hands. The barbs hooking his white coat.

McLeish pointed to the screen. 'It's him. He's playing games with me. He's been playing me all along.'

The pipework clanged and banged around his ears, echoing with more whispers of his school days.

'Go away,' he shouted, clasping his hands over his ears. 'It gets louder every day.'

He's weedy, he's smelly, he's got no friends.
He hides in wardrobes, he's round the bend.

***

'Where's Timothy Levin?' Bryony asked the porter in Timothy's room.

'I haven't seen him since this time yesterday.' He had little to do, so moved out with his caddy, leaving Eric and Bryony confused. Bryony stood by the painting easel and faced Eric.

'I'm sorry about this, but I can't think where else he could be. His medication would have been this time yesterday, and I presume he was present for that,' she pondered.

'Could he be with Dr McLeish?' asked Eric.

'We can always check,' Bryony replied, looking down at the picture displayed on the easel, not for the first time struck by the accuracy and detail. She recognised the man who was loading a box into a van, but was unable to place him.

'He's scared of that man.'

They wheeled round to see Caulk standing at the entrance, biting her fingernails and staring hard back at them.

'The doctor?' asked Bryony.

'The doctor's a bad man.'

'In what way?' asked Eric.

'But he's very scared of that man.' She nodded towards the easel.

Both Eric and Bryony studied the picture.

'Does he work here?' Bryony asked Julie.

'Sometimes,' Caulk replied guardedly.

'Christ,' said Eric. He smacked his forehead. 'That name.' He pointed to the edge of the drawing that had the front of the van vanishing off the page. The letters showed the company vehicle logo etched clearly but unfinished. 'ENDEAV…'

'That's the van that was at the fire. At Bells Road last week – at Timothy's house.' He recollected the vehicle he saw out of the corner of his eye when he'd approached the rear entrance of the chemist. Then the pain of what happened next.

'Endeavour,' finished Bryony. 'The pharmaceutical couriers for the facility.'

'Endeavour,' repeated Eric, 'that's it, Endeavour. We need to find Timothy.'

'If he's not here I'll have to report him missing,' said Bryony.

'I know where he might be,' revealed Caulk. Her instinct now told her that she could trust these two. Today she was in a better place. 'But you can't tell the doctor.'

Chapter 42

Ashley slumped in a lazy seating position inside Gorleston police station. He'd been fretting over the database in front of him for over two days. The list of all the companies registered in the UK was vast, even the cut-down search for Norfolk and Suffolk still came in at around 5,000. He reduced the search further to those starting with 'D' which filtered down the results to 100 or so.

This morning he focused on the phone manuscript from four different network operators over a half-hour period of the crime. Burnt had ordered Ashley to scan the list as a background task and to make sure it went unnoticed. Ashley had welcome news and was about to pick up the phone. Laughter bellowed from the corridor. He sneaked over to the open door and poked his nose out to see two constables reviving an old story. He quietly pushed the door to.

Burnt was making little progress doing door-to-door on any known offenders. The same 'I know nuffin',' from potential informants. He eased to a stop on a cobbled street adjacent to Gorleston seafront.

Gorleston-on-Sea, ramshackle, like its neighbour Great Yarmouth. An imposing seafront, overlooked by mansions carved into flatlets for those on benefits.

'Please let it be good news, Ashley. I'm losing the will here.' He removed his Ray-Bans and scratched at his stubble.

'Could be. I've been cross-checking the phone transcript you sent me.'

'Cross checking Veronica Esherwood, more like.'

Ashley fidgeted. 'I've marked up a few phone numbers from the transcript you gave me.'

'Okay.'

'There was one number called just before the time of the Airwave hack that was used repeatedly afterwards. I marked up all the calls linked to that first number. There is a definite link between four numbers.'

'Sounds good.'

'As suspected, they're all with unregistered SIM cards.'

'Even better. Could be burners. We need names to go with the numbers. Remember, it's between you and me. What about the vehicle at Bells Road?'

'There were a few grey vans. I'll have a completed company list by the end of today, so I should be able to start enquiries on Monday.'

'And the photofit?'

'It's been circulated and is going in today's *EDP*.'

'Good work, stick with it. You're making better progress than I am.'

Burnt killed the call. Ashley replaced the phone then checked his watch. He smiled, a glint appeared in his eye. He wheeled round in his chair and yanked open the bottom drawer of the grey case-notes filing cabinet. And plucked out a new pair of suede Tom Baker shoes. He placed them down, admired them briefly, then slipped his feet in, sighing in comfort. He did a couple of laps of the office, then went over to the suit hung on the back of the door that was just for court appearances and slipped the rose-pink Burberry shirt off the hanger. A lunch date with Veronica.

This was therapy for Burnt. Taking his mind off what gnawed away deep in his stomach. Jackie. Could he trust her? Course he could. Then he needed to prove it. *Don't follow up on every phone call. Accept that she meets men. She takes the kids to school, to play dates, swimming lessons, she meets a lot of dads.* And he knew where they lived – and what they were thinking.

Had he misheard the location for Bells Road? Was he 100 per cent sure he was given the wrong address? Or was he too consumed with jealousy to hear?

The night he left his car to take in the fresh air, like he always did when he needed to be alone. When he wanted to think, to get things clear in his mind. Wanted to work on what he was going to say to this Rodney who was sexting his missus.

And needed to leave the car at the other end of the street so the chump couldn't report him.

He remembered turning at a mural of Nelson, the fire growing in his belly. Past the off-licence, swerving an early starter in skin-tight T-shirt and jeans gripping a Buckfast, and onto Deneside. Remembered checking his phone, making sure he had the right address. Then he texted Rodney from Jackie's phone, fingers trembling. Told him she wanted him and was all alone in the Albion. And nestled into the backyard of a terrace stinking of cats, with the gate pushed in,

Turned his radio off and prayed he was wrong.

Maybe he was. Hadn't given this Rodney enough time to explain himself.

He opened his contact list. Filtered on all names ending with a question mark. His code for guys on his hit list. Guys he could lose it with.

Then pressed delete. Paused when the phone asked him to confirm sending the seven numbers to the ashes. He accepted.

Back to work.

Burnt heaved himself out of the car with a sigh. It was his seventh call this morning, and although it was already eleven o'clock, he fully expected it to be the middle of the night for the residents.

Just maybe a desperate user-cum-snitch was willing to spill something. Most of the crims he spoke to were due in court, this he could use as a bargaining tool to push them to turn informers. Usually their partners answered the door. Hollow-eyed, edgy, baby under arm to use as defence.

Best use of a baby if you're a crack addict. It can get you a sympathy vote when you're up against it. And when social services take it away, your partner can supply you with another one.

This door-to-door was emotional for Burnt, and personal. He'd had a lot of experience with addicts – his parents.

When he turned over a den or carried out an arrest, saw the mother holding a fragile bundle close to her body to protect herself, it cut deep. He saw himself of over thirty years ago, defenceless. To see the mother protecting her partner just to keep her habit, sickened him.

He could trace his mother, had the resource at his fingertips, but it was a burden he had been putting off. Some days he was stirred into tracking her down, but he soon found a distraction. Did he owe her anything? No, but that didn't mean he shouldn't find her. He owed his grandparents everything, but it was now too late to thank them, too late to apologise for all those teenage years of rebellion. What would he do when he found her? What would he say? He would only have questions. Was his father worth protecting, worth the beatings, the humiliation? Just for a dirty smoke.

Chapter 43

'You sure this is the house?' asked Graham.

'Yep. This is it,' said Drew.

The three boys stared at the burnt-out shell of Timothy's former home. Graham, determined to recapture what was taken from him the night before, didn't have the army to confront the bikers who had mugged him the previous night, but reckoned an easier solution might not be far away. Said to Tom and Drew as they made it to Timothy's house that if the psycho bitch in white was a dealer, and she wanted to protect Timothy so much, they must be in business together.

Told them the burnt-out house was used to store and weigh out packs of drugs. Drew nodded hungrily, Tom rubbed his bare arms in the morning sun.

Overnight, Graham had become obsessed with finding more of the powder. The potential to make heaps of cash was snatched from him, he was so close. There must be more, and this was a good a place as any to start.

Graham led the pair through the alleyway, round the back of the terraced house where they could see the rear entrance boarded up and marked with 'police aware' stickers. They spotted a partial opening, a section of plywood hanging off a nail, a hole big enough to wriggle through.

Tom pointed. 'I don't want to go in there. It's creepy.'

Graham said, 'There's three of us, and I have this,' then unzipped his windcheater halfway to reveal the butt of his blade. 'Now stop being a wimp and follow me.'

Tom searched the neighbours' windows for an excuse. Hoping someone would spot them, tell them to clear off before they call the police.

Drew pulled his strained T-shirt over his belly, pushed up the sleeves of his jacket, remembering the buzz he got last night when they chased Timothy out of town. Couldn't wait to give him a kicking.

But still fearful of Graham, who every day seemed to be progressing into a meaner and nastier character, last night's embarrassment only serving to centre his attention on revenge.

Graham licked his busted lips that still burnt, more with shame. He took a beating from the bikers last night, then was outdone by the cranky bitch in a doctor's uniform. He sat up in bed all night, wired, plotting, chewing it over on a wrap of speed Spike gave him for compensation.

Graham pulled back the plywood and slipped in first. Then Tom, Drew squeezing through last.

Once inside, the sense of exhilaration returned. Graham rifling through drawers in the kitchen, ordered the others to check for loose floorboards. Drew, excited, soon became distracted and started flinging crockery against the walls, kicking at the unhinged cupboards, stoking himself for conflict.

'Shut the fuck up. We need to be quiet.'

Drew stopped, drawer in hand, and threw it to the floor.

'There's no one here, let's go,' tried Tom.

Graham ignored him, pulled his blade and trod through the threshold to the living room, tearing away the yellow barrier tape. The pair followed to the base of the stairs in the hallway.

Timothy woke with a start on his mother's mattress. At first forgetting where he was, then gasping as spiders ran over his feet – still the mind games. His head thumped, the crashing plates and shouting that woke him now stopped. Then his heart hammered – a voice he recognised.

He jumped up, switched on the lantern, leapt out of the bedroom to the landing and held out the light. Three figures at the bottom of the stairs, faces covered with wolf masks, staring up at him, long noses sniffing the air. One wearing a grin.

Chapter 44

Timothy dashed back to the bedroom as Graham leapt up the stairs. The broken staircase snared each of the boys in turn as their feet fell through the slats.

Timothy, now at the window, pulled at the chipboard then clambered through the open gap, holding the frame for support. He squinted into the blinding sunlight, then down at the drop, grabbed the guttering and stepped onto the outside window ledge. The three boys stumbled into the bedroom as he shinned down the drainpipe.

Graham tripped over the lantern and cursed out loud as he lay sprawled on the floor. Picking himself up, he turned to tear back down the stairs but clashed with Tom, who head-butted him on the nose. This added more fuel to the fire – eluded by the wimpy kid once more. He lashed out and scalped Tom with the lantern.

'Go after him and find out where the stash is. I'll do a scoop here.' Blood dripped from his nose, the lip busted the night before wept over his chin.

Tom fled. If he was quick he could make this work, have a word with Timothy on his own, get a story together, appease his brother – before Drew got to them.

Graham swept the back of his hand across his nose, then reached into his pocket for a knife. 'Take this. Scare him and make him fess up.'

Drew hesitated, then shaped up and took the blade. 'Sure,' he said with a shrug. He knew he wouldn't have to use it, just to brandish it would be enough, and it was something he knew Tom was too scared to do. This would gain him a bit more respect.

'Quick,' urged Graham, 'We'll meet back at our house.'

Empowered, Drew pushed the blade into his inside pocket and clambered back down the stairs after Tom, who was by now tearing to the back door.

Timothy darted across the road, turning in time to see Tom emerge from the arched access at the side of his house. The chase continued for a few minutes, with Timothy pulling further away. Tom saw the gazelle dart down an alley and called him, looking behind to check how far behind Drew was. Saw him slowing to a walk.

Timothy turned into a cobbled yard and jumped a retaining wall to the embankment. He heard screams behind.

The wide gorge of greenery, overgrown and unkempt, has a long, snaking valley that cuts the small seaside town in half. The embankment is home to anything that nobody wants, from empty beer cans and magazines to fridge freezers. A good place for Len's Motors to dump the tires he can't afford to recycle legitimately.

The bonnet of an old Fiat Punto lay along the twisting causeway. A supermodel looked out of a *Vogue* magazine, pouting for attention, now crumpled, torn and forgotten, only rodents showing interest.

Timothy tore down the hillside, the long grass whipping against his legs. He dodged the garbage and leapt over a pile of fly posters. Curving around the car bonnet, he reached the basin of the gorge and looked over his shoulder to see the predator with a wolf's head gunning for him. He made to the underside of the bridge. And stopped.

This is where I always come. This is where I should take the beating. Not at home, not in front of my mother. I know this place well enough, where every bit of junk is in this clutter. I hear their calls as I canter on down to the base of the embankment and under the bridge. But there must be no more running. I'm always running away. The grasses are talking to me.

'It's time, Timothy, it's time.'

I can't just keep running. I'm not leaving anything behind, it's always there when I stop. It's still in my head, I can't run from memories.

It's time for the beating, and then it will be over. Then I can go back to my dreams. I'm used to them now, they help me forget and teach me to weave and slip in between the cracks in the tarmac, teach me where to steal and to scavenge. I can dissolve into the holes with the weeds. If I stare hard enough, the earth shows me small diamonds that glisten in the darkness, telling me their secrets, they tell me where to go and where to hide.

I hide too much.

'Oi, Tim!' called Tom, 'slow down.' He turned to see how far away Drew was, see how much time he had. Timothy was propped against the inside of the arch, hands in pockets, head bowed. Tom got close.

'Look, Tim, we haven't got long, and Graz won't let this lie without something to show for it. Are there any drugs in the house?' He was panting, hunched over.

No answer, no eye contact. Still the distorted faces that made his stomach turn. He pinned his stare to the ground.

Tom looked back, saw Drew appear at the top of the embankment. 'Tim, there's no time, talk to me for God sake.' Tom, almost dancing on the spot like a child who needed a pee, pleaded once more, 'Okay, at least tell us where that woman lives, ya know the one in the white coat. Give us something to go on.'

Drew ambling closer. Timothy, silent, couldn't look up.

Tom tried again. 'Graz is in a right rage. Let's make some shit up.' Now almost shouting he turned again, saw Drew wearing a grin, gripping his coat.

Tom whispered through gritted teeth, 'Run, Tim, run.'

'Nice place you got, mind if I move in?' piped Drew, only yards away, picking his way through the undergrowth.

Tom edged closer to Tim, out of earshot of Drew. 'Please, Tim, just go, he'll never catch up with ya.'

He couldn't make out Tim under the hoodie, his loose hair swept over his face, didn't know if he could even hear him, just wanted to help him. Could feel Drew's panting breath.

'Fess up, freak,' barked Drew, over Tom's shoulder.

'It's okay. I got this,' Tom pleaded, head half-turned. Then stopped, mouth open, watched Drew draw a blade.

'Let's cut this freak open.'

'No,' shouted Tom. He held out a palm to Drew and rested the other on Tim's shoulder. Then desperately pushed at Timothy. 'Go, quick, please, just go.' Tom didn't know whether to scream to the heavens or lie down and cry, he just wanted it all to stop. Wanted his brother to give up with the fighting, Drew with the trying to be big. Wanted his mother back home – and Dad to care again. Tears formed. Levin needed help, not a beating. Tom realised he connected more with this loony kid than anyone else he knew.

Wolves, two of them. Watching, circling, teeth bared, dripping saliva. Snarling and sneering at each other. They sense my terror – smell my fear like an open wound.

The grasses hissed.

'You are going to be slaughtered, Timothy. It's time to act.'

Timothy yanked out the whalebone and flew at the nearest wolf. Tom stumbled backwards and tripped to the ground, bewildered by the strange weapon.

Before he could fight, shout or scream, Timothy dived on top of him and drove the sabre-shaped blade into his neck.

Drew stepped back. Blood sprayed the arch of the bridge and doused the boys. Timothy gripped the weapon, pinning Tom to the floor.

The grasses hissed at him. *Don't stop. Don't give him another chance.*

Tom writhed and kicked in despair, and within seconds his suffering was over.

The final thing Tom saw were two holes to a bottomless pit – t he glazed eyes of the last person he ever expected to be his slaughterer.

Tom's body went numb, he gave up the fight. Despair turned to relief as the pain subsided. He entered darkness. The gazelle, for once, victorious.

The grasses stopped hissing.

Timothy pulled away from the body and stood, fixing Drew with an empty stare, leaving the whalebone jutting out from Tom's neck. Drew's face altered from a wolf, to a piglet, to a human. A frightened boy.

Drew was locked by Timothy's gaze, he stood open-mouthed as the full gravity of the killing hit him. Stepping back and whispering something inaudible as the blood drained from his face. He spewed over his trainers, shook, dropped the knife, and looked around in the vague hope for help. He tried to scream. Only a rasp. He looked down at Tom whose blank, expressionless face offered no answers.

Timothy no longer had a weapon, but that was no comfort for Drew. He felt stuck, gripped by the scene, held under Levin's spell. Levin's black empty eyes. Even if he got away, how would he explain what happened, much could he tell? It was too much to think about, all happened too quick. It was not supposed to end like this. Tim never fought back.

He tore himself away from Levin's cold gaze and ran, tripped briefly, picked himself up, and stumbled head-on into a stranger. He knocked the elderly gent off his feet, righted himself and took off, whimpering an apology.

Eric stood up and edged towards Timothy, scanning for witnesses.

***

Graham tore at the floorboards with a screwdriver he'd found in the utility room. Clothes lay strewn across the floor, upturned cabinets emptied and the remains of the sofa ripped to shreds. He kicked a bin across the room and stormed downstairs to the kitchen. He'd covered the house twice and found nothing. He gave up and fished out the tiny wrap of speed Spike had free-issued him. He licked the remaining powder and grimaced. Needed to stay alert. No sleep for over twenty-four hours and a busy day ahead – to hunt down the bikers and the pack of Halloween. He'd been naive but was determined to make up for it. He would wait for nightfall, then raid them. Tooled up, masked up, and scare the crap out of them – just needed to find where they lived. Spike.

Chapter 45

Julie Caulk perched on the edge of the bridge, staring at the scene on the embankment. She recognised the fat boy running up the hill, had thrown his bike into the river only the night before. Was unable to reach Timothy in time to help, could only watch the drama unfold.

Fortunately, her presence alone was enough to divert attention from the sight below. A large lorry rattled past her and, as she felt the harsh draft of noisy air rush around her ears, she made brief eye contact with Drew, gave him a crafty smile. He returned a startled look as he stepped into the road, red-faced and panting. Before turning his attention to the equally surprised face of a Polish lorry driver.

Stefan was late with his delivery of twenty tonnes of drill pipe to Gapton Hall Industrial Estate, and getting into quite a sweat. He drove over the bridge while meddling with his satnav, trying to get the damned thing to speak to him in his native tongue. Technology wasn't his forte. Drew and Stefan locked eye to eye for a moment as Drew stepped into the road. Stefan swore at his device in Polish while it told him to make a U-turn wherever possible.

Drew, no longer a wolf but a rabbit, was too late to change direction. As for the sixteen-stone orangutan behind the wheel, he had no chance of slowing in time, so he just pressed his foot on the air brakes and muttered a brief Polish prayer.

Drew bounced off the side of the oncoming lorry, and his broken body hit the tarmac as the large load screeched to a halt.

Silence.

The driver would take the blame, but it was simple physics that killed Drew – momentum is equal to mass times velocity.

There was plenty of both and, if Drew had had time to consider his departure, he would maybe have seen some irony in his least favourite subject.

The locals turned and gasped as the screeching tires and the thump of Drew's body cut through the air.

A crowd gathered round the lifeless boy. Someone called the emergency services, others attempted first aid, but this was of no use to the teenager.

Drew was identified by a passer-by, and locals interrogated the foreign driver before the police arrived at the scene of the accident. Stefan had wolves of his own to deal with, his licence wasn't completely legal, and he had been driving for more than the required time without stopping, the vehicle's tachograph proof of that. In due course Stefan Lunge would have to meet a very big wolf – a magistrate.

***

'Christ,' shouted Eric. He was in a flap. Caulk had said where she expected to find Timothy, if he wasn't at his burnt out home he would be at the embankment. Eric's house backed onto the valley, so he chose this first for his search.

'Timothy. Go back to mine,' he ordered. 'You know how to find it, go the back way and avoid the streets. The back door's open. Get changed, there're clothes in the spare room.'

He was thinking out loud. It had been agonising to watch from afar. He had rushed across the embankment, unable to get to the scene in time to stop the carnage. And felt compelled to cover for Timothy.

'I guess it's all over,' muttered the boy, looking down at his hands.

'It wasn't your fault, Timothy. They had knives, they attacked you. I saw it. But we may not need to tell them anything.' Again, scanning the embankment. 'We'll talk later. Just go. I need to call the police.' Eric needed to buy the boy some time or, better still, erase him from the crime scene.

They both heard the screech of brakes from the large vehicle over the bridge. Eric guessed what had happened, but had no idea if it was fatal. Timothy crouched down against the wall, dazed. Put his bloodstained hands to his face and shook his head. 'What have I done?' He looked over to the corpse. 'I've taken a life.'

'Get up and go,' Eric urged again. And tried another ploy. 'Do you want to find your mother's killers? If so, get to my house and stay there – and hide.'

Timothy stared cold at Eric, sprang to his feet and bolted.

Eric let Madge lap at Tom Hacket's blood. It was best to muddy the crime scene as much as possible. He didn't know that you should keep clear, he was just an old man and was trying to restrain his cocker spaniel.

He made sure his footprints replaced Timothy's, stooped over the corpse with the murder weapon jutting out from its neck. The memories from ten years previously flooded back, the fateful patrol that had cost Gary Levin his life. Eric had so far been unable to fulfil his promise to look after Gary's wife and her kid, but he could try to make amends now.

He crouched over the lifeless body, pulled out the whalebone, and wiped the blood on his coat. Tucked it in his pocket.

Was about to phone the police, but paused, phone in hand when he spotted the knife Drew had dropped. This would work better. Could he do it?

'Blank it out, Eric,' he whispered to himself.

He grabbed the blade, did a quick sweep of the field, cowered over the corpse, then drove it into Tom Hacket's neck until it hit bone. He fought back the urge to spew, grimacing at Tom Hacket, muttering a prayer. Then wiped his prints and stood up to call 999.

The chubby boy had run straight into him after stabbing the boy on the floor. Two kids having a fight, one ran off scared at what he had done. That would be his story. It would be Eric's word against his. Just hoped this would explain the blood on his coat.

Chapter 46

It had taken some time to summon up enough courage to make a getaway. The illusions had been so vivid he had spent twenty-four hours rooted to his chair in misery. Finally persuaded by Leeman, McLeish grabbed the last remaining bag of MR11 from his locker-room and necked a mouthful.

Within a few minutes the remedy eased the visuals, though unfortunately not for long. Getting to his car without questions from his colleagues was easier than expected. He had inadvertently chosen a quiet time to make his escape.

He left Yarmouth and made for the Acle Straight. And fled to his father's holiday home in North Norfolk, it was an ideal bolthole.

But the journey was becoming difficult, the Halloween starting to close in on him. His stomach churned and he gagged, sicking small white deposits down his front as he drove along. He dared not turn the radio on, but the dulcet humming of the vehicle started to play tricks on him, moaning in his ears. Then the visuals returned.

The Acle Straight can seem an endlessly long road even to those who are sober. McLeish felt as though he was on a conveyor belt to oblivion, the red morning sky on the horizon waiting patiently to swallow him.

He was startled at the wheel by an overtaking lorry blaring its horn. He jumped in his seat and checked his speed. Twenty-five miles an hour. He glanced in his rear-view mirror at the stream of cars accumulating behind him, no doubt cursing at being stuck behind a Sunday driver.

'I can run faster than this,' said Timothy from the back seat.

'Feel free to get out whenever you want. You weren't invited.' McLeish dabbed at the bag of MR11 on the passenger seat. Hoped Timothy, whose flesh fell off his bones, would disappear from the rear-view mirror.

'Are we going on holiday?'

'Christ. You too, Miss Primrose. Having quite a day trip, aren't we?' McLeish burst into laughter, glanced at a family in a passing car who stared him down in disbelief.

He shouted to them, 'Sorry, the kids in the back are nothing but trouble.'

He shovelled in more MR11, and waited for the bats dancing around the vehicle to vanish. Then put his foot down until the speedo registered sixty.

Twenty minutes later the black SUV was snaking its way up the A140 towards Cromer, a little too close to Norwich for McLeish's liking. After the hiccup on Friday night he didn't want to go near the city, but he was in no state to navigate an alternative route. Slugs crawled up his legs and ants scurried over his hands as he gripped the steering wheel tighter. He negotiated each bend with a new distraction, the pair in the back wouldn't stop bickering. *Not much further*, he told himself as sweat trickled down his forehead into his eyes. He mopped his face and skidded around another corner as he hit mud. Then scooped up the now near empty bag of MR11 powder and attempted to neck the remains as he took the next bend one-handed.

Julie Caulk sprung from the backseat, white coat on, wild eyes in the mirror. He felt her breath on his neck. 'We don't need you anymore. We can look after ourselves, good*bye* doctor,' she scowled, grabbing the steering wheel. McLeish yanked it back.

The SUV bounced onto the opposite side of the road and came head-to-head with a horse. He only had time to pray that it was an illusion – he drove through it.

The horse buckled. Its legs smashed through the windscreen as the rider flew over the roof of the car into a grass verge.

The three in the back disappeared and left him to plummet into the dyke.

The beast in its pain and confusion whinnied and kicked out as it lay stuck over the bonnet of the SUV. McLeish scurried out of the vehicle, threw up and fell backwards into the peat.

In desperation, he attempted to take to the road and run the remainder of the way, until a lucky but incensed horse-rider met him head on. She wasted no time, tearing into McLeish with whip and heels, who curled up on the ground screaming for her to stop. She only paused the beating to call a vet, and it wasn't long before a local dialled the police.

Chapter 47

'How you feeling?' Eric asked for the umpteenth time. He placed a hot mug of tea in front of Timothy and propped himself against the kitchen unit. Eyeing the plastic clock that ticked too loud.

Timothy pushed the empty breakfast plate to one side, cupped his hands around the mug and took a gulp. The bacon and egg soon went down, the first thing he'd eaten in a week. Finally, an appetite. He had hidden upstairs all evening and through the night, waiting for the police to take him away. They showed while he sat shaking like a junkie on the bed in the spare room, expecting any minute for the door to burst open, Eric to turn him in. Never happened, Eric gave them a story.

The hallucinations were over, had been since ramming the sharpened bone into Tom Hacket's neck. He shuddered at the recall. Another sad image to add to his collection of dark memories.

'Who was he?'

'I don't know. But if anyone finds out, it was self-defence. And I'll just have to change my story,' said Eric, tapping on the work surface. The wrinkles under his eyes looked scratched on with black ink. He turned to the dishes to keep himself busy while Madge nipped at his feet, hoping for scraps.

Timothy carried on, feeling if there was one person due an explanation, it was Eric. 'I just don't know what made me do it. It was like I was being hunted. I gave up running away, ready to take a beating, get it over with.' He sat back and folded his arms, swamped in Mario's spare clothes. Threw another shiver. 'Then, I just snapped. All this whispering in my ears all night and all day. First it was the sea when I was at the beach, then the grasses at the embankment. Crazy.' He shook his head and gulped down the rest of his tea.

'You feeling over it now?' Madge nagged Eric some more.

'God, yeah. Every face was some sort of monster. All different and kind of always changing. Like everything I've ever drew coming to haunt me. It was mental.'

When Eric got back to the house after the knifing, the first thing he did was clean the murder weapon. Knowing the police would be round anytime soon he guessed it would not look amiss in his bureau. It would fit right in, better than in his bin or anywhere close to the house – who knew how thorough the search would be. They could comb the whole embankment, have 100 officers swarming round looking for evidence, or some do-gooder could hand it in.

So he put it on display, prominent, staring them in the face, as though it had been there for forever.

The same thoughts bounced around his head like an overactive tennis ball that hit the same spot over and over. He now knew who caused the fire at Bells Road and who killed Timothy's mother. But he had a coat covered with blood, had falsified evidence, and a killer in his house. And still had a kilo of crap behind a breezeblock in his garage that Mario left days ago. The pair of them were in a whole world of trouble.

He had paced the house all night like a wired cat while Timothy shook in terror telling him about the hospital, about how he had found his mother's killer. Then Eric listened to him screaming in his sleep.

Eric jumped up, swore at Madge, kicked her out into the garden with a punctured football, and slammed the door on her. The soiled clothes and drugs that could send him down for the rest of his life sat at his feet like an immoveable object.

When Mario had turned up at his house a few days earlier to explain the trouble he was in, Eric took the package and said he'd front the cash. He never got to ditch the drugs. Thought maybe he should hand it in, say he suspected the police but never worked out how to voice it. It never went any further. Instead, he put it in his garage behind a loose breezeblock. He added the bloody clothes to it just before the stubby copper turned up.

'First things first. I'm gonna dump this crap,' he said, hooking the Bag For Life round the throat, 'then take you to the hospital.'

Timothy stiffened. 'No. I can't, please. Not that mad doctor again.'

Eric held out a palm. 'You won't have to go near him. We file a complaint. You explain everything he's done. I sign you out and you come and stay with me. But right now, you're reported missing. Just say you slept under the pier for two nights and I say you turned up at mine this mornin'. Too late to say you were here last night, I told the coppers I was alone yesterday.' Eric wrapped the package tight and placed it on the work surface. Madge scratched at the back door.

Timothy shrank into his seat and shivered. Scooped Mario's black sports jacket off the back of the chair and slipped it on. Couldn't keep the chill off.

Bryony had said she would be at work all weekend and for Eric to call if he found Timothy. Eric hadn't spoken to her since yesterday, didn't want to tell her what he had seen.

He grabbed his car keys, said it was time to go, pretended it was all going to be alright. Then his phone rang.

He released the bag, pocketed his keys and moved to the hallway to take the call. DS Griffin. Wanted to question him, give his account of the previous day, said some new evidence had come to light. Told him to show up at Lowestoft Road immediately – or they could send a car for him.

He swallowed hard, coughed the lump from his throat as he wandered into the living room and agreed to be there within half an hour. Hung up, committed his story to memory, whispering through it as he returned to the hallway to place the phone back in its cradle. Instinctively, he looked to the bureau, like he had every time he paced past it for the last twelve hours. His heart skipped a beat – the bone had vanished.

Timothy? He walked to the kitchen. No one. The back door was ajar and the bag of soiled clothes – gone. Eric rushed outside and shouted for Timothy, ran to the embankment, nowhere to be seen. Damned himself for mentioning the hospital.

He made back to the house and grabbed his coat. Madge pleaded at his feet for her mid-morning walk. He opened the box of dog treats on top of the fridge and pulled out a large deer horn, placed it between her teeth and gave her a brief stroke behind the ears.

'That will keep you busy for a few hours, girl, you might need to get used to it.'

Then left the house to meet his fate with the police.

Chapter 48

Timothy stood at the rear entrance to Seafield Close, hands deep in a borrowed jacket clenching the murder weapon, not for comfort anymore, but quiet determination. The hospital loomed, grey and large.

For the first time in days Timothy felt lucid, but he carried the guilt like a backpack of lead. The tears had come and gone, leaving a quiet but raw anger in the pit of his stomach.

He would have waited for the police and taken whatever punishment was due, but once he'd run he knew it was too late to hand himself in. That would implicate Eric. It was best to take the weapon and the clothes and deal with it on his own – it was time to confront his mother's killer. He should have done this before now, but needed time to recover, time away from that prison – from that doctor.

Caulk said Endeavour would be here this morning. If it all went wrong he would make sure he joined his mother, but just maybe his plan would succeed. Etched on his mind was Ronnie's face. He squeezed the whalebone, denting the palm of his hand.

Vehicles came and went, each driver flashing their IDs, the barrier obediently swinging open. He recognised some of the orderlies, saw Bryony trundle to the gates in a Nissan Micra, McLeish jumping into his car in a hurry and tearing out of the exit. He shuddered and retreated into the alley.

He was just stamping the cold out of his feet when Endeavour turned the corner from Dickens Lane. They halted to let the gates open and coasted to the rear carpark. Timothy watched the two couriers open the rear doors and empty the van. And seized the moment to hurry across the road, circle the side entrance, then jog across the grass to the rear carpark of the hospital.

Finally slowing to a breathless walk, he got to the van as the two couriers entered the building. The rear doors were open and there was no one in the front seats. He peeped inside. Saw a bag of power tools and a box on a pallet with thin steel binding holding it tight.

His heart pumped.

The plan was to jump them when they returned, drive the whalebone into the thug's stomach, tell him it was from his mother. That was feeling less likely. Yesterday was different, not just the hallucinations and whispering rushes, but because then he was cornered, threatened. This as cold blood.

A crumpled tarpaulin behind the driver's seat caught his eye. This could work better, when they were driving. He had another thought, something that could sort it for good. For everyone. He pulled out the bag of soiled clothes from under his jacket and placed it beneath the tarpaulin, climbed in next to it and covered himself.

And waited.

The pair stomped back to the van, muttering between themselves, one of them barking at the other to hurry. The last pallet of supplies was hoisted out onto the carpark and the van shook as they slammed the doors. He clenched the whalebone and reached into the bag of clothes to grip the pack of powder. 'Soon, Mother,' he whispered, 'soon.'

'Be careful, Timothy.'

'I will.'

He let his mother in. She lay spooned behind him, clutching him, helping him drift away like she always did. The engine growled into life, and Timothy slipped off, seizing the opportunity to be with his mother for a little longer. For the last time.

Chapter 49

Hard beats pounded from the speakers of Mario's works van. The three stooges, as ordered, had arrived at the remote woodland retreat with the cash.

'What time is it now?' Frodo yawned, still jaded.

'Ten-thirty. They should be here by now,' snapped Jeff, who hadn't slept for a week. He sat biting his nails, knees up to his chin, head to toe in black.

It used to be Gothy Jeff, still the short spiky hair and silver cross in the left ear, the Sisters of Mercy tattoo covered these days. But since landing a job at Wilson's chemist, the blanched white apron over a stubborn goth dress code hadn't done his street cred any favours. So now they called him nerdy Jeff.

He twitched in time with the beats, much to the amusement of the other two who hadn't had any problem sleeping.

'Simmer down,' insisted Mario from the driver's seat, plucking a roll-up from behind his ear and squeezing the car lighter. 'Give it another ten mins and then we'll phone your contact.' He sat back with his feet up on the dash and lit the fag. Blew a couple of hoops.

'This pounding jungle music isn't helping.'

'It's drum 'n' bass,' corrected Mario.

Jeff tightened his grip round his shins and rocked back and forth. 'What's the bloody difference?'

Frodo and Mario shook their heads at one another in disapproval. They made no comment but gave each other a knowing look, it was one of the reasons they called him 'nerdy' Jeff.

'I'll put some ambient on,' levelled Mario.

Another ten minutes passed and there was still no sign. A thousand pounds in cash felt like a lead weight in Jeff's pocket, albeit donated by Mario's uncle.

'Are you sure we've got the right place?'

'There's only one Fritton Wood, and this is the only carpark. So, yes, we've got the right place. If he wants the money, he'll be here. I just can't wait to see what this cop looks like, by the way. I'm taking a photo, for sure, and sending it in.'

'No you're fuckin' not.'

Frodo laughed. 'He's joking.'

Jeff had much more to lose from this than the other two, was told so by the CID who'd knocked on his door a week earlier.

The three fell quiet. A large van pulled into the parking bay opposite.

'That's a funny vehicle for CID. He must be getting someone else to do his dirty work,' said Frodo.

'Quite a criminal expert these days, aren't we, Master Frodo.'

'I'm gaining experience all the time, Mario.'

'Can you pair stop it? I've got to hand over the money to this pair of crooks. Look at the state of them. What are they going to do?'

They looked at the contents of the Endeavour van.

'It's easy. Hand it over, wait for them to count it, apologise for the misinformation, explain these things happen, blah blah,' Mario said as if he had done this 100 times. 'Then Frodo and I drive off at high speed and leave them to put a bullet in the back of your head.'

'Christ. Some friend you are.'

'Who sorted the cash?' Mario reminded him. 'And we didn't have to sell one gram, it went straight into the bin, and a kind donation from my uncle means the streets are clean. You can hand over feeling guilt free, with a halo above your head – which of course you'll need, seeing as you're going to heaven in five minutes.'

They stopped. The Endeavour doors opened. Two guys climbed out of the charcoal van and approached. One was tall, chiselled, the other, short and stocky with bulging eyes and pouty lips. The two thoroughbreds marched towards them. Mario was beginning to realise just how ugly this could all get.

The stooges took this as the cue, they got out, tried the casual look. Jeff attempted to bore holes into the crooks, cracked his knuckles and arched his back with an exaggerated stretch. He would be about seven stone wet through so looked more like Iggy Pop on the stage. Frodo made some introductions. None were necessary, there were no pleasantries from the thugs, just a nod. Frodo's 'Nice morning, isn't it?' babbling was lost in the tumbleweed.

'Not here,' said Frank, as he stopped Jeff going into his inside pocket a bit too soon. As he motioned to follow him away from the car park, they walked to the woods. 'Alone,' he said over his shoulder, meaning that Mario and Frodo would have to wait with Ronnie, who had a lingering odour to go with his appearance.

As Frank and Jeff walked away to exchange the cash, Frodo attempted to warm the cold atmosphere, so took his pouch of tobacco out of his pocket and offered it to Ronnie, clumsily tipping it over him. It helped clear the air.

'I need to take a leak,' said Mario. He took big strides to the back of the Endeavour van. Out of sight, he stopped and seized the opportunity to do a little favour for Eric who was owed more than a registration plate for his £1,000 input and efforts. The others were also unaware of Mario's scheme.

Had better make it quick.

Mario pulled out the micro-tracking device he'd purchased the previous day, along with a tube of adhesive compound. He quickly squelched as much compound as he could onto the device, waited as long as he dared for it to dry, then placed it under the driver-side rear wheel arch as firmly as he could.

Then ditched the rest of the compound and packaging under the van, rubbed spilt glue down his trousers and sauntered back to Frodo, doing his best to keep it casual. He asked for a light.

Ronnie, who now seemed to be chatting away to Frodo, didn't notice a thing. *Hope he isn't recruiting*, thought Mario. Better still, he saw Jeff returning, and the tall guy with the chiselled grey face like it was carved from stone, heading to the Endeavour van, implying the transaction was complete, and all had gone okay. All of them were unaware that the powder they had paid for was in the back of the van – with Timothy.

Brief nods – the meeting was over. Mario relit his half-smoked roll up and climbed back into his works vehicle.

'Thank God for that,' exhaled Jeff as he squeezed into the middle seat.

'I told you it would be easy. It went okay, didn't it?' said Mario.

'Sort of,' replied Jeff with a sheepish look.

'What do you mean – *sort of*?' asked Frodo as they watched the dust settle behind Endeavour.

'Well, he seemed happy enough, I think he was surprised we'd pushed it that quick, to be honest.'

'And?'

Jeff opened his leather jacket, the inside zipper open and bulging. 'He's given me another pack.'

'Why on earth did you take it?' asked Mario, coughing on his fag.

'He said I had to, or I'd be up to my neck.'

'There's no way we can get that much cash again. Eric isn't a bottomless money pit. This game will go on forever. You're going to have to do one – go missing or something – because this isn't happening again.' Mario whacked up the tunes and pulled away.

Endeavour turned south on the main road, Mario headed back to Yarmouth.

'Seems like an easy life being a drug dealer,' said Frodo eventually.

'That stinkin' stooge your best pal now, is he?'

'No, I'm just saying, like. You pick up, you distribute, etcetera, it all seems very straightforward to me.'

'It's very straightforward when you're sitting on your arse all day for five years at a time, behind bars.'

'I suppose so,' conceded Frodo, who was thinking of the limited career choices ahead.

Chapter 50

'Griffin speaking.'

He knew this could be only one of three people. The clam-phone rarely came out of Griffin's jacket. Pre-paid in cash and unregistered. The call was traceable, but there was no link either to him or to Leeman on the other end.

'We need to talk.'

'Can you elaborate?'

'The doctor's lost it.'

'Lost what?'

'The plot.'

Griffin clenched his teeth, waiting for a uniform with a mug of tea to pass. Then hissed, 'Meaning?'

'Meaning completely gaga, chasing fairies, dancing on moonbeams, overdosed on tiger's blood, whatever you like to call it. He's taken too much of his own medicine if you ask me. Well, actually it's my medicine, which is why I don't touch any of it.'

Leeman was in his bathroom staring into the mirror, nowhere to pace, chose his moment while his other half was hoovering the stairs.

'I'll speak to him.'

'He's buckled. I told him to leave town. I think he has a holiday home up the coast, he said he would hide out there until recovered – not that he ever will. I phoned St Nicholas Hospital, pretending to be his father, and requested he came home, saying it was a family emergency. This will buy him a bit of time, at least. He'll take MR11 to overcome the psychosis, but if he has taken as much Halloween as I think he has, it could be bad news.'

'MR11 is the remedy, right?' whispered Griffin, the clam gripped tight to his ear, looking around the hallway for eavesdroppers.

Leeman turned to face the shower curtain left open to stop the mildew, a woman's touch. 'Up to a point. Even so, he could spew our names. It could link us even though people may think he's deranged.

'Christ. What an idiot.'

Griffin paused. A uniform passed, so he pushed one hand in his trouser pocket and rocked on his heels, blathered about a court date till the uniform was out of earshot then he got back to the problem.

'Okay, I think it's time to cut our two little elves loose. About time I cracked this drug ring, although it's a bit earlier than we'd planned, I know.'

'Chuck 'em under the bus for all I care. I guess that's going to impact on me?'

'Too right, but we'll sort that when we have to. You're going to have to prep your girlie for this.'

'She doesn't need to know, I'll do all the talking. It will be you who interviews us, right?' Leeman knew Pooch would be shocked at the revelations if he had to explain things to her. That would ruin his chances of getting a ring on her finger.

'I'll make sure it's me.'

They hung up. Griffin waded back into the interrogation room where Eric sat with a face like a tombstone, arms outstretched on the table, tapping out a rhythm with his index. A habit he had developed, to help keep memory of the answers he'd given so far. Eric thought it had gone okay. As far as interrogations went, he'd had worse, much worse.

'Well, thank you for your time and cooperation, Mr Haines. You can collect your house keys from the front desk, that's all the questions we have – for now.'

Eric tried not to show any relief, but he felt like running, and was escorted out by a bored uniform they called Wingnut.

'That was a little shorter than I was expecting.'

'I know, thought it best we wait until we find what's come back from the search, and keep it polite for now. Then we'll have him back in tomorrow, cross reference his story and push a bit harder – keep him on edge.'

'Okay,' agreed Ross, 'let's see if Burnt and Ashley have anything for us.'

'I've had a buzz from a scumbag on the street. It might be nothing, but you never know.'

'What have you got?'

'An ID on the vehicle at the Bells Road fire. I'd like to follow up with it straight away, sir.'

'Okay. You need a constable with you?'

'I'd rather do it alone. As soon as he sees a uniform he'll clam up. If I'm in civvies, he's more likely to spill.'

Ross held on to the chair he was tucking under the desk. Eyed Griffin. 'As you wish. Everything okay?'

'Fine,' said Griffin, a little too quickly, 'just want to get this mess out the way.'

'Indeed. You contact me if you get anything. If we can wrap this one up, we can allocate all the resources we have to the Hacket murder.'

Griffin delayed leaving the interview room, fussing over the folder and evidence bag containing Haines's coat, waiting for Ross to exit. Then made a call.

He flicked open the clam, pressed speed dial four. 'We need to talk, face-to-face. Something's come up. And it's urgent.'

'I don't care,' insisted Griffin, cutting Frank Allen short. 'Turn back and go to the lockup.' He paused while Frank grumbled.

'Good,' he replied, looking at his watch. Two pm. 'I'll be there in half an hour, wait there and don't take any more calls.'

Chapter 51

*J*ust call the station, Bryony thought. She had registered Timothy as missing, but that was not why she wanted to speak to Burnt. It was trickier than that. How could she say it? 'My boss who happens to be the lead psychiatrist at the hospital where I work has gone cuckoo, and I think the couriers burnt Timothy's house down.' She would get a drug test herself for comments like that, end up on the other side of the medicine counter at the hospital.

And where was Eric? Why hadn't he phoned? He was the one person she could trust. Between them they had discovered there might be something amiss, something sinister. She needed help – yes, it was time to inform the police.

Be brave, she told herself. *Call Great Yarmouth Police Station.* It wasn't an emergency, no need for 999, *let's not make a drama*.

She was standing in for Stamford at reception for half an hour, sighing at the scores of files, the endless paperwork trail that seemed to go around in circles, the big push to go digital pushed to the back of the queue for another month. Then she reached over and scooped up the phone from the cradle.

A helpful duty officer answered. Bryony took a deep breath and thought carefully about how to phrase what she wanted to say, scratching at her shocked fringe, biting her bottom lip.

'It's Bryony Joy from St Nicholas mental health institute. I would like to speak to someone about a fire that took place at a chemist last week, I think I might have some information.'

The duty officer patched her through. The flycatcher picked up.

***

Griffin and Burnt passed each other in the foyer. Griffin briefly made eye contact while hurrying towards his exit.

'Someone's in a hurry,' Burnt remarked.

'Not really, just following up on a tip-off. It's probably nothing,' Griffin said, trying not to break his stride.

'You need Ashley?' asked Burnt, nodding over his shoulder.

'No, it's no big deal.'

'As you wish.'

The flycatcher stopped Burnt as he passed the reception. Not the most glamorous pseudonym, but apt. She manned the desk when sitting in for the duty officer while he was off-shift or busying himself. It gave her freedom to cluck at the younger men as they went by, make them squirm.

The catcher had a real knack for making the coolest of customers turn pink. She had the appearance of a warthog in make-up. She tried her best, had tipped fifty, and had the complexion of red sandpaper and teeth like a piranha. This week she was wearing her bleached hair in a bun, but it could have been a Mohican for all the difference it made.

'Hey, Burnt baby,' she shouted, loud enough for every male in the vicinity to look up – and turn away in relief.

'I need to see the super …' he attempted, trotting past.

'You didn't say that last night,' she laughed. Saw the panic in his face. 'But let's not go into that. There's competition for me on the other end of the line. It sounds like a real damsel in distress,' she continued, holding her hand over the mouthpiece, 'I'm obviously not enough for ya.'

She bellowed with laughter once more, held out the phone for Burnt.

'Ashley, you take this. I need to catch up with Ross.' Burnt dodged the desk, leaving the young DC with the flycatcher. Ashley had no choice.

'The younger the better,' she cooed.

He took the phone, trying to avoid eye contact but failing to evade the lashings of Fantasia perfume. He cleared his throat before speaking. 'Detective Constable Ashley.'

Bryony delivered her speech. Said she had suspicions about an Endeavour employee, that he might have been involved in the fire a week ago, and that she had concerns about a doctor at the hospital. Phrased it as best she could, but knew she sounded more like a little old woman lost in the shopping mall.

'No problem,' Ashley replied. Endeavour, could that be mistaken for Demeanour? 'I'll be over to take formal statements and interview the staff. No, don't apologise, we always take any information seriously. Thank you for your call.'

Bryony hung up, overwhelmed, hadn't expected such a positive response. Then looked up in disbelief at Timothy's double.

'Hello, I'm Fiona Pendle. I'm here to see Dr Alexander McLeish.'

Chapter 52

Eric Haines's head was bursting with questions. Where was Timothy? Should he phone Bryony? What would he tell her? Which of the police could he trust? He was striding away from the police station towards home when a rusty diesel van drew up alongside him.

'Your taxi, sir,' chirped Mario, easing to a standstill, the passenger window open.

'Well, you'll have to work on your looks, although the timing is perfect,' said Eric, as he climbed into Mario's works van.

'A man of your age at the police station,' tutted Mario, then checked his mirror and pulled away.

'Just helping the friendly arm of the law, Mario.'

Mario had phoned him as Eric was leaving the station, said he had news.

'I thought you might want to know,' said Mario with a wink.

'Know what? Oh bloody hell, I forgot all about that. You didn't go, did you?'

'Yeah, it was a breeze.' Mario tapped his steering wheel in time to the beats as he trundled the high street.

'Christ, your mother would bloody kill me. It was for your hobbits to deliver, not you. Christ, you might've been killed.'

'Calm down, it was a snitch.'

Eric rubbed his face, turned down the tunes. 'How can you drive to this noise? Can't hear myself think. Don't know what I was doing, fronting money to bloody gangsters, I'm too old for this crap.'

'Don't worry. I have something for you, a registration number.'

'Really? That's great. It gives us something to go on.' He climbed out of his coat and opened the window.

'It's only a number plate. You know I was in the SAS, right?' Mario grinned at his uncle while steering with two fingers on the wheel.

'Bloody hell, here we go.'

'But there's something else.'

'Oh?' Eric was expecting some bad news.

'I've put a tracker on the vehicle, under the wheel arch, actually.'

They pulled from the lights. Mario, now beaming, didn't give the full story, about there being another pack to shift, gave the good news only. Maybe he would sell this one on as Frodo had said and duck the next meeting. Jeff would have to get out of town and find a new job. As long as it wasn't as a bloody chemist.

'Yep, it has a built-in GPS that shows where the vehicle is. All I need to do is log on to find out.'

'Really? My God, that must have cost you a fortune.'

'Fifty quid.' Mario had forgotten how out of touch his uncle was.

'How did you do that?' Eric asked, eyes wide. Mario then filled him in on the details of the drop.

'The battery will only last a few hours, though, so whatever we do it's got to be quick.'

'So now we log onto a computer?' asked Eric. 'There's one at the library.'

Mario had to laugh out loud. 'That's Stone Age. All we need is this,' he said, pointing to his mobile phone in the cradle on the dash.

'You're going to phone them?'

'No.' Mario laughed again. 'The tracker tells me their coordinates, their postcode and street name, and right now it shows me they are in Yarmouth. Look.' Mario pointed to the phone showing a live feed of a map displaying an animated 'X' moving along the road.

Mario was amazed at how little his uncle knew of the modern world.

'Oh, and it stores up the history of where they've been as well.' He gave Eric a twitch of his monobrow as he gripped the steering wheel and jumped a set of lights.

The retired squaddie was dumbfounded. 'Magic moonbeams on a stick,' he said in disbelief. The screen had his attention.

'At first they seemed to be heading to the A12. Probably London, because of their strong cockney accents like, but no. They then stopped, turned around and came back to the coast. They must like it around here. I think I might get a job in the police force,' said Mario.

Eric rolled his eyes, but was nevertheless impressed. Then guilt overwhelmed him. It could be dangerous, and the fragile plan was getting kookier by the minute. He would have been happy with just a number plate and ID of the car.

Eric expected the van to go to the hospital. At that point he would phone the police and tell them anonymously about the couriers, the drivers and the possible illegal freight – oblivious of the fact that Timothy was hiding in the back under a tarpaulin.

They traced the flashing cursor on the phone, which lured them towards the seafront. Mario slammed on the brakes as the lights turned red.

'Watch the road,' insisted Eric as a car hooted from behind. But Eric was as transfixed by the blinking cursor on the screen as Mario. Had only just got the hang of his Nokia 6210 and texting – this was a whole different world.

'How does it know?' continued Eric, captivated.

'GPS.'

'We had portable GPS packs when I was in the army, but they were fifty times the size, you would have to strap them to your back, they weighed a tonne. It wasn't that long ago, really.'

'Moore's Law,' Mario pointed out.

'Whose?'

Mario explained to his uncle one of the few things he'd remembered from his university days. 'Moore's law. Way back in the fifties, when integrated circuits were invented. This guy,

Gordon Moore, the co-founder of Intel, predicted that every couple of years the numbers of transistors that could be fitted into a circuit would double. They can make the wafers thinner and thinner each year, as they improve the technology. Thing is, the trend has never stopped, it still holds true. Year after year. Amazing really.'

'So you learnt more than just how to roll a joint at university?'

'Not much more.'

Mario put his foot down, trying to catch up to the flashing green cursor. Eric wanted to know more about the world that had flown past him at great speed without stopping, but the phone once again caught their attention.

'They've stopped,' they said in unison. The flashing cursor stood still, the glyph on the upper corner of the phone changed from a green traffic light to a red exclamation mark.

Eric was gripped by the phone.

'At Nelson's monument,' confirmed Mario, tapping at the screen to get more details while driving one-handed. 'It's at that little business park,' he added, swerving as he tried to navigate.

'Not what I was expecting,' said Eric. 'I guessed they would be heading to the hospital. Be careful.'

Chapter 53

'Can you open it?' asked Ashley.

He stood outside McLeish's office with Bryony, Timothy's aunt Fiona Pendle, and a janitor, whom Ashley hoped would let them in without having to kick the door down.

The janitor shrugged. 'Sure, if you want me to.' He rummaged in his toolbox for a keyset, happy to try out his lock-picking skills.

Bryony turned to Mrs Pendle to apologise for the third time but stopped short of attempting to explain that this was 'all most unusual'. She was becoming inured to surprises in the hospital, but thought there might be one more on the other side of this door. Having to explain that Mrs Pendle's nephew had gone missing from the hospital was bad enough, part of her didn't want to know what was happening to McLeish. He hadn't returned any of her calls but sent a rambling email that morning about the pressure of the job being too much. And with what Caulk had told her she felt the need to inform the police.

Two minutes passed as the janitor tried various picks and techniques. He stuck his tongue out while he probed and scraped at the lock. Bryony attempted to make conversation, unwittingly playing with her hair and scratching at her hands. Pendle was a knockout. It was rare for Bryony to have a crush on anyone, there were few that could turn her head. But Fiona Pendle had an air of confidence that made Bryony look on in awe. She immediately adored her, almost giggled when she spoke, even went a little pink. Couldn't help but hold her gaze, to get an eyeful of her smooth tanned skin, those high cheekbones, and bedroom eyes. Decked out too. Slim suit, delicate jewellery, not showy, more understated. Plain classy.

Ashley checked his phone. He was keen to have a snoop, and this was a good excuse to scour the doctor's room before jumping to conclusions about the Demeanour/Endeavour vehicle.

Fiona knew stamping her feet would do no good, it wasn't the student's fault. Poor girl was overworked, she thought. She clasped her Gucci handbag patiently in front of her with both hands, held her chin up to take in the surroundings. There was a lot going on inside her head, but little given away.

'Ah ha. That's the one,' said the pudgy janitor, congratulating himself. He opened the door and stood aside smiling, as if waiting for a reward.

Ashley brushed past him. Got as far as the computer desk and stopped. White dust scattered across the desk, and on the floor – more crystals sparkling around his shoes. He stepped back, 'Don't touch anything. Miss Joy, is there any reason why medication would be taken or administered in this room?'

'No.'

'Crikey, you guys have some fun round here don't you?' cracked Fiona.

'Okay. From now on, this is a crime scene, and will need forensic examination. Please stand back. I will need formal statements from all of you.' Ashley turned to the janitor. 'Find some barrier tape and cordon off the entrance. This room is only to be accessed by police officers.'

***

'So now what?' asked Mario. They sat across the street, captivated by the stationary Endeavour van as though it might suddenly burst into flames.

Eric rubbed at his eyes. 'We make an anonymous call to the police, giving the address of a van, say it's holding drugs, explain we suspect illegal activity in this lockup. Well, something like that, anyway.'

'Okay. And wait for the fuzz to show?' said Mario with a smile, enjoying playing cops and robbers.

'I guess so.'

Eric put on his glasses, marked down the plate. Then took out his phone and was about to hit 999 when someone familiar pulled up next to Endeavour. Eric paused, shrank into his seat.

'You know that guy?' asked Mario.

'Know him? He's just questioned me.'

They watched Griffin getting out his car, sweep his hand through his hair, and saunter into the lockup while flicking the creases out of his jacket.

'I think we've found our bent copper,' said Mario, bouncing on his seat.

'I think you're right, Sherlock. Let's see what he leaves with before making the call.'

Chapter 54

Griffin had to duck slightly under the side door that led him to Frank, who was sitting casually at the steel table pulling on a cigarette, Ronnie tidying around him.

Griffin scanned the partially lit garage. 'Just the two of you?' he asked. This meeting was their first. Showing his face on this side of the criminal fence wasn't something Griffin took lightly.

'That's right. Were you expecting someone else?' replied Frank, still rattled at having to track back up the A12.

Griffin made no reply, he wasn't here to answer questions. He considered the quiet lockup. 'Is there just the one exit at the front?'

'Uh-uh,' Frank replied, a little quieter. He sat up slowly and stamped on his fag-butt. 'You guys cased it in the first place, remember?' He frowned at Griffin, the lines on his face long and deep.

'I'm asking just in case there's a bit of heat, that's all. Things have got a bit out of hand lately.'

'Last week you mean?' Frank asked, hoping not to have to explain the fiasco for the third time. Again, no answer. Griffin now with his back to Frank, was looking to the mezzanine.

'It was me who bought you time to get out, you know,' Griffin continued. 'That was a real mess, but that's not all.' He turned to face Frank, hands in pockets.

'How much have we got here?' he asked with a shrug, sticking out his chin.

'There's a few kilos of Halloween, and that's about it. All the rest's delivered. And there's £1,000 in cash, in the safe.'

'Mmm.'

Ronnie picked up a broom. Kept his head down, and as far away as he could.

Griffin narrowed his eyes at Frank. 'Have you got a piece on you now?

'It's out the back – just in case.'

'Show me,' demanded Griffin.

Ronnie edged away from the pair. Sweeping imaginary dust.

Frank shook his head, sighed, and paced over to the kitchen in the back room. Got down on his knees, yanked away the skirting under the kitchen unit with a *tut*, and searched for the pistol. After a couple of sweeps with his arm, he found it, wrapped in cloth. Uncovered it, gripped the cold steel loosely, and showed it, palm up.

'That should do us,' said Griffin to himself.

Frank cocked his head, gave him a quizzical look. Griffin stood in the doorway between the main area and the back room, with Frank at the sink unit, gun in hand. To make this work, Griffin needed to see both at once. He looked over his shoulder to Ronnie who was at the far end of the warehouse near the door, swiping away with the broom. Too close to the door? It was now or never.

Griffin beamed a shark grin, plucked out the Glock 26 from his inside pocket, and pumped one into Frank's chest. The bullet ripped through Frank. His legs crumbled.

Then he hit the floor, writhing in the spreading pool of red.

The shooting had taken Griffin by surprise. He had been looking forward to this, and felt well prepped for it. But Frank Allen's demise took him aback.

The booming noise of the gun echoed round the lockup, and Frank's agonising cry gave Ronnie the couple of seconds he needed to flee.

One thing Ronnie had learned from his life of crime was the ability to spot when a meeting was going to kick off. Griffin's presence alone was a warning. As soon as Ronnie heard the shot, he dropped the broom and bolted as a second splintered the doorframe.

Griffin had set up Frank nicely, his fingerprints were on the gun, and he had been pointing it at the detective. He had been following up an anonymous tip-off, and expecting a dead end, considered it unnecessary to bring back-up. His gun needed justifying, he had signed it out two weeks previously, and forgotten to hand it in after shooting practice.

Griffin knew the timing would have to be perfect. He would have to take them both at once, thought he'd got it right, but that small hesitation had cost him a witness. Although no one would believe the criminal. Griffin could link him to the Bells Road fire and drug trafficking, there was no problem there, especially with his string of convictions. It would be unprofessional to run out into the street shooting wildly, he had just defended himself and anything else would be suspicious.

He looked down at the twitching body while he made an emergency call. He gave the name and the registration plate of the Endeavour van as Frank Allen gave up on life.

Once the spasms had stopped, DS Griffin reached into Frank Allen's pocket for his phone, checked the history list, and yanked out the battery. Then he put on a pair of latex gloves and picked the weapon off the floor, turned 180 degrees, pointed it behind where he was standing and fired into the rooftop.

After placing the gun next to Frank's side, he left the building as calm as when he walked in.

Chapter 55

Ronnie came scuttling out of the side door and dived into the van. Eric dropped his phone, fumbled to pick it up. Hit 999, swearing to himself at getting distracted by more techno-babble from his nephew. That's when they received the second shock of the morning – Timothy Levin's face in the rear window of the van as it reversed into the road.

'Follow them,' Eric ordered.

'What's he doing there?' asked Mario, not expecting an answer.

Eric gave the vehicle description to the emergency control room officer, while Mario tried to keep up with the swerving Endeavour van. Just as he hung up, his phone rang. He looked down at the name. *Bryony*. Eric felt obliged to answer, although not sure how to explain what was happening. He had promised to contact her if he found Timothy, could he pretend he hadn't seen Timothy until now? He let it ring out.

Mario kept close. Endeavour almost stopped, then jerked away again. Eric called Bryony, tried his best to explain where Timothy was.

***

A steady stream of traffic on Haven Bridge. Pedestrians pulled their collars up around their ears to keep out the easterly wind. Caulk strolled along the bridge and, unlike most of the others in the vicinity, stopped at the apex and looked down the Yare where it snaked out to sea. This place held memories for her, dark ones. It was where she'd tried to end it all.

But not today, or ever again, which was why she would test herself, by standing at the same spot to prove how far she had come, and how much stronger she was now in dealing with what life could throw at her. After pausing to reflect she returned to her task of finding Timothy, but was distracted.

Chapter 56

Timothy knew this was the moment. He glanced out of the rear window for any sign of police – there were none. He could do this quickly and make his escape. He opened the pack of Halloween and crawled up behind the driver.

Ronnie looked in the rear-view mirror. Before he could speak, Timothy had both hands over Ronnie's mouth with the pack in between his fingers. Ronnie could do nothing other than try to breathe in and gulp down while at the same time steering the van. The open packet held firmly over his nose and mouth left him with little option.

Ronnie swerved, braked, swallowed, and choked as the crystal powder pellets made their way down his throat. Timothy held firm, gripping Ronnie's head against the seat rest, the pair locked eye to eye via the rear-view mirror.

'Keep driving,' Timothy ordered.

He eased his grip when Ronnie's resistance stopped, then clambered over to the passenger seat. Had a few words for this man. Ronnie's life would never be the same again, Timothy was sure of that. He sat in the passenger seat and spoke candidly to the doomed driver whose gaze darted between the road and Timothy.

White pills peppered Ronnie's coveralls. He expected the worst, but self-preservation told him he might be able to talk his way out of what was coming.

'Keep your eyes on the road,' said Timothy. 'You know the first part isn't too bad, you'll feel quite energetic and good about the world,' he smiled.

'I know,' said Ronnie, who after last week's incident had vowed to himself never to touch the stuff again. That time he'd had only a dab – this would drive him out of his mind. His vision was already becoming bleary as he drove along the dockside towards Haven Bridge.

'But then it goes wrong, all very wrong. Your body goes hollow and moves by itself as you look at it from the outside. You watch your empty shell limping along. If you close your eyes, it gets worse. Everything changes, all the things you have ever feared start to show themselves to you, and start punishing you. Then you start to hate yourself for being the bad person you are, and the hurting starts because of the things you've done, or in my case not done. But I'm making up for it now. You see I didn't do enough, did I, Mr whatever-your-name-is who killed my mother?' Timothy fixed his stare at Ronnie.

'It wasn't my fault. I didn't know it would send me potty.' Ronnie started to ramble, trying to reason with the boy. 'I tried the stuff, and it freaked me out. And your mother came at me … and well …' But he knew it was hopeless, trying to explain why he'd taken a life, killed the boy's mother.

'Why were you there? Why did you take this stuff? Why kill my mother?' Ronnie gripped the steering wheel harder, foam forming on his lips. The crystals around his face burning holes in his skin.

Timothy began to pull up his sleeves. 'With me there was no choice, I was force-fed this white stuff – I never asked for it. I was ready to meet my mother, and maybe I still will. After it had cleared a bit, though it never truly goes away, it sometimes flashes back at you – she came to me. There I was, sitting in the dark and trying to die, and she came to me and told me: "It's not your fault," she said.'

Timothy revealed his freshly scarred arms to Ronnie.

'I punished myself, I still hate myself for not saving her and always will. I sat there in her burnt-out bedroom and tried to join her, but then she told me … I'm not sure how, but she said it wasn't what she wanted. My mother's not ready to see me yet – she wants to meet you though.'

He touched the weapon in his pocket. Ronnie eyed it, sweat running down his face.

'It should be you who's joining her. It was your decision to break in and burn our home down, to change everything, to take her away and to ruin my life forever. You need to explain that to her.'

'Now hold on,' started Ronnie, trying to keep his eyes on the road. But with his vision becoming ever more blurred, he knew he couldn't stop whatever was coming. The demons were creeping up in front of him, perched on the bonnet and licking their lips.

'It's not my fault,' he cried. 'I can't help it if I'm like this, I didn't choose this. I had a life forced on me that I never wanted. I had no choice. This life has never been an option. It's been handed down,' he attempted, his voice getting louder. 'Some fuckers get given business or money or somefin', but no, not me – I get a life of crime.' He burst into tears as he turned onto the bridge.

'It's me who's left with no choice,' replied Timothy.

One demon too many jumped out in front of Ronnie. His stomach turned and the bile rose in his throat.

The van careered over to the opposite road of the bridge, clipped a bumper then rammed into the steel handrail. Trapping Timothy.

Cars swerved and beeped their horns, there was nothing left the broken criminal could do but reassert his innocence.

'I didn't choose this,' he screamed, trying to plead his case, head in hands to the jury of snakes at the window. Satan beside him.

'My father was a crim, my grandfather worse, my stepfather isn't worth talking about. It goes on – it's like a chain. That's it, a chain.'

Ronnie was crying, blank looks from the ugly faces licking the window gave the verdict of death. Claws tapped at the glass.

'It gets handed down to the next poor sod in line, but don't worry, it stops with me. I've got no offspring, so it's the end of the chain right here.'

He poured out his heart, crying to a now jeering crowd who laughed heartily, drinking goblets of blood in celebration. His throat tightened, his heart pounded through his chest, getting louder in Ronnie's ears like a beating drum.

Ronnie choked and his face turned blue, the veins getting larger as they started to protrude from under his skin. They imploded, leaving a blue-webbed scarred face staring out of the window at the onlookers. Blood ran down his nose, and after a few faint whispers, the bulging, bloodshot eyes stopped blinking, and stared wide open, taking in the last view of terror as his heart surrendered.

***

There was no time to take statements from the two women. DS Ross interrupted Ashley who could hardly believe his ears – a shooting on Great Yarmouth seafront.

'Ashley, proceed at once to Nelson monument. Griffin is there awaiting back-up, the perpetrators have left location, so it's expected to be safe, but use caution. Burnt is on his way to Haven Bridge where the perps have been in a collision, the vehicle belongs to a company called Endeavour.'

Ashley hung up, and explained why he had to cut the interview short, although it was not necessary, the pair could hear Ross barking down the phone. Bryony looked at Fiona in disbelief, and then her mobile rang. It was Eric – at last.

Ashley made down the stairs, holding the banister with one hand. At the ground floor he sped at the exit to shoulder-barge the door open without breaking speed. He smashed into it and bounced back. A bemused security guard looked over his paper at Ashley who was floored, rubbing his arm.

'It's locked,' he said, biting into an apple, smiling with his eyes.

Fiona Pendle came scuttling down the stairs behind as the guard buzzed the door open. She flew through the exit, almost leaping over Ashley as he crouched on the floor. Bryony wanted to do the same, but feeling a duty of care stopped at the feet of the detective.

'You okay?'

'I think I've snapped my collarbone.'

Chapter 57

When Burnt arrived, the bridge was in gridlock. A police van was parked across the causeway to prevent traffic moving to or from the incident. Burnt pulled up behind them and updated control.

The Endeavour van, bonnet pushed through the railings, looked like it could topple into the Yare. Burnt requested water rescue to dispatch a speedboat and moor near the bridge. Ordered the uniforms to move all the public away and cordon off the scene. Then leant across the front seat of the police van, grabbed the PA handset and instructed the public to exit the bridge on foot. Forcing drivers to abandon their vehicles.

No one had left the van. Burnt narrowed his eyes, made out two figures behind the cracked glass. If there was a hostage, he would need to tread carefully.

Amongst the crowd stood Eric and Mario, separated by constables making a human chain and requesting everyone move away.

Burnt updated control over the radio, then switched back to the PA and requested the driver to step out of the van. He repeated the instruction. The bridge fell silent.

Only Timothy knew why the perpetrator wouldn't get out of the vehicle. He'd had plenty of time to plant yesterday's murder weapon on Ronnie. He wiped his prints and placed the whalebone in the dead man's overall pocket.

'Take this with you,' he whispered, 'you'll need it.'

Then he put the remains of the powder together with the bag of bloodstained clothes in the back of the van.

Barely able to see through the fissured windows, he made out pixelated police cornering the van on three sides.

He thought how best to get out. Not wanting to crawl on top of the corpse, he kicked through the passenger window with his right foot.

The crowd gasped when they heard shattering glass. Burnt yelled at the uniforms to stop.

Timothy peered into the Yare. Wished he'd learnt to swim. Then gripped the door frame and hauled himself up onto the handrail. He looked down, his stomach turned and he slipped, but he just about caught the inside roof handle of the van and steadied himself. Then he took in the crowd.

Burnt froze. Recognised Levin, and the jacket that had been hanging up at Eric Haines's house only a day before – the same white sports logo. *This is whom Haines is protecting. Timothy is Eric's nephew*, he assumed, remembering the good luck card found in the bedroom. At the same time Mario was wondering why Timothy was wearing his jacket.

***

Fiona abandoned her hire car near the town hall. She would get closer to the scene on foot. She legged it to the barriers in time to see Timothy teetering on the edge of the handrail. He stepped onto the bonnet, looking for a clear spot to jump onto the road.

Fiona could hold back no longer. She pushed up against the interlocked arms of the police. 'Timothy,' she hollered.

Her sister was right, the boy looked just like her. Timothy considered the crowd, picked out his mother's face. Thought the nightmares were returning.

'Mother?' he called in surprise, and stepped back into fresh air, his arms flailing around him as he plunged into the Yare.

'Christ,' cried Fiona.

'Hell,' snapped Burnt. He hollered down the radio to the water rescue service, requesting a utility speedboat for a second time.

Fiona turned to run back to the edge of the bridge – and slammed into another onlooker, nearly knocking her off her feet.

'I'm sorry.'

Caulk waved away the apology. 'I know where he might turn up, but we have to be quick.'

'Really?' said Fiona, ready to believe anything.

'Yes. We must leave – now.'

Caulk pointed to a parked taxi on the south side of the bridge where the driver was watching the pantomime unfold. Fiona followed Caulk and pulled out fifty pounds from her purse to guarantee the taxi driver would ask no questions – and break all speed limits.

Eric wasted no time. He ripped off his coat and launched himself off the edge of the handrail, plunging into the cold North Sea.

Mario stood rooted to the spot watching in wonder, but needed to avoid questions, as he still had a kilo of Halloween in his pocket. As soon as his uncle surfaced he edged to his van.

Onlookers and police watched two bodies bob around and float away to the harbour's mouth. Eric trod water, searching for Timothy, paddling around as the tide dragged him away. A speedboat gunning towards him.

Timothy gulped in salt water, wretched, and lost his breath as he was gripped by the current.

Eric dived deep, but it was hopeless. There was no visibility, just putrid yellow stinging his eyes. He surfaced and screamed Timothy's name as the coastguard moored alongside him. He was hauled onto the boat.

Eric lay spewing while two support divers finished kitting themselves for a dive.

Timothy shouted his mother's name and held on to the last memory he had of her. He relaxed his body, felt the tide pull him away.

His mother came close, whispered in his ear, held him.

He felt his ribs crack as he smashed into something steel. Then convulsed, and his head recoiled as the invisible object battered him.

The river Yare opens out to the sea with a kink in the harbour where a small steel service ladder from the jetty gives access. This part of the dock is where Timothy held on to. He crawled to the surface and gripped the slime-covered steel. He could not pull himself out of the water, his drenched clothes weighed on him, his ribs were battered, and blood seeped from his scalp.

He held on tight, hooking his heel round the ladder. There were several rungs to mount before he would reach the apex. He grabbed the slippery steel, and pushed himself up, but slipped and had to grip with one hand as he slumped back to the water.

Then a face appeared. 'Take my hand,' said Caulk.

Timothy held out one arm weakly, trying to keep hold of the ladder with the other.

Caulk launched herself over the side of the ladder and lowered herself until she was waist deep in the water. She gripped his hand and yanked him towards her. Fiona leant over the sea wall and hauled him over the side.

The bemused taxi driver sat back in his car, happy with the easiest fifty quid fare he had ever taken.

Fiona hugged her nephew in relief, tears pouring down her face. She should have done this years ago – this was her blood.

'No, I'm not your mother. I'm your aunt,' she explained, wiping his face and trying to smooth down his hair, kissing at his forehead. 'I will take good care of you, but we need to go. I've seen enough madness in this crackpot town to last me a lifetime.'

She turned to Caulk. 'Sorry. But … how did you know?'

Timothy shivered, nestled into Fiona while Caulk explained herself.

'It's simple,' she said, shrugging, 'I jumped from the same place two years ago. Somehow I got lucky and ended up bashing right into that ladder below.'

She nodded over her shoulder. 'I guess someone up there threw me a line. That's when I realised, everyone needs a lifeline. I need to help people.'

Fiona felt her heart would break in half. Nevertheless, she held strong, had to get out of this place, and fast. The thanks could come later.

They scurried from the harbour's edge towards the taxi. Timothy limping, supported by Fiona who barked at the taxi driver, 'I need an alternative route out of this town. Not that bridge.'

'Sorry, darlin,' not like that,' he said, pointing to Timothy.

'Five hundred pounds. And switch that bloody radio off.'

Chapter 58

The hot summer rain poured over Griffin and Ashley. Vivaldi sounded from the hallway as Griffin pressed the doorbell. A figure grew behind the frosted glass, unlocked the door, opened it wide and stood aside. Mid-twenties, hair tied back, holding a Shiatzu puppy with a pink bow and a studded silver collar. She was a looker, thought Griffin, that was for sure, the old boy had done well there. Although there was probably nothing between the ears.

'Miss Jennifer Tyke, I presume?' inquired Griffin.

'Yeah, that's me. Come in.' Strong London accent.

They followed Miss Tyke through to the lounge, both admiring her rear view. Prints with a twenties theme hung on the wall, a butler in a tux pouring champagne for a lady on a beach, sitting carefree in the wind, a group of knobs partying to excess despite the weather. The gaff was immaculate, cream shag pile carpet looked like it had never been walked on. Couch never sat on.

No sooner were they seated and the pleasantries complete, teas and coffees refused, than Leeman entered. His freshly showered hair was still damp after his Tuesday afternoon squash session. He gave his wide-grinned happy-to-help face.

The *Eastern Daily Press* beamed up at them from the coffee table, showing the hero cop headline of Sunday's escapades. Griffin showing all his teeth. A drug ring unveiled and the streets rid of thousands of pounds' worth of contraband, with one of the gang a suspect in the murder of an ongoing enquiry.

Quite a rap. Ashley rubbed at his bandaged shoulder; *shame the boy is still missing*.

The revelations had shocked Miss Tyke. A constable had knocked on her door Sunday evening asking her to confirm the registration plate of the works vehicle. Two hours later CID were round with more questions. She hadn't known anything untoward was happening with her business. This ignorance had been the beauty of the set-up – Leeman's girlfriend wasn't lying when she answered the questions.

Griffin recapped that Endeavour employees were involved in drug trafficking and murder.

'I'm sorry,' interrupted Leeman. 'It's all my fault. I really should have paid more attention to who my partner was employing,' he said, scratching his ever-expanding bald spot, belly pushing through his striped shirt.

Crystal shook in the display cabinet behind him as a truck rattled past.

'Although it's her business, I do help on the commercial side. I mean we should have carried out a more thorough search of the individuals we employ. To be honest, the goods we courier aren't expected to be that much value to anyone other than the client. You know, mechanical and electronic parts from distributors to small engineering facilities and the like, mainly within the offshore industry. We're just trying to compete with the big boys, which is tough when working in East Anglia, our competitors are global. We've tried to broaden our business geographically, which is why we've employed people from further south. But we didn't think it necessary to undertake character checks. If they had a clean driving licence and a legitimate reference we considered this to be enough for what is, essentially, a delivery man's job,' he concluded, edging to his partner, offering an arm.

She gripped her puppy, kissed its forehead, adjusted the pink bow. The company was hers – on paper, although she hardly lifted a finger. There was usually a pickup and delivery to organise once a week, which was always legitimate, Leeman had made sure of that. If ever investigated, then a squeaky-clean trail of the small enterprise was there for all to see, just ticking over in an age where the larger courier companies cherry-picked most of the work. There were separate bank accounts for the receipts for Pharma supplies that had no link to Endeavour, but to an offshore account called BetaPharm.

'I hardly spoke to this guy, Frank Allen,' blurted Miss Tyke. 'I would just get an enquiry, either over the phone or by email, from a customer asking for a pickup.' She rocked her baby peeking out from between her breasts. 'Then I would send out an email and create an invoice the next day,' she said, looking to Harry as she almost crushed her puppy.

Ashley wished he could do the questioning, but he was under orders to keep tight-lipped. His shoulder throbbed. Griffin countered with some spoon-fed lines that Leeman hoovered up on her behalf. And gave instructions for Endeavour to prepare their business records for review. There would also be damages to pay to Great Yarmouth Council, which Leeman and Tyke fully acknowledged.

'It has been a lesson for us, for sure. We'll have to take more care in future,' said Leeman, as Griffin and Ashley stood up to leave.

Ashley burst out, 'So you never tracked your van's progress?'

The puppy growled.

What harm could it do? He needed to clarify something that had been needling away at him, and this was as good a question as any to confirm it. 'I mean, whenever I have a parcel delivered at home, there's a tracking order issued that I can follow online.'

He looked squarely at Tyke, but knew the answer would come from her other half – who paused a little too long. Tyke looked at Leeman, not knowing if the answer was yes or no.

'I'm afraid we can't compete at that level, it's expensive,' he said with a smile, folding his arms. 'We must consider the fitting, the maintenance, the website, and suchlike. We're small scale. That's how we manage to make ourselves affordable. After all, that's our motto; we endeavour to serve what others leave behind,' said with a wink, making his hand like a pistol and aiming at Ashley, trying out a well-rehearsed catchphrase.

'I see,' said Ashley, ignoring the pointed stares from Griffin. 'It's just that there was a tracking device located on the vehicle, but obviously not put there by yourselves.'

This was news to Leeman. He looked briefly towards Griffin as if for an answer. The look alone was enough for Ashley.

The forensic team had not formally released this information, Veronica leaked it to Burnt and Ashley. She performed the post mortem on the two victims from Sunday's incident and had her doubts about Griffin's story. She was at the recovery depot when forensics had made the vital find on the vehicle only hours ago. Although not officially acting in her capacity as a pathologist, Veronica as ever could not resist the urge to accompany the forensic team who were carrying out a second inspection on the perpetrators' vehicle, in preparation for briefing SI Ross.

It was a quiet drive back to HQ.

Chapter 59

'This is a serious accusation, Burnt.'

'And not one I take lightly, sir.'

The pair sat head-locked in Ross's office at HQ, Burnt trying to reason with his superintendent.

'It's just too much of a coincidence,' continued Burnt, on the edge of his seat.

'DS Griffin has a lot of contacts, that's for sure,' conceded Ross. 'We'll have a thorough investigation and you'll have time to voice your concerns.'

'But we need to do it now, before he can cook up a story.' Burnt leaned forward, almost tipping the seat. Nodded towards the annotated transcript in front of Ross. Three pages of thumbed printout, worn and well read. Burnt stood and paced the floor.

'Four phone numbers, all in contact with each other,' he put finger to palm, 'all at crucial times in the investigation so far. Look at the location of the calls. One of the numbers was within the proximity of Lowestoft Road police station.'

'And have you checked the registration of the phone numbers with the service provider?'

'Yes. All four are unregistered, which makes it even more suspicious. Burner phones.'

'That's not enough to go on, Adam.'

Burnt's body fell still. 'But that's not all.'

'Go on.'

'One of the numbers went offline around the same time Griffin turned up at the lockup where he uncovered the drug ring.' He stopped and prodded at a smudged, highlighted number with his chubby index finger.

'That's nowhere near enough.'

Back to the pacing. He knew it wasn't going to be easy. 'I also asked forensics to check for fingerprints on the deceased, Frank Allen. Guess what, Griffin's prints are all over him. I think he was searching for his mobile after shooting him.'

'It's not uncommon to frisk a perpetrator, whether killed or not,' insisted Ross, creases across his brow. 'Are you serious, Burnt?'

'Hear me out. I think I might be able to prove that one of those numbers belongs to Griffin. As long as no one knows McLeish is in custody.'

'How?'

He tapped the entry with the question mark. 'I want to call one of the remaining two numbers. I haven't done this so far as I don't want to make the owners suspicious.'

'If all this were true I would expect the phones to be trashed by now.'

'I agree, they would be – but could be the owners of these numbers are waiting to hear from McLeish?'

He let it hang.

Ross leant back and rubbed at his eyebrows. 'Okay, Griffin will be back soon,' he said with a sigh. 'We'll run through the events before any formal meeting, but let's just see what he has to say.'

Ross sat with the weight of the Norfolk police's reputation on his shoulders. 'And if you're wrong?'

'I'll put my hands up and apologise all round. I'm sure there are a few DI's around here who'll have a chuckle at my expense.'

Ross smiled. 'You haven't exactly embraced the locals, have you, Burnt?'

'I've tried, in my own way.' He knew that either way this could be career suicide. If he were correct, colleagues would loathe him. If wrong, he would be ridiculed. Nevertheless, justice was just that.

Ross tapped at the keypad of his desk-phone, asked Griffin to come to his office as soon as he arrived at HQ.

Griffin assured him he would be there in five minutes. Burnt stood and paced again. He had always found Griffin slippery, someone who would dodge every question. And when there was information he had to share, Burnt would be the last to know.

Griffin's strong ties in the area made him popular with everyone, Ross included. There was always someone who knew Griffin's aunt or nephew. People just took to the local boy who was making a good career for himself. It was easier to make Griffin an ally in comparison to an invader from the Midlands.

The pair sat in silence, the air getting thicker, the background hum of typing and paper shuffling from adjacent rooms filling the airwaves. Burnt scanned the spotless office, struck as always by Ross's tidiness. Reference books lined the shelves, the desk displaying only essential items for his work, not so much as a chocolate bar wrapper or coffee cup stain. Two beaming faces sat on a fishing boat baked in sunshine next to his monitor.

The raised voices of a few DIs congratulating Griffin made Burnt's stomach churn. This was going to be tough. He craned his neck to see the DS high-fiving a colleague in the corridor. Ashley following, head bowed.

Griffin strolled in and shot a smile at Ross. Took the one remaining seat in the office. Ashley followed behind and stood by the door, pushing it to, awkwardly.

'How's the arm, Ashley?' asked Ross.

Ashley looked at the floor. 'I'll live,' he muttered.

'All in the line of duty,' said Ross.

'I wouldn't expect an OBE, though,' piped up Burnt.

Ross sat upright, gave his serious face. Didn't want this to be an interrogation, and Griffin deserved time to make his report. But anomalies needed explaining.

'First, I would like to compliment all three of you on what has been a tough week. But before we start the official debrief tomorrow, I want to go over everything we have so far.'

Meaning no minutes.

'To start with, who killed Tom Hacket?'

Griffin was first. 'Ronnie Lesley, but I expect Frank Allen was present.'

'What was the motive?' asked Ross, already holding up the palm of his hand to Burnt who was ready to jump out of his seat.

'The Hacket brothers owed them money for the contraband they were supplying. I think it's as simple as that.'

'Go on.'

'The new drug we have identified, Halloween, was handed in by someone who claims to have purchased it from Graham Hacket at the Oakwoods.'

'The Hells Angel?'

'Outcast, but pretty much the same thing. The powder matches the same found on Ronnie Lesley in the Endeavour van, and at the business unit I discovered. Although I've no proof regarding Graham Hacket.'

Griffin, sat back, flicked his blond hair from his eyes, made a steeple with his fingers. He spoke directly to Ross like he was the only person in the room. He was the only one Griffin needed to convince.

'The murder weapon and blood-stained clothes with a DNA match for Tom Hacket, also discovered in the Endeavour vehicle.'

Burnt butted in, stopped his flow before Griffin could get too far. 'It was the same weapon I saw at Haines's house the day before.'

'You can't prove that,' replied Griffin, not even turning his head. Griffin remained calm, as ever.

Burnt got clammy. Then reminded everyone of the evidence he took from the scene on Sunday when they had searched the premises. 'So what about the bone I took to forensics? Haines just throws his proud artefact to the dog as a toy?'

'That was a deer horn, found at any pet store, and confirmed by forensics,' said Griffin, smiling at Ross.

Burnt felt certain the bone would shed some light on the case; he wasn't aware it had come back from analysis. If not whalebone, it still didn't explain what Burnt saw Saturday afternoon in Haines's bureau, and there was no explanation for the fact that the piece was missing the next day when he had searched the premises.

'Okay, so why the hell was Levin in the vehicle?' exclaimed Burnt, out of his chair again.

'Recruited, would be my conjecture. A mentally unstable boy goes missing from a mental health facility. The report described drug abuse and no family. Roaming the streets, he bumps into the perpetrators. I don't think we will ever truly know.'

'He was wearing the same jacket I saw hung up at Haines's house.'

Griffin raised no more than an eyebrow. 'Again, where is the proof?'

Burnt sighed; he was losing the battle and was relying on the phone numbers to win Ross's confidence.

'Plausible so far … and the Endeavour employers?' asked Ross.

Griffin shrugged. 'They were completely unaware of any of their employees' activities, who tied in legitimate courier work together with their dealing.'

'And Harry Arthur Leeman is a chemist for Zenacare, which is very convenient when there's a new drug on the street,' said Burnt, looking to Ross for support.

'The director actually. And that doesn't make him a cook – or a crook,' scoffed Griffin, smiling towards Ross.

Ross looked to the transcript of phone numbers on his desk. 'Can you explain why you had a firearm at the altercation at Monument Road on Sunday?'

'That I must apologise for,' said Griffin, showing the palms of his hands. 'I forgot to sign it back two weeks previously after firearms practice. It was in my glovebox, and I don't know why, I just got a bad feeling so took it into the workshop. This will not happen again, I promise. But the mistake saved my life.'

'Quite. That will need to be in the report.'

Burnt pressed the speed-dial saved into his phone. He was sure the number he had dialled belonged to Griffin and just needed to hear it ring. Ten agonising seconds passed. Griffin continued, in that smooth smug voice, about the evidence they had so far, how it would be a straightforward posthumous conviction for the CPS.

Burnt sighed. Anger melted to despair, annoyance for thinking Griffin would be so stupid. The phones they'd used were long gone.

The police had McLeish's handset that matched one of the four numbers, but without a link there would be no evidence against Griffin. He sat back. Ross looked over, eyebrows raised – did Burnt still want to accuse Griffin of corruption within the force?

Time for plan B.

Burnt texted a single message to Veronica Esherwood who was sitting in the forensic wing of the building, with McLeish's phone in front of her. Burnt had prepped her and she was happy to help. She too had doubts about Griffin.

Veronica read the text, and immediately phoned the suspect number – this time from McLeish's phone. It was possible that the cohorts had blocked all numbers other than the four they wanted to contact.

'One minute, gentlemen,' said Griffin, standing up to leave the room. The rumble in his pocket went unnoticed by Ross and Ashley, but Burnt stood up to face Griffin while blocking the door.

'Do you recognise these numbers, Simon?' asked Burnt, leaning across the desk and spinning the printout of calls to face them.

Griffin paused, a flicker of uncertainty crossing his face. He hesitated, looking at Ross for support. 'Why?' His voice had a tremor.

Burnt continued with a hint of sarcasm. 'Please answer your phone, don't let me stop you.'

Griffin's face flushed. 'What phone?'

'The one in your pocket, vibrating like a whore's dildo,' said Burnt.

Ross gave raised eyebrows. His favourite DS seemed to have something to cover up.

'Answer your phone, DS Griffin,' said Ross, standing up and leaning across his desk.

Griffin slowly reached to his pocket, buying himself as much time as possible. It stopped vibrating as he gripped it. Relieved, he glanced at the transcript. Said, 'Can't say I do. Should I?'

'These numbers were called at crucial times when the crimes were committed.'

'Have you traced them?' asked Griffin, putting the transcript down and edging away from the desk, phone in hand, squeezing it a little too tightly. It started to vibrate again, and this time Veronica caught everyone's attention, stood at the doorway clearing her throat. Gave a wry smile as she wiggled McLeish's phone between thumb and forefinger.

Burnt said, 'A clam. A bit old school, isn't it? Were you expecting a call from Dr Alexander McLeish by any chance?'

'I don't know what you mean …' stammered Griffin.

'Give me the damn phone and explain yourself, Griffin,' said Ross.

Burnt swooped the handset from Griffin and handed it to Ross, who leafed through the caller list to check against the transcript.

Burnt continued with his reasoning, blocking Griffin's exit. 'You see, someone used this phone at crucial points over the last week or so, like the time when a hoax call was made to emergency services for the Bells Road fire. I think that whoever took that call organised a hoax over Airwave. It was one that I took, and one that sent me to the wrong location.'

'What a load of crap,' said Griffin, backing away. 'So McLeish tries to phone me, what the hell does that prove?'

He looked at Ross, who was making a call himself from the clam. He put it onto answerphone and placed it on the table. It rang three times.

'Went well, I thought.'

Burnt was first. 'Am I speaking to Harry Arthur Leeman?'

Silence.

'Initials HAL, chemist and inventor of HAL31?'

The line went dead.

'DS Griffin, I am placing you under arrest,' said Ross.

'This is bullshit,' Griffin stammered, fists by his side. 'I brought down a drug ring, and this is the thanks I get? Christ, can't you see the bigger picture? I'm lining this guy up for a bust. I've been working on this for months, and you've blown it.'

A crowd gathered outside the open office behind Veronica.

'No. You've blown it,' he shouted to Burnt, pointing a finger. 'Ever since you came on the scene this place has gone downhill, what do you know about real police work? You spend half your time beating up every Tom, Dick and Harry that ogles your missus.' He looked to Ross for help. Back to Burnt. 'That's why you messed up at Bells Road. Too busy knocking crap out some cretin whose been shaggin' your missus for the past year. Just admit it. You messed up,' he shouted, his pointed finger trembling.

In one swift Aikido move, Burnt took hold of Griffin's outstretched hand, twisted it, and jumped behind him in one step. He yanked Griffin's arm up behind his back, dropped him to his knees and pushed hard from behind, squashing Griffin's face to the table. Twisted harder till they all heard a crack. Griffin yelped.

By now, staff from the corridors were bursting through the door, forcing Veronica into the centre of the room who took her turn to ask a question.

'One thing's been niggling me,' she said, perching on the edge of Ross's desk and staring down at Griffin's reddened face. 'There were three gunshots fired one after the other on Sunday at the Monument Road lockup.' She paused, handing Ross McLeish's phone who was still checking all numbers on the transcript. 'Witness accounts state that there were two shots in quick succession, and a third about ten seconds later.' She waited for it to sink in. 'That does not match your description of what happened. Why the big gap?'

She didn't wait for an answer, and probably would not have got one, as Griffin was muttering obscenities under his breath at Burnt who was handcuffing him to the table leg.

'Also, the shot that you claim was fired by the perpetrator, according to forensic evidence, was carried out less than three feet from you. You were very lucky he missed.' She looked down at Griffin. 'As I have said, I work closely with forensics. Oh, and one more thing. Frank Allen's fingerprints were not on the trigger of the gun, yet he had no gloves on when discovered with the firearm in his hand. There were, however, minute particles of latex found. I think these inconsistencies need to be resolved,' she said. Turned to face Ross, who looked shocked.

'I want a solicitor,' rasped Griffin.

'Oh don't tell me,' said Burnt, willing to guess who owned the phone with the last remaining questionable number from the transcript. 'Gregory Ravel, by any chance?'

Chapter 60

One month later

Madge wagged her tail, licked her lips in anticipation. Pavlov's dog, thought Eric, what a simple discovery – how could someone be remembered in history for discovering something so obvious? He churned over the dark meat in the bowl, turning his nose away from the foul smell while the spaniel clawed at his legs. He had taken puppy-training classes, mainly for his sanity, to keep his mind off things – and to stop the bloody thing biting at his ankles all the time. Failed on both counts.

With the bowl now on the floor and the can in recycling, he returned to his latest spiritual book, *Long Walk to Freedom.* Stretching his legs at the kitchen table, crossed at the ankles, he opened the earmark, and gave a yawn.

The letterbox pinged.

After a sigh, Eric padded through the hallway and scooped up the pack of mail. Flyers, circulars, the local gazette – and a postcard. Back at the table, he leafed through them, discarding each in turn. Who did he know on holiday? A beach view at dusk. Flipped it over, noticed the Singapore postage stamp.

Uncle Eric,

Hope you are well. I read you jumped in after me. We are lucky to be alive.

I've found peace a long way away in the red-hot sun. The nightmares have finally gone, and there're no wolves here.

Thank-you for protecting me. I shall never forget it.

Take care.
Tim

'Christ.'

Eric's vision blurred. He circled the table, ran his hand over his hair, fanned the card through his fingers, suddenly animated, buzzing while Madge chased the steel bowl. How the hell did he do it? Didn't Bryony say the aunt lived in Singapore?

An urge to tell Bryony, somebody – anybody – overcame him. But what good would it do? To give someone a secret, a weight around their shoulders – who needs that? The police had pleaded for information from the public to help discover the boy, and like everyone else, Eric had assumed the tide had swept Timothy out to sea where he drowned.

No reason to enlighten them.

Madge came in for a snuggle. Eric knelt and picked her up, whispered that it was all better now, stroking her behind the ear, pacing around the table with a smile on his face for the first time in weeks.

A mugshot on the front of the gazette stopped him.

'Hero cop held in custody. The proclaimed "hero of the streets" abused his position and perverted the cause of justice.'

Eric opened it out while clutching at Madge, and read on, the grin growing wider.

There were no follow-up enquiries after Timothy went missing. Not at his door anyway. He spent a week in hospital, took ill with pneumonia. CID came for a statement soon as he was well enough, then Mario bounded onto the ward, bursting at the seams to give him the news, told him that the two thugs they shadowed were responsible for Tom Hacket's murder. Eric just nodded from behind the starched sheets – he could keep a secret.

So could Caulk. She took a job with the Samaritans, her first in fifteen years. She'd got the right credentials, a listener with previous. The calls varied, some suicidal, others just needed a chat, and the occasional hoax call.

She loved it.

The job wasn't that hard to find. It was voluntary, no academic skills needed, just the ability to listen and empathise. Only a reference required, and the shining recommendation sent from the CEO of a major oil and gas firm in Singapore sealed it. A small but steady trickle of money from the same offshore company allowed Julie to rent a flat and live again. She didn't need much else, this wasn't just surviving, it was a new start.

Mario had also decided on a fresh start. While driving down South Town Road he contemplated his future. He had a moral dilemma; should he do the right thing or make some money, easy money? Frodo would always choose the money, he was an opportunist. As for Jeff, he just thanked his lucky stars he was still in one piece.

They knew they would not be hearing from the thugs they'd met at Fritton Woods ever again, so the package of powder handed to them was theirs to sell.

Mario made up his mind. Pulled up beside Haven Bridge on Steam Mill Lane. No more deliberating. He walked to the water's edge, tucked up against the underside of the bridge, and did a quick scan. He leant up against the waist-high concrete barrier for a moment, reached into his pocket and pulled out the cellophane-wrapped kilogramme of Halloween. Tossed it into the Yare. Waited for the undramatic splash.

'It's only money,' he whispered to the river, surprised by the enormous feeling of relief.

With that off his mind he could concentrate on him and Lola from now on, he wasn't going to take any more liberties. Her mother had come to stay at the flat for a week, which had prompted him to move the package from under the spare bed – not that Lola had known it was there in the first place. If her mother had found it he guessed it really would have been the end.

Frodo had recommended using Lola's mother as an unsuspecting mule to Mario's relatives in northern Italy. Mario had considered this only briefly.

The falling out with Lola was water under the bridge, which is where the package was now, making its way to the bottom of the riverbed, pushed and dragged by the tide, swirling around in the dock water. It came to rest between the spokes of an abandoned bicycle.

That left one more.

And it now belonged to Graham Hacket who had also made a new start – as a dealer. The desire to retrieve it from the Outcasts had killed his brother, to give up the search would be in vain. Hacket's naivety was replaced with cunning – his guilt masked with spite.

He camped outside the address Spike had given him. At three am drilled out the lock and bust in, wolf mask on, covering his features, held the drill to the guy's throat. There was no resistance, the scabby couple were happy to get rid of it. Had sat sobbing in the flat at the nightmares that tortured them for days. Handed it over to the boy-cum-man in a wolf-mask.

Graham, just out of school, could now kick-start his career. The local press and TV kindly promoting his merchandise.

Chapter 61

'Visitor,' shouted the guard through the open vent. McLeish could barely hear him over the noise of the neighbouring cells. Next door was always rowdy. He had a single cell for now, his hearing put back another month.

McLeish pushed his trembling hands through the partition for cuffing. Once clamped, the door unlocked with a scrape of steel. McLeish shuffled onto the mezzanine, cowering. It was a long walk to the visitors' room on the ground floor.

He hated leaving his cell.

'Doctor, help me,' they jeered. His walks of shame were fun for the inmates. A doctor turned bad was almost as good as a copper that turned.

'I need you, doctor, in my bed, now.' Whistles, this time from three cells down from an unpopular rapist. 'Doctors, they're my favourite.' More laughter as he edged past, head bent.

Next floor down was a little quieter. Where the inmates just gave him the convict glare. All in single cells, lifers, not interested in leaving, had given up trying to persuade anyone to trust them. Psychopathic opportunists.

McLeish would struggle with life in a mental health prison and he knew it.

Finally, at the visitor room. A secure unit split in half by a concrete wall with a meter square of toughened glass in the centre, scratched and blurred. A strip light flickered.

He sat, hands on knees, peering through the glass. Surprised by his guest, expecting the police. Distracted by the bugs that were climbing the walls.

'Hello, Bryony,' he said, rubbing at his arms. 'Have you come to analyse me?'

The intercom echoed, carrying a ring.

'Sort of.'

She wanted to know how coherent the doctor was. Needed to see him face to face one last time.

Her placement at the hospital had come to a sudden end, along with the jobs of all the staff. The residents despatched to hospitals with facility wards. Bryony needed closure on what had ended so abruptly.

St Nicholas Hospital had been the last of its kind, certainly on that scale, and it was now just a matter of time before the council sold the land to property developers.

The simple question was, *why?* But McLeish's answers came with babble, quickly losing the thread of the conversation.

He started to defend himself, explaining how he was trying to do something great for the world, that he had transformed the hospital, but had made one single mistake. He'd overdosed on a drug he was trialling to rid the world of the torment that so many suffered with mental health problems. The creation of the Halloween drug had been necessary to prove the remedy, MR11.

One generic all-conquering medicine used worldwide, with him as its ambitious innovator.

Still the inflated ego, Bryony thought, but now it was imbued with incoherent chatter. Side-tracked by the bugs that gathered round to listen, their knees crossed and with glasses on, taking notes with their minute pencils and pads of paper.

She scribbled it into her own notebook, pointless as it was, an attempt to make sense of it all. Concluded that McLeish had severe short-term attention deficit due to his drug habit.

The discoveries had shocked Bryony and many others. There had been the trialling contraband medication on unsuspecting patients, including minors. Abusing his position, using unlawful suppliers, as well as maintaining a drug habit paid for by the NHS, almost killing a prostitute by lethal injection and abandoning her.

Add money laundering to the list, and McLeish was in for a tough trial – if he was fit to stand. Bryony guessed he was not sane enough to stand up in court. She could feel no sympathy for the man who was supposed to be her mentor, even when he broke down crying. There was little to say.

She nodded to the guard, stood, zipped her Parka to her neck, and strolled away from McLeish who was scratching at his neck, wiping his hands, ridding himself of whatever creatures had made their way into his mind.

'At least you know how your patients felt,' was all she could say, almost a whisper, feeling a lump in her throat as she left the room. Disgusted.

McLeish contemplated this, smiled at a private joke, then was pulled from his reverie as the guard unlocked the door with a clunk.

'Quite a popular one today, aren't we, McLeish? You've got a phone call. Come on.'

No. Not his father, again. He called to berate him, to tell him how his son had ruined the family reputation. That his mother would turn in her grave. And to urge him to stop pretending and stand trial, like a man for once.

At first McLeish had asked for help, maybe in the vain hope his father could pull some strings.

McLeish stood by the phone, waiting for the verbal abuse.

'Alexander McLeish speaking,' he attempted.

'Do you dream when you're awake, doctor?'

'Who is this?'

'For me it was Vikings. Do you wake up sweating and sick, never sure if it's a dream or not?'

'Is this …'

'Don't trust anyone.'

'Timothy?'

'You thought I was dead? I wished I was when I was in that hospital.'

'Levin?'

'It's hard to know who your friends are when you're in prison.'

'Are you okay?'

'Much better, now that I'm far away from you.'

'Where? Where are you?' stammered McLeish.

'One bit of advice – watch out for wolves.'

The line went dead. McLeish shuddered and hung up, turning to the guard with a shrug.

He shuffled along the corridor, head bowed. The noise in the prison unbearable. Constant shouts, screams, fighting and bickering. He could not contemplate the next few weeks here, let alone years. Up the sets of stairs, past cell doors thumped and kicked from the inside. Looks of anguish from most, mocking smiles from some, and deathly faces from others.

The guardrails were six feet high, with mesh that extended further, daylight poking through the ceiling slats. Past more cells, limping along and trying to ignore the howling of fellow inmates. What they would do when they got their hands on him.

He was three cells from his own when one of McLeish's admirers spat at him. 'You'll get more than that later,' he shouted. The guard moved over to rack the vent with his baton.

'I can't do this,' McLeish whispered. He turned to face the line of cells. 'I can't do this,' he repeated, louder. They started to jeer and chant his name.

'The doctor needs some medicine,' shouted one.

The guards were barking at the prisoners to pipe down, banging at the steel doors. McLeish took his chance, grabbed at the steel-fenced guardrail and scaled it. The handcuffs didn't stop him, using two hands at a time, he clambered upwards, listening to the roars behind him willing him on, some banging on the cell doors, some clapping in encouragement.

The guard turned to see McLeish already six feet high. He tried to grab at his feet but came away with his plimsolls. With his toes free, it made it easier for McLeish who, now consumed with energy, allowed him to dig into the mesh to spur him on. Hadn't someone once called him Spiderman? Yes, he was good at this, and for a moment felt elated as he got to the apex of the fence and looked down at the jeering hordes of faces through the cell windows. Popular once more. He pumped his fist in triumph as he looked around to face the crowd. He had everyone's attention, but with the guard now scaling the fence after him, he knew he didn't have long. He straddled the apex.

'Is this what you want to see?' he shouted.

'We've got a jumper.' one of them screamed. The asylum was now raucous with chanting. 'Jump! Jump! Jump!' they goaded.

McLeish leapt from the apex of the fence and plummeted to the concrete floor three storeys below.

There were howls from the cells, faces pressed up against the vents, the quieter ones sniggering. The building intoxicated.

McLeish saw a black open mouth coming out of the floor to devour him. Sharp fangs with dripping saliva gripped his body as he met concrete.

Chapter 62

'Colonel Mustard, in the drawing room, with the candlestick.' Adam opened the cards in the centre of the game board to reveal the answers, smiling in self-assurance.

His children looked on in anticipation. 'Yep,' he confirmed, with a grin, displaying the cards face up on the table. He sat back on the couch as the two boys jumped on him by way of celebration, causing the father of two to spill beer. Winked at Jackie. Beat her again.

'How come you always know the killer, Daddy?' asked his oldest, fidgeting into his father's side.

'He's an Inceptor,' declared the younger of the two boys, pointing a finger at the ceiling. 'A Detective Inceptor.'

'That's right, it's my job,' Burnt replied, gulping back the remains of the glass.

'Beating two under-sixes at Cluedo doesn't make you Sherlock,' insisted Jackie, cramming the board away with a grumble.

'It was three against one,' he countered, putting an arm round each of his boys.

Jackie threw her arms around in the air theatrically. 'Oh, and against all odds, the lone wolf once again triumphed over evil,' she joked.

'Something like that.' Adam looked to his children and whispered, 'I think Mummy is a bit grumpy she didn't win.'

'Watch it.' Jackie put her hands on her hips. Showing cleavage. 'Mr Newly-promoted detective inspector had better not get too cocky, or there will be no dessert.' She winked at her husband, nodded upstairs, the subtle hint missed by the kids.

She took to the kitchen as the oven timer alarm sounded. The chocolate brownies were ready. Burnt shooed the kids away.

They leapt up and trotted to the kitchen, dressed in Thomas Tank pyjamas.

DI Burnt wrenched himself from the couch and followed his family, stopping at the open page of the gazette where an unflattering photo of DS Griffin stared up at him. A trial date had been set, giving the local tabloid an excuse to embarrass the police yet again.

'It takes a wolf to catch a wolf,' whispered Burnt.

The phone on the table rumbled. Flashed a message. He unlocked it and scrolled to the note. Withheld number.

She still playing around? You still trust her? Then where was she yesterday? Ask her that. Sex addict that one
  BTW I'm suing Norfolk police
  See you in court
  G

Burnt locked the phone, hid it in his pocket. Took a deep breath. That fuse, once again lit.

***

James Ashley sat bolt upright, drenched in sweat, the sheets clinging to him. Made Veronica jump. A repeat of how he woke her most nights.

'The same dream?' she asked, pulling back the covers, slipping out of bed to use the bathroom.

'The same dream,' he confirmed.

He took the pint glass from his bedside table and drained it, then lay back to stare into the ceiling. Put his palms over his eyes – what he would give to remove that image from his mind. To un-see it. The same one that hid until he slept.

The eyes, always the hollow, pleading eyes. Following him, pleading for justice he couldn't give.

The end

Acknowledgements

It has been a long road to publication since typing those first few words and I have received encouragement from my friends and family all the way. Some, I feel the need to say special thanks to:

Firstly Paul Kedward, for reading draft one of many, providing feedback, and enduring my endless babbling, usually on the climbing wall. Also, to Julie Bakewell for the education into the dark-side. Next, to Laurence King for his mentoring and razor-like critique, 'If you can do without it – cut it,' will be etched forever on my mind.

I also want to thank Betsy and the gang at Bloodhound. Taking on debut writers is something few publishers are prepared to do, and to do it so wholeheartedly leaves me humbled. Thanks all, for making my work real.

Special thanks to Kathryn – you never know how much someone means to you until life gets tough.

Finally, love to Freya, Ben and Nessie.

Printed in Great Britain
by Amazon